STRANGE REPORTS
FROM SECTOR M

STRANGE REPORTS FROM SECTOR M

Matt Carson

ISBN-13: 9781974511877
ISBN-10: 1974511871

To my Dad—all those word games as a kid really paid off. I'm sure, I'm positive, and I ascertain the difference between the two.

So what exactly is this thing, and why are we getting strange reports from it, huh?

Allow me to explain: The first reference to Sector M in my work can be found in the final story of this very book, a novella called "The Foeman's Chain." Originally, the idea was a sector of space on the peripheries of civilization, a wilderland or untamed frontier given only a cursory survey. In my own headcannon, the explorers of this space had labeled every system with a word starting with the letter— you guessed it—"M." While I don't remember consciously deciding to go with the first letter of my first name, I'm sure that played a part in it.

When I was able to build a dedicated writing office, I decorated it with all my little muses. I have a number of different versions of Optimus Prime scattered around the room. On my desk, the Egyptian sphinx stares across from a Warthog from *Halo*, manned by the gladiatorial robots from *Real Steel*. I have miniature starships from *Star Wars* and *Star Trek*, a closet for all my renaissance garb, and lots of shelving to hold my reference books. Many of the knickknacks and toys I have on display are survivors from my childhood. Because of these relics, and the externalization of my many fandoms, the office became known as the "Museum of Matt" and "Sector Matt." That naturally morphed into "Sector M." This is my creative space, my Doctor Strange-esque *sanctum sanctorum*. The majority of stories in this anthology were brainstormed and written right there.

When it came time to brand my author and creative enterprises, I didn't just want to go with my name. Twitter is littered with handles like "John Doe Author," and that always strikes me as a little weird and desperate. So, Sector M was the obvious choice. It's the umbrella under which I do all my creative stuff, the headspace I occupy more often than not, and the lens through which I view the world.

And it can be a strange place.

So when I say this book is named *Strange Reports from Sector M*, what I'm really saying is *Some Weird Things Rattling Around in Matt's Brain Have Made Their Way onto the Page, Again.*

WHAT'S THIS BOOK ABOUT?

Let's set some expectations early on, yeah? Most of the stories here have some sort of science-fiction element to them, though there is a sprinkling of urban fantasy/horror. Many have a heavy military influence, but all of them have some anthropological or sociological theme(s) to them.

Also, be aware that I make up words. English is great for doing that. If there isn't a word that fits what I'm trying to say, or a form that captures what I mean, I make up something new. Now you know...and knowing is half the battle!

The stories get longer the deeper you go. I start with some really short pieces, and work my way up to short stories of a more traditional length. Towards the back I have two stories in the novelette/novella length, depending on which definition you use.

I preface each of the stories with any notes and thoughts on what brought the story about. I'll keep these "liner note" sections brief, but if you're curious about my thought process, and the questions I pondered, check 'em out. Or you can skip them entirely. I won't judge.

Finally, let's talk about an overarching theme. Originally, there was no theme other than that the stories are all mine. There wasn't any other unifying motif to them. Some of these stories took place in a shared universe, but were still islands unto themselves. As I started to put these stories side by side, however, certain patterns began to emerge. I won't spoil it for you; I'll leave it for you, the reader, to pick them out for yourself.

Or maybe there is no greater theme, and I'm just imagining things.

I do that a lot. :)

Enjoy!

Si vales, valeo.

-Matt Carson
May, 2017

Table of Contents

The Really Short Stuff

Growing up in rural East Texas you could not get away from commercials hawking car dealerships on TV. Chief among them was a place called Westway Ford, which still exists. Their mascot was originally a Yosemite Sam looka-like, who would shoot the letters spelling out "Westway Ford" on a billboard at the end of their TV spots. Later, he was replaced by a new guy, Joe Greed. Joe was about as over-the-top as you could get. Clad in a white "oil baron" business suit and white hat covered with green dollar signs, he sported a pair of oversized glasses (Elton John in scale) also with dollar signs over the lens.

Years later, I was paging through a magazine at the doctor's office and ran across a big pharma advertisement. You know the kind—the ones with three pages of small text, following a color ad of older folks laughing. When I read the line consult your physician before use, *I mistakenly read it as* consult your <u>physicist</u> before use.

Those two things combined in my head. What if there was a Slartibartfast kind of guy out there who bombastically advertised a service that would seem impossible to us? All I needed then was to write in the voice of Slim Pickens and Honest Al was born.

Honest Al's Used Star Emporium

Howdy, folks! Is your star past its prime? Is it about expand its outer layer and destroy your favorite planet, or collapse into an unsightly black hole? Well don't just settle for a sad, saggy star when you can get your hands on a brilliant, raging ball of fusion today!

Come on down to Honest Al's Used Star Emporium, where we service all your stellar needs! We've got white ones, red ones, blue ones, yellow ones! Need anything along the main sequence? We got 'em! You want Pulsars?[1] We got 'em! Hypergiants?[2] No problem! Whatever you need, Al has you covered…guar-raan-teeeed! We'll just lasso (-whip

---

1 Extreme rotational intervals and greater-than-average EM emissions may cause death in some sapients. Use only as directed.

2 Stellar radius on very large models may exceed existing orbital paths. Luminosity may also exceed standard tolerances. Consult your physicist before use.

cracks-) that pre-owned star of your dreams and precipitate it wherever you want![3]

Don't want to part with your old star? Well, you don't have to! Our stellar physicists, gravitic specialists, and hydrogen recombinationists are standing by to breathe new life into your old star, giving it the same zip and radiological output as when it was young!

I'm so sure that we can reignite or reinvigorate any star that we'll do it for the low, low price of 19,999,999,999,999 ,999,999,999.99!?[4] That's IN-SANE! You won't find prices this low anywhere else in the Virgo Supercluster, folks, or my name isn't Honest Al!

So fly, teleport, or psychically manifest yourself on over to Honest Al's Used Star Emporium today, and put a little light in your life! You know our jingle, sing it with me now:

You know the stars will be your pal...when you trust in Hon-nest Al!

---

3 Not responsible for any property damages resulting from unexpected gravity waves, stellar expansion that encompasses habitable real-estate, mass displacement, or loss of orbital stability.

4 Does not include installation costs, local, or galactic taxes, or any other applicable fees. Financing available and underwritten by the First Galactic Central Bank of Nexus. Honest Al is a subsidiary of Star Makers, LLC. Void where prohibited.

I can thank my aunt and her record collection for introducing me to Blues and Motown at an early age, particularly Smokey Robinson.

In later years, I came to appreciate a whole musical genre that centered itself around regretting your actions, heartbreak, and lamenting the course of your life, even more than Country music.

We all the sing the blues at some point in our lives. As our ideals of body image and beauty become increasingly unachievable, and our technological sophistication grows to spread it, how long before we have a digital Pygmalion moment?

Holographic Blues

I've got those holographic blues, baby,
And they've gone and got me down.
I've got them holographic blues, baby,
And I just can't shut 'em down.

It all started with the protons, yeah,
And it's driving this poor boy insane.
I say, it started with the protons, yeah,
And it's driving this poor boy insane.
Well, it's all gone down and bad, yeah,
Left me cryin' in the rain.

I've got those holographic blues, baby,
Lord have mercy on my soul.
I've got them holographic blues, baby,
This woman ain't got no soul.

Now she's shining on the grid-light (yes, she is)
And I can't even look at her face.
Yes, she's shining on the grid-light, yeah,
And I can't even look at her face.
Well, she's more than any woman could be,
Lord, deliver me from this place.

I've got those holographic blues, baby,
Though I'm tryin' to keep it real.
I've got them holographic blues, yeah,
'Cause what I want ain't real.

We all must stare down our own mortality at some point, and the same is true for just about any literary character. All things end.

To me, a character is never so true as when they stare death right in the face. It's when there's no escape, no way out, no hope, that we truly see them for who they are.

We only see Cahill in this one scene, his last, but I really empathize with the guy. He's seen so much darkness in his life, and even when a sexy Anubis comes by to collect him, and give him a rather pleasant send-off, he still finds it hard to let go.

Fade to Black

f I step into the next room, I'm dead. I thought I was ready for this, that I had let go of everything that might prevent me from crossing that threshold, but now that the moment is here, I'm rooted to this cheap armchair, looking death square in the face.

Opposite me sits my executioner. No, that's not the right word, more like my facilitator or assistant. In any case, the one who will end my life. Jack Kevorkian, she ain't. This is Los Angeles, the biggest collection of beauty queens, movie stars, and models the world over, but I ain't never seen one like *this*.

Her bare legs, below the hem of her red satin dress, belong to a dancer or figure skater, and end in stylish red pumps. The opposite direction, above her slender waist, is just as glorious, with a face that is exactly as it should be, framed by long black hair. Perfect. Perfect like a dark angel sent to claim me.

Step through that door, and it's over, just fade to black.

"Before we begin, do you have any questions?" she asks in a voice as sultry as Marilyn Monroe and Betty Page's love child.

"Yeah," I say. "So you're the real deal, huh? No poseur or wannabe, you're actually—"

"A vampire?" she finishes. "Yes, I am. Do you believe me?"

I do. I don't know why, but I do.

"You touched a lot of lives during your service to the city, Mr. Cahill. That's why I am here, as a final thank you."

"*Final* is right."

She lifts one of her perfect eyebrows. Suddenly she is holding my hand, even though I didn't see her bridge the space between us.

"Tell me, how many months do you have left?"

"Eight," I say, "if I'm lucky. Doc says it's more like six, even with treatments. It's already in my lymph nodes."

It's Leukemia, in case you're wondering. Damn thing must be contagious, because it killed my Evelyn just eight years ago. She didn't go quickly, either. I watched her shrivel into a grey thing I barely recognized. She prayed every day for death the last two months. God, that hurt.

Despite what I've faced in thirty years on the force, perhaps I'm a coward at heart. I'm not sure I can go through what she did: dying by inches, waiting, begging, for the end to come.

The raven-haired woman squeezes my hand, and it's warm and friendly.

"There's nothing wrong with facing death on your own terms," she says. "I've seen it more times than you can imagine, but it can be beautiful if you let it. You need not fear it, not with me." Her words wash over me like a cool ocean wave.

There are a lot of worse ways to die than in the arms of a beautiful woman. Hell, that's the whole reason she's here, to take me to the other side in the kindest way possible.

"Will it...hurt when it happens?" I ask like a sheepish teenager.

"No," she says. "We will have tonight to celebrate your life, you and I."

She leans forward and I can't seem to tell whether her eyes are brown or blue.

"And when the time comes, I will sing you off to sleep."

I close my eyes, knowing that this is my last day. Men all over the world, even ones who weren't already dying, would kill each other to die by this woman's side. I'm dead already.

I stand up. She stands up with me.

"Would you like to watch me undress?" she asks, and I nod. She moves with liquid grace into the other room. I follow, one step, then another. I'm almost at the threshold, my hand even rests on the doorframe.

They say that when your death is near, that your life flashes before your eyes. That never happened any of the other times I faced my end. All those golden childhood memories of my father and mother when they were young, now worn away with time; the sigh of the ocean as I walked barefoot on the beach, hand-in-hand with Eve, filled with an indescribable peace; the first time I worked a murder scene, and the victim was a twelve-year-old girl; hearing the rain titter and tatter on the roof of the old farm house; the smell of rich black soil, of flowers in bloom, and freshly cut grass; seeing my own blood stain my kevlar vest, curiously detached, as I felt my life drain away from two tiny bullet holes; the sting of loves lost and won, hearts broken and renewed, it was all there.

It wasn't much, but it was my life.

I step through into the other room.

And I'm crying. *Me*, of all people.

But she is there to kiss away the tears.

It's the end.

Curtains.

Fade to black.

I'm a sucker for "found footage" movies. This story is my attempt to do something like that in print. How much of a world can you build from just a transcript? What assumptions are made about the characters? How much will the reader read between the lines and fill in the gaps on their own?

Also, I'm fascinated by the trope of psychic manifestations in science fiction, particularly from the collective unconscious of a group of people. What if the sum total of our frustrations, fears, and sorrows were given form?

I AM RAGE

[Decryption of Recovered Text Sample 1-7743-A:]

Vanderhold: What I am looking at?

Messier: Combat footage from the 806th in the First Commonwealth, the Trambler Incident.

Vanderhold: Really, Manny? We're wasting time with this again? Do you have any idea…

Messier (interrupting): Just watch it, okay? We pulled this off one of the Totenkopf Lancers. Looks he was right on the front line when it happened. Poor bastard.

Vanderhold: Just look at it. It's an obvious fake.

Messier: That's just it, Jules; it's not. I ran the auth codes a dozen times. The footage is legit.

Vanderhold: Freeze it there. Back up a tad. *There.* Tell me, what do you see?

Messier: A guy ripping open a main battle tank with his bare hands. It looks impossible, I know, but…

<u>Vanderhold</u>: I don't care how high on our combat stimps you are, no one is strong enough to do that, okay? *No. One.* Maybe they used holography, or something. And there, do you see that tattered cloak? It's straight out of the old movie *Akira*, just with a hood. Reverse the feed. Yeah, okay, stop. Look, the incendiary shell the tank fired stops in mid-air, just like the movie. They didn't even bother to change it. Someone's mixing genres a bit, but it's an elaborate fake.

<u>Messier</u>: Well, *something* took out the 806th and demolished the Trambler building.

<u>Vanderhold</u>: Yeah, a bomb. A bogeyman didn't do that, so go find me the ones who did. Use whatever methods you need. You have my full authorization. Squeeze, Manny. *Squeeze.*

<u>Messier</u>: Look, I don't think it's that simple. Trambler is only a kilometer from PSION. Tell me you don't think there could be a connection. I mean, you've read the reports—we're making real progress—

<u>Vanderhold</u> (nervous laughter): You remember the part about that we don't talk about PSION in front of anyone? Ha-ha, yeah, I think you should go now. Go find out who did this. Really, go.

[End of Sample]

[Decryption of Recovered Text Sample 1-7743-B:]

<u>Messier</u>: Whoa, who's the new guy? Where's your usual stenographer?

<u>Vanderhold</u>: She went on leave unexpectedly, I'm afraid. Family business or something.

<u>Messier</u>: Jesus, Jules...really?

<u>Vanderhold</u>: Nature of the beast, I'm afraid. You have something for me?

<u>Messier</u>: You could say that. He's popped up in three more places. All outliers this time, but no survivors. Not one, at least among ours. Seems like he let some of our lab-rats go before he gave it the axe. Years of research out the airlock.

<u>Vanderhold</u>: The cockroaches are easy enough to replace. Check with our street dealers. They have plenty of stock on the hook. Researchers are a little harder, but on the whole, no big loss.

<u>Messier</u>: He left us a message this time. We have his voice.

<u>Vanderhold</u>: Play it.

<u>Unknown Voice</u>: *I...AM...RAAAAGE!*

<u>Messier</u>: I just about pissed my pants the first time I heard it.

<u>Vanderhold</u>: Grow a pair, okay? That's one of our military voders, just pumped up with a bit more bass.

They target the fear centers of the brain to reduce a cockroach's bowels to water, to be more pliant. Break up riots, that sort of thing. What? What's that look?

Messier: I thought that, too. What's more, I knew *you* would think that, too. I had it analyzed to uncover the voice beneath it.

Vanderhold: And?

Messier: We didn't find just one. We stopped counting around two million.

(Long Pause)

Vanderhold: Oh, that's not good.

Messier: Finally, you see the light.

Vanderhold: Get me a specialist for this. The entire network, Manny, you have your pick from anywhere. Make it happen.

Messier: I'm on it.

[End of Sample]

[Decryption of Recovered Text Sample 1-7743-C:]

Messier: They are calling him the Revenant now. We've seen poorer neighborhoods dressing up in a similar fashion and trashing company assets. He's approaching folk-hero status, you know.

Vanderhold: I trust they didn't prove quite as bulletproof as this fellow?

Messier: Er, no. We put down the entire dorm-ward, just to be sure.

<u>Vanderhold</u>: Good. Ah, it seems our honored guest is here. Come in, come in!

<u>Thorwald</u>: Major-General Heward Thorwald at your service, your Excellency. I must say, it's an honor to finally meet you in person. I've heard so much about the way you—

<u>Vanderhold</u>: Can we save the ass-kissing for another time, hmm? Tell me what you plan to do about our little problem.

<u>Thorwald</u>: Um yes, Excellency. Analysis has his next targets pretty much on lock. He's circling the perimeter. They think he's slowly working his way to the Nexus, here. We know where he's going to strike next, so I plan to collect the entire corps of Death's Head assault mechs to wait for him. There's no running from their matter-transducers once they lock on. Our friend will light up like a Christmas tree as he's burned from the inside out. We'll leave the staff in place, just so he doesn't show up to an empty building. Wouldn't want to spoil the game.

<u>Vanderhold</u>: I like it. Manny, check with HR, will you? If we have any problem children on the books, have them transferred to that building, just in case. Two birds, one stone, and all.

<u>Messier</u>: Sure, okay.

<u>Vanderhold</u>: When do you plan to spring the trap, then?

Thorwald: Two days. I can say without bravado that the next time he shows his face, we will absolutely murder his sorry ass...Your Excellency.

Vanderhold: I like it. Run with it.

[End of Sample]

[Transcription from Recovered Audio Sample 1-7743-C2:]

Messier: Well, the service was nice. I think he would have liked the flowers.

Vanderhold: I don't see how you could keep a straight face during all that.

Messier: What do you mean?

Vanderhold: He failed. He was barely a real person when he *had* a purpose. He proved himself no better than the cockroaches your men give the boot. His widow on the other hand...

Messier: Oh, please, not *that* again.

Vanderhold: Flesh is meant to serve, and then be discarded. Make the necessary arrangements.

Messier: Make them yourself—*gaah*. We still have a really big problem, if you haven't forgotten. And he's getting stronger. He doesn't use his hands anymore. Just *poof*. Men, vehicles, half a city block. *Gone*.

Vanderhold: I'm hearing a lot about the problem, but nothing about the solution. You just need to work *smarter*, Manny.

Messier: What the—? *My life is on the line here, too.* Don't you think I'm doing everything I can?!

<u>Vanderhold</u>: Clearly, you're not. Fine, if I have to do your job for you...what's his next target? Thorwald gave you that, at least?

<u>Messier</u>: A bank.

<u>Vanderhold</u>: Hmmm...ramp up the shields for containment and put a Mark-24 in the vault. Check with HR and find a button-pusher. Standard coercion contract. Am I being plain enough for you, *Mister* Messier? Maybe you should write this down.

<u>Messier</u>: No, I got it. Jesus, Jules.

[End of Sample]

[Transcribed from Recovered Audio Sample 1-7743-D:]

<u>Messier</u> (Comm Filter): Oh, god—he's here! All units, open fire! Artillery, bring the fire (gunfire, screaming, metal screeching). No, no, no...

<u>Vanderhold</u>: Listen to me, Manny. You *hold* that lobby, you hear me? I will recycle everyone you know and own. I'll make it *hurt*, do you—

<u>Messier</u> (Comm Filter): Die! Die! (gunfire) Why won't you *die*?! No, stay—stay away, I— (brief scream, static).

<u>Vanderhold</u>: Manny? Status report! Manny? Answer me.

<u>Unknown Voice</u> (Comm Filter): Hello, Jules. Pleasant day?

<u>Vanderhold</u>: Go to hell!

Unknown Voice (Comm Filter): I'll be up in a moment. Then, there will only be the two of us.

Vanderhold: Look, maybe we can cut...(interrupted by loud explosion). Aaaah! That elevator cost over three mil, asshole!

Unknown Voice: That's the least of your worries now.

Vanderhold: Wait, how are you doing this? That's impossible! I...I...(bones breaking, faint whimpers) What...what are you?

Unknown Voice: I am the testament to all your sins. I am the voice of all your victims. I am all of those who cried out, not in vengeance, but in rage as the jaws of the manifold trap closed around them. Look upon me, now, Jules. *LOOK. AT. ME.*

Vanderhold: You don't have a face. Oh, god...

Unknown Voice: You didn't give them a face, so I have none.

Vanderhold: If you're gonna kill me, get on with it. I *hate* heroic monologues.

Unknown Voice: *Regina, forgive me. Regina, forgive me. I love you.* Those were his last thoughts as he cried over the detonator. Did you know his name?

Vanderhold: What?

Unknown Voice: So many names. So many final thoughts, at your hand, or others like you. And now there is only you and I. Shall I make introductions?

<u>Vanderhold</u>: No, get your hands off of me!
<u>Unknown Voice</u> (whispers): *I am rage.*
(Prolonged screaming.)
[End of Sample]

One thing right up front—this story is not about any one conflict. Draw any parallels you like to real world events, but this story wasn't written about any of them.

There are two things at play here, even in this small a space. First, is it better for people to lose their identities and still be alive, or should free will reign, even if it will only further compound generations of bloodshed? Which is the better alternative?

Second, does any one group truly have the authority to pass judgment on another, en masse*?*

The Burden of Memory

"M r. President?" General Kline prompted.

The Planetary President of Argos turned from the window, where he had been surveying the neat, manicured lawn of the Capitol Mansion. So clean and tidy, beautiful even, but a distraction from the situation at hand.

"There can be no peaceful resolution, then?" the President asked, settling behind his enormous glass desk. His question had been to the General, but his Secretary of Foreign Affairs answered instead.

"The talks at Bamut have broken down entirely," she said. "The Umishi and Learan ambassadors stormed out, both spewing an impressive string of curses, insults, and casting aspersions on the character of each other's mothers. And within the hour—"

"Both sides mobilized their forces," General Kline interrupted. "Full ground armor, air support, and sea units on both sides of the disputed isthmus." She shifted in her seat, straightening. "No nukes or biologicals that we can detect as yet, but everything else they can field, including a call for reservists."

The President accepted this. The weight of it pressed down on his shoulders and the back of his neck. Both of his hands down to the fingers tingled with pins and needles.

"We've been down this road before, though. Any chance they're just rattling the saber? Trying to loosen sanctions, or counting coup?" The President scanned his cabinet, but their expressions told him the tale. He settled on his Vice President, who regarded him with grim resolve.

"Not this time, Mr. President," the VP answered. "Both sides will be out for blood. The Magenta Papers have seen to that. The Learan will not accept such a monumental insult to the Great Founder, and the Umishi must match their intensity in order to survive."

The President nodded. His VP had grown up in the war-torn districts of the disputed zone, though he had abandoned much of their ways since his childhood. The VP had proven invaluable in navigating the cycles of rising tensions, gamesmanship, and détente in the conflict zone.

"Expected casualties?" The President queried.

"Simulations project twenty-thousand or more within the first twenty-seven hours. The numbers taper off slightly as the initial airstrikes subside, but climb again rapidly as ground armor comes into play. Given a month of sustained hostilities, we're looking at half a million dead or wounded, divided between both factions."

"And our ability to intervene with our own forces?"

The General smiled thinly, "As I am sure Foreign Affairs will advise you, it is an election year. Boots on the ground will cost the Party greatly come this Gamelion.

However, we have two divisions of conventional units that could force a peace."

"But not maintain it," the VP said.

The President let the comment pass. "And what about unconventional forces, General? I refuse to believe that the only options here are complete inaction or forceful intervention. We need a third option, people."

General Kline looked up at him. "There is Lethe-17, Mr. President. Efficacy trials have succeeded far beyond anything we could have hoped, and our current stockpile is more than enough to affect so small an area, globally speaking. I can have it loaded into ICBMs and ready for deployment inside eighteen hours."

The Secretary tensed and crossed her arms. "Wait, are we really considering this a viable option? Once they are infected, the effect is permanent."

"That's rather the point," the Vice President said. "And it may be the only way that peace may ever reign in the region."

"Thank you, everyone," the President said, dismissing them. "Kieran, a moment, please," he added as the VP stood up. Everyone else filed out, and it was just the two of them.

"Do we really have the right to take that from them? Their memories, their personalities, the total extinction of both cultures? Sure, they'll still be living and breathing, but will it really be them in the end?"

The VP took off his glasses, holding them up to the light, squinting. "When the Learan Officiam took my father, I couldn't understand why. It was his own government, and he was a patriot. They killed and imprisoned not only the Umishi, but those who didn't profess enough fervor for our Great Founder. Only when I went to University did I see the truth of the matter: the war will never end of its own accord. It's an unverifiable land grant from a long-dead Emperor versus an unsubstantiated birthright from a rogue state. While that serves to frame the conflict, the real problem is not what happened six hundred years ago, but the blood that is spilled today, which perpetuates the violence further into the future. The cycle must be broken."

"But is this the answer? A tabula rasa?"

The VP put his glasses back on. "What can one do for two peoples so burdened by their own memories, except relieve them of them? Perhaps with guidance they can rebuild without the endless personal vendettas that will keep the flames burning forever."

He was right, and the President knew it. He had always believed that those who could intervene had the moral imperative to do so, but that idea had suffered horribly during the years of his administration. He had given in one too many times, made one too many compromises. Perhaps this was his chance to make his mark, to end the deadliest and most prolonged conflict in Argosian history. Even if it cost him the next election, he could make sure no more children grew up fearing for their lives and safety.

The President pressed a button on his desk. "General?"

Kline answered from her collar comm. "Mr. President?"

"Move forward with Lethe-17. Use it all, and don't make any more."

"Yes, sir!" Kline said and the President cut the connection.

"You won't have to push the button alone," the VP said. "We'll usher in this new age of peace together."

▲ ▲ ▲

Twenty-two hours later, the President finished his breakfast, kissed both of his children, as well as his darling wife, and went down to the White Room. He had doubled the Mansion's guard on the perimeter the night before, and tripled it at all the entrances.

His first clue that something was wrong was the absence of guards at the door to his office. The second was when the barrel of a gauss pistol jabbed into the back of his spine as he turned to leave.

"Move," the voice behind him said, prompting him into the office. "Security has been disabled, as well as surveillance. Take a seat."

The President took a guest seat before his own desk. Odd, to see it now from this angle.

"What are you doing, Kieran?" the President demanded, starting to stand, but the pistol trained at his head persuaded him not to follow through.

"Answer me, dammit!"

The VP came around the President's desk to the special console Kline had installed for the launch. He sat down in the President's massive oak and leather chair, but the weapon never wavered.

"Don't worry, my friend. I do not intend to stop the launch, only…alter it slightly." His free hand danced across the console. "Ah, excellent. The good General did install my biometrics in case you let me do the honors."

The President saw the changes in targeting parameters, and his heart went into his throat.

"You're going to detonate them in the upper troposphere!"

"Indeed. And once it settles into the jet stream, we shall all have our taste of Lethe-17. The chemical agent is pervasive. The Learan, Umishi, you, me, and all of Argos will know the peace of forgetfulness."

"You're insane," the President said, face flushed a bright red. "Why? Tell me, *why*?!"

The VP smiled, but there was no mirth to it. "Now it feels real to you, doesn't it? It's one thing to promulgate your authority and agenda upon others from afar, but quite another to be on the receiving end of it, eh?"

The VP finished his changes and pressed the launch button without hesitation.

"But to answer your question, it's because this administration doesn't get to pick and choose which cultures endure and which ones are snuffed out. We are all sons and daughters of Argos, all part of this one island in space, Mr. President. We stand or fall together."

"You bastard! You…you—" The President choked on his words.

"Awww now, don't be cross with me, Adrian," the VP said. "Pretty soon you won't remember why I'm holding this gun on you, just as I won't recall the necessity that drove me to it. We shall all be reset in moments, Mr. President."

The VP smiled, and this time it shone like never before.

"Who knows, perhaps you and I will be friends."

I first came across the term "Lookback Time" in college, in one of my astronomy classes. I never looked at the night sky in the same way again. There's just something serene about being able to look into the far-distant past with so little effort.

This one's also about heroes. When someone demonstrates uncommon valor on a grand stage, what happens to them after the fact? What expectations do we place upon them, either fairly or unfairly?

Now some could argue that this entry is not a story at all. There is a conflict of sorts, but not one that requires a hard, decisive resolution. In that sense, it's more an extra-long pensée, *or a thought expressed in literary form.*

This is a moment in an old man's life, a reflection of what has happened between the time he saw a supernova as younger man, and how his life has changed when the light from that star catches up with him decades later.

Looking Back

The night sky is never what it seems. An observer might chance to look up at the glittering starscape and behold faraway suns, nebulae, and galaxies, all spread out among the heavens like gemstones spilled upon black velvet, all sublime, breathtaking, humbling, and absolutely deceitful.

In the untold eons it might take for light from those distant glimmers to reach our eyes, billions of them could have burned out, fused together, or ceased to exist entirely. You never see what is in that dark veil, only what was. In essence, to look at the night sky is to look back in time. The farther the light of a distant star, the farther back in time you can see.

Those of us who study the heavens call this phenomenon "lookback time."

- Dr. Yeva Talbot, host of *Kosmos: An Ascendant Journey*

The thought of traveling starlight, even now reaching out towards him from the past, occupied the mind of Sigurd Ulf-Halvarsen, on this night of all nights in his life.

The crowd had assembled around him on the lawn of the Heimdall Observatory, but the far-seeing lens would not be necessary. The sky had obliged for the occasion, rolling back the cloudy curtains to allow the spectacle to unfold before the eyes of the twenty thousand observers there, and hundreds of thousands more elsewhere who were staring into the sky tonight.

Those who clustered around Sigurd were almost entirely the children of survivors from the Midgard Exodus. There were few, so very few, who remained alive from that time, few who remembered the hellish voyage, the cramped quarters, the life-support pushed to the raw, bleeding edges of its capacity to escape the violent death of Midgard's primary.

Sigurd closed his eyes, letting his mind drift back to that time, now fifty-two years past, memories as clear and vivid as the day they were made. He had worn the uniform of a Captain of the Aesthir Navy in those days, ably commanding the cruiser, *Valkyrie* in the name of his Jarl.

He felt a small hand tug at his tunic. A girl of six stood there with a look of bottled up anticipation.

"Granpapa, Granpapa!" she said with excitement she could barely contain.

"Yes, child?"

"It's almost time! Can I stand by you when the sky blooms? Can I, *please?*"

Sigurd took her small hand in his, now gnarled and weathered with age, though still strong despite. "Of course, Tallia. I would have it no other way." He gave her a wink and her face lit up with a smile that was missing her two front teeth.

"I love you, Granpapa! Everyone here loves you! They all say so! You're their hero! You're *my* hero!"

She gave him a hug, then plopped down beside his chair. No wind, earthquake, or act of gods or men would tear her from his side.

Not tonight.

Tonight, the light from Midgard's exploding sun would complete its inexorable, fifty-two year journey to reach them on Valhalla Prime. Tonight, Sigurd would be touched again by the same rays of light that he had felt in those desperate hours of his younger days.

He breathed in the fresh night air that seemed at once gentle and palpable as it played across his face and the back of his neck. The event was fast approaching.

By most measures, Sigurd had lived a long, normal life. He had come from humble beginnings from among the Miners of Ivald, lived and loved and, in time, had become the great-grandfather of Tallia, whom he never passed up a chance to spoil rotten. She had her Grandpapa tightly wrapped around her little finger, but Sigurd did not mind. He would not live to see her grow into adulthood, but that was simply the way of things.

Practically all aspects of his upbringing had been ordinary, a pattern played out a hundred million times in the lives of other men the universe over, save one. One day, more than half a century ago, Sigurd Ulf-Halvarsen had saved the entire population of a planet.

On patrol in the Midgard system aboard *Valkyrie*, he had picked up the signs that the sun that warmed the planet was on the verge of going supernova. Why the star's imminent death had escaped the notice of the colonists on the planet was still a subject of speculation, and Sigurd had heard any number of theories through the intervening years.

On his own initiative, then-Captain Halvarsen had commandeered three superlarge ore tankers belonging to the Gjaller Combine, and ordered them to dump their holds of precious odinium ore, a cargo worth trillions.

In seventeen hours he performed a miracle as he evacuated all seventy thousand colonists with only four ships. Perhaps for the rest of his life before and after that event he was normal, but for seventeen hours, he was a god.

After the Exodus, he had left the Navy and taken a job at a promising food production company based on Valhalla Prime. He had married his sweetheart, Vivienne, and, together, they had brought two wonderful sons into the world. It seemed as though Sigurd's story was close to the proverbial 'happy ending' myth that the media continued to push upon people.

Life, however, was not that simple.

The Gjaller Combine had done their best to destroy him financially for the losses he had caused them. Every few years lawyers would come sniffing around his door, looking for ways, ranging from ingenious to devious, to recoup some part of the damages. Advocacy groups and private donations had kept him afloat during those turbulent times. The government had probably kept the Combine from completely bankrupting him, but they hadn't attempted to help him in any other way. Even his veteran's benefits were a hassle to get, no matter what role he had once played, however briefly, upon the universe's stage.

When his oldest son, Rolf, was of age, he joined the Navy, looking to distinguish himself and escape from the shadow of his father. Sigurd had protested the decision. Space and warships were a dangerous business, he'd said, many who joined never came back. Ignoring the pleading of his parents, Rolf joined the Naval Academy. Great things were expected of him, and, in time, Rolf had proven himself to be a talented and dutiful young officer. That is, right up until the time when his shuttle crashed into a mountain on his way to a new assignment.

The family was devastated. There were times when Vivienne couldn't stop crying, and others when she seemed detached and distant, running at times hot or cold. His younger son, Lars, had taken the loss of his big brother particularly hard, being only sixteen at the time of the tragedy. The natural target of his anger was, of course, his father, without whom Rolf might still be alive. Rolf's death set in motion a series of barricades that Lars would construct around his heart until he became all but estranged from his parents, calling seldom and writing infrequently.

Years passed, and with it, some wounds were healed. Silver hairs began to creep into Sigurd's once reddish-blonde beard. Lars became a father in his own right, visiting more often, letting his children know their grandfather, but remaining aloof during those times, speaking little and saying nothing.

Vivienne died some years later, leaving another hole in his heart. But, he had consoled himself with the thought that their love, for all its occasional ups and downs, had been real and enduring. It still glowed bright and true in his heart even these many years later. The greatest part of him, it seemed, had passed beyond the veil. He carried on, buoyed by the smile of his great-granddaughter.

Still, his past meant little as life doled out its slings and arrows. His one great deed was slowly being forgotten as new generations could only read about it in a chapter in their history class. There were times when he wondered if the Exodus was remembered at all. Had the event that decided tens of thousands of lives been so obscured by time in just five short decades?

Then there were the handshakes and the polite confusion to remind him that it hadn't. While it was always flattering, there was always *that look* that followed. Sigurd never exactly knew what they were expecting, perhaps they thought he would be taller, not as old, a titan, a man-god who had chosen to live among mere mortals. When they found just a man returning their handshake, it was something of a paradox for them to resolve, the deed and the man.

They wanted him to be more, never knowing that he had been swept away in events beyond his control and managed to rise to the occasion. That seventeen-hour snapshot of his life had not made him smarter, wiser, or greater than any other person, but somehow everyone naturally assumed that it had.

Sigurd looked up towards a corner of the sky where Midgard burned bright and clear. The strongest observatories, including Heimdall, could still see Midgard just as it had been before its sudden end. All you had to do was look up to look back.

The assembled multitude stirred as the event drew nigh. Beside him, Tallia glowed as she spied a figure walking up behind Sigurd's chair. Looking up, he found the face of a man looking at him through Vivienne's clear blue eyes.

"Father," the man said.

"Lars? I didn't think you'd come."

"I suppose that was the greatest incentive of all." Lars sat down next to his father. "Am I unwelcome?"

"No, of course not. You never were."

Lars was on the verge of saying something, but was searching for a way to begin. Sigurd could see him start and stop, unsure and emotionally naked as he had been so long ago. The old man gently rested a hand on his son's shoulder. Fortified by the strength he found there, Lars found his voice.

"I've been thinking about the past lately," he said. "You might say that I've seen things in a new light." He cast his eyes to sky.

"What's on your mind? Please, tell me."

The barriers threatened to return, to end his course before it began, but Lars pressed onward.

"All those years ago, when I used to hear people talk about what you did, it wasn't concrete enough, it wasn't real. Tonight is when we'll see the proof that it was."

He dropped his head.

"I know I've spent more years than I care to count blaming you for Rolf, however unfair that might have been. The pain became a habit, and habits, once formed, are hard to give up. It became familiar, an anchor. I would sneer when people would call you a hero. Heroes were meant to be larger than life, and you," he looked Sigurd in the eye, "were just my father."

Sigurd felt the old pain surfacing, scarred wounds attempting to reopen. Lars continued.

"But, I realize now that I've been living in the past. It's taken me this long to understand something that people who've never met you know the world over." He placed his hand on his father's.

"You *did* save those people, thousands are alive who wouldn't have been otherwise, and that makes you a hero, father, as surely as the stars shine in the heavens. For that, I just wanted to tell you tonight, of all nights, that I love you, and that I'm...proud to be your son."

Tears rolled down Sigurd's face, gathering in wet streaks along his beard.

He swept his son into a hug, feeling Lars's cheek resting against his shoulder as he had done as a child. There was no greater gift for a father than to be able to put his arms around his child and feel them return the embrace. His son's eyes were pressed together as the warm beads escaped and streamed ever downward.

A light sprang up in their midst, seeming almost like the blossom of fireworks only one that did not fade away. Tallia tugged at Sigurd's shirt again.

"Grandpapa! It's starting!" the little girl beamed.

Sigurd looked up to see that a corner of the sky was blazing in a starburst of brilliant white. A collective gasp went through the crowd, followed by roaring cheers that seemed to roll like continuous thunder.

"Can you ever forgive me, father?" Lars asked, his eyes pleading. "There's so much that I wa—"

"Sh-h-h-h-h-h," Sigurd said softly. There were so many things he had lost since last the light of Midgard had touched him, but looking at Tallia, and now at Lars, his heart soared at what he had gained. No matter how well the past might be preserved in memory or starlight, it was the present that had always been of the greatest importance. Sigurd cast his eyes skyward, his world now put to rights.

He squeezed his son's hand, and felt Lars return the gesture with love.

"Don't look back, son," Sigurd said. "Don't look back."

There's really no two ways about it: This story came about as a way to cope with my grand-mother's death. About three years after she passed, the grief and loss hit me again, and hard. You never quite get over the loss of a loved one; you just learn to live with it. Well, out of the blue, I was emotionally reset to the time when it happened. No surprises, it was just as hard as the first go round.

I wrote this as a way of getting it off my chest, about losing something incredibly precious and close to you, while powerless to stop it. I rarely write anything resembling urban fantasy, but this was the form it took when I put my hands to the keyboard.

And the Song Goes On

The angel in my arms was dying, and all I could do was watch. She may not have had wings or a golden halo around her head, but that was the only word that could even hope to describe her. I grasped her hand, intertwining our fingers as we huddled near the towering mausoleum.

Her grip was weak. It shouldn't have been; I'd seen those hands rip concrete and steel and supernatural flesh apart with equal ease. Now, that strength was fading—just one more thing that victory had cost her. Too soon, it would be more. I could hear that ethereal song that radiated from her growing quieter and more distant.

Even at that moment, with the inevitability of events playing out before my eyes, my mind could not accept what was happening. Here was a being of light, immortal and imperishable, who should have never counted her tomorrows, dying because of us. And by us, I mean humans, Earth. She had saved it, but at so great a cost that I wondered if the lives of every human past, present, and future were worth her life alone. I still ask myself that, and perhaps I always will.

She struggled to speak. I brushed back strands of silver-gold hair from her forehead, slick with rain and demon blood.

"I'm afraid of it," she whispered to me. "Dying. H-how do you live with it, hanging over you all your life? "

"I don't know, we just do," I answered. *Brilliant.* For once, she sought wisdom from me and that's the best I could do. What did I know? I was just a gawky kid who—manfully, I might add—played the harp really well.

"I didn't think I could do it," she continued. "When the time came, I wasn't sure if I would have the strength, knowing—" She didn't have to finish the sentence.

"But you did. It's done. You saved us all, every soul," I said, and my jaw quivered as I spoke. "That was you, all you."

Her face contorted, but then the look of pain passed like an ocean wave. Her luminous blue eyes regarded me steadily.

"Because you gave me the courage."

At that I was undone. I was the only witness to the passing of something pure and ineffable, something death was never meant to claim, and she was thanking me? Generations of humanity should have lined up, single file, to thank *her* for what she had done that night. But I now lived in a universe of impossibilities, one where the deathless died, and an insignificant race upon one planet, around one sun, in one galaxy, would survive.

Through the haze, I felt her hand tighten with some of her old strength.

"The song continues in you, Liam," she said. "You must share it. Promise me that you will."

"I promise."

What else could I say but that?

I felt a tremor go through her body, and I knew it was time. My breath froze in my lungs and didn't want to come out again. I was scared as hell. She may have taken the form of a woman, but I could never have had a better father-figure than her.

"Liam," she said, so softly I could barely hear it. Her eyes closed. "Liam…"

Her song reached a final crescendo, and then she was gone.

A being of immeasurable grace and light, and her last words were my name. Yeah, that stays with you.

I'd like to say that this was the end of my tale, that it ended with me crying in the rain. It would have been, except for what happened next.

A man appeared next to one of the funeral monuments that was in the shape of, you guessed it, an angel. He was tall and dark-haired. That was about all I could make out. His face was lost in shadow. It suddenly felt like I was standing next to a high-tension wire. I could *feel* the power contained within him, radiating out like an invisible sun.

"Such a thing has not happened since the forging of the stars," the stranger said. "Stand aside, mortal." He took a step towards us. I eased Varathiel to the ground, and drew her sword from the muddy puddle where it had fallen. To my eyes it looked like a silver katana with angelic etchings down the blade. The symbols leapt to life with a cold blue luminance. It felt perfect and nearly weightless in my hand.

"*Don't you touch her!*" I snarled at the godlike being in front of me. I'm pretty sure there was a snot bubble coming out of my nose. I couldn't have looked less intimidating if I had tried. Still, I was between him and her, and I was not moving.

The man looked at me, at least I'm pretty sure that's what he was doing.

"Release her," he said with a voice like contained thunder. "Your will holds her vessel to this place, to this moment."

I knew I was dead. If the being in front of me wished it, all the combat training in the world wouldn't change anything. At the same time it didn't matter.

"Get off my Earth," I said, raising the sword into the most pathetic high guard ever. "Now."

"I wish only to take her home."

"She *is* home. She gave her life for it when the rest of you shining *asshats* abandoned her."

He took another step.

"Not one more, or—"

"—or what?" he finished for me.

"We'll find out."

To my surprise, he stopped. He was so still he might have been a statue.

"Very well," he said. "It is decided."

"Yeah," I said in sheer defiance, perhaps too quickly. "Um, what is?"

"She chose you to inherit her song, a gift never before bestowed upon a mortal."

The runes on the blade blazed to life, like each one had a spotlight burning behind it. Then I heard the song return, *her* song. No, that wasn't right—there was something new to added it. My mind expanded. New vistas and possibilities opened before my eyes. The stars burned in the sky like living things, the wind brought its own song to my ears. I could hear the dead dreaming as they slept in their coffins. I lifted my sight to the man and saw a white-gold column of flames standing in his place.

And the sword, I knew it was mine, as surely as if I'd practiced with it every day of my life.

"It is done," he said, his voice now filled with new dimensions. "The song burns eternal."

He turned to go.

"Wait." I called after him, but not with words. "What do I do now?"

The raging pillar of crackling cosmic flames paused.

"Become worthy of it," it said, and then was gone.

And that's how I came to be the guardian of the Earth. It wasn't because I was worthy of the gift she imparted to me that night, or that I ever will be, but because the song goes on.

Now it lives in me.

I had a college anthropology professor say something in class that really stuck with me:

"Sure, the Greeks built temples to the gods of their pantheon, worshipping them and making earnest sacrifices, but the collective stories fulfilled another purpose. They were, in many ways, like comic books are today. Most people didn't travel, but they craved stories of adventure, heroism, and faraway lands, just as we do. Herakles (Hercules) has more in common with Superman than you might think."

This started the wheels turning in my head. What if characters we know to be fictional nowadays are taken as real in the future, perhaps even venerated or deified? What might be the result? How would those adherents to the faith resolve the inherent contradictions of so miraculous a pantheon?

That Lynda Carter happens to be my first TV crush is, um, entirely incidental.

The Mundanity
of Miracles

"What troubles you, Sister?" the new Reverend Mother asked as Sister Diana prayed. "I see a look of confusion on your face, or one might even say one of—"

"Doubt," Diana finished for her. The younger Sister stood up from lighting the incense before the triple icons of the Lady of Stars. "Yes, that is true. I am in crisis."

"Please," the Reverend Mother prompted. "What is on your heart?"

Diana wished that her Order had the puffy bell sleeves to hide her hands, but those of her path wore a *chiton* from Terra Prime's ancient past. Still, she crossed her bare, muscular arms beneath her breasts in thought.

"I was brought up Solarian," she began, "and I continue to celebrate the birth of stars and mourn them at their collapse or supernova. I have my double doctorate in astronomy and astrophysics, but my mother gave me one of the seven secret names of the Carter. There was no way I would not choose her as my guiding patron."

"And she is a strong one," the Reverend Mother said, pointing at the three statues, depicting the Carter's three aspects: Oracle, Executive, and Warrior. "I would have chosen her for my own patron if Lady Zorel had not called me first."

Sister Diana nodded, "And the two were sisters-in-arms, and fought side by side in many battles, but you see that is part of my quandary, Reverend Mother. While it is known that Lady Zorel was a celestial visitor to Terra Prime, the Carter was a native and a mortal. Yet, how can I possibly resolve all the things the Carter supposedly did in a single life-span, which at the time was no more than a century?"

"Ah," the Reverend Mother said, "And you cannot help but wonder if some of the stories of her heroism and bravery have been exaggerated over the millennia of retelling."

"It runs deeper than that, Mother," Diana said, dropping her head. "It states clearly in Themyscira 17:26 that the Carter chose an *invisible* jet as her personal conveyance when we know that Terrans did not have such technology until much later. In Amazons 6:14, it says that the Carter 'was so hot that she melted the polar ice caps.'" Diana looked up to meet the Reverend Mother's gaze, almost pleading. "How can that be possible? Her body temperature would need to be thousands of times that of normal, and we have no clear record of the ice caps melting all at once like that."

Diana sighed heavily. "I'm having difficulty taking passages like that in the *Book of Wonders* as literal truth." In some circles, her words would have been blasphemy, but here in the Imperial capital she was allowed free discourse without recrimination.

The Reverend Mother laughed, which made her long red cape billow behind her.

"Then don't, my child," the older woman said. "The miraculous parts of the Carter's legacy are truly the most mundane, and the least useful to us. Many have tried to lift commuter transports with their bare hands or deflect projectiles using golden bracelets, but to my knowledge they have all failed. If she could do such things, we are unable to emulate them, so why try? What is more important is the example she has given you. Tell me, child, what has the Carter taught you about life?"

Diana's face reddened at the cheekbones. Such a basic question, but infinitely complex! She gestured to the three icons on the altar, each in its turn. The first statue was dressed exactly as Diana, flowing dark hair in a classical updo.

"The Oracle teaches me to be wise, thoughtful, and forgiving of others' faults," Diana said. "She counsels me to be calm in the face of ignorance, and to leave the universe a better place than I found it. The Warrior teaches me that I should be strong, physically and spiritually, and that the defenseless should be protected. 'Justice will come,' she says, 'as long the righteous hold to their convictions.'"

The Warrior, always the middle icon of the trio, wore a curious outfit consisting of a golden tiara, red knee boots, and blue hip shorts emblazoned with stars, from which she took her epithet.

"The Executive," she pointed to the aspect dressed in a skirt and jacket with black rim glasses and a stylish pony-tail, "teaches me to be kind, competent, and savvy in all arenas. She assures me that I can be both beautiful and intelligent, while diminishing neither."

"An answer almost verbatim from the *Book of Wonders*," the Reverend Mother said. "But let us delve deeper. Let us say for the sake of argument that one aspect of her story, say her truth-compelling lasso were absent from her narrative. Would that change the example she has set before you?"

Diana tilted her head to the side in thought, "No Reverend Mother, it would not."

"Quite right, and neither would it have mattered to the trillions of young women who have honored her as a patron in the seven millennia since her life. The Carter would have still shown them how to be women of power and importance, beautiful and fearless, regardless of if she could stop a bullet cold, or if she fought next to the Bat-Knight as it is said she did with Lady Zorel."

"And what of the Glim-zah?" Diana replied. "They worship the Bat-Knight as though he were one of their own race which found its way to Terra Prime. They flatly deny that their Winged Lord ever associated with My Lady or yours, despite the multitude of textual evidence that he did."

"And they are free to do so," the Reverend Mother countered, "as long as they harm no one in that belief." The older woman put her fists on her hips, splaying out her elbows on either side, which gave her a dramatic air. "Only if they decide to hurt themselves or others to prove it should the belief be reexamined. The Synod were Solarians as well, but their literal interpretation of the *Book of Suns*, compelled them to appease every violent solar flare by shooting people into stars as a blood sacrifice. And we know now that this came of a mistranslation between ancient Portuguese and Standard Imperial Russian."

Sister Diana's face became troubled, and the Reverend Mother laid a hand on her shoulder in comfort.

"Look, we cannot know for certain what went on back then on our home world, or know who interacted with whom, and to what extent. It was too long ago, and the records from that era are sloppy, incomplete, and inconsistent."

"And yet we model our lives off of truths taken from that dark and backwards age," Sister Diana said. "Are we fools to do so?"

"That is for each one of us to decide for ourselves," the Reverend Mother said, then shrugged. "Strip away the divine, the ineffable, and the impossible from our two patrons, and they are still worthy of consideration. They are role-models beyond compare, noble examples that we might aspire to, and I don't believe the presence or absence of either freezing breath or purple healing rays makes one iota of difference when the scales are balanced."

The Reverend Mother looked upon the young sister's distress with tenderness, just as maternally as her title implied.

"We must all resolve the world around us to the world we wish it to be," the Reverend Mother told her. "That is how the Solarian faith came about in the first place, and how I believe our patrons would want us to approach them, not out of ignorance or fear, but out of enlightenment. If you can do that in the Carter's service, then you need not fear an infinite number of crises like this one."

The younger Sister nodded, eyes fixed upon the Oracle, Executive, and Warrior.

"Thank you, Reverend Mother. I will ponder your words."

The older Sister nodded and swept from the room, a wave of crimson billowing behind her. Sister Diana knelt again before the icons, and prayed silently.

Oh, Lady of the Stars, who could make a hawk a dove, and stop a war with love, who makes liars tell the truth, I must humbly admit that I cannot bring myself to believe in everything taught about you. Yet you have filled me with such purpose and inspiration as I cannot describe. Whether you are real, and hearing these words now, or if you never existed and I am merely talking to myself, you have forever changed my life for the better, and I am thankful. All my hopes are pinned on you.

May wonders never cease.

The Not-So-Short Stuff

Lilly Sun, perhaps the most powerful character I've ever created, sprang out of the many conversations I had with my uncle. When we would visit, we would sit in worn armchairs and spend hours summarizing the books we had read recently. There we would make recommendations on whether the other one should read those titles. These conversations often ended with a trip to the bookstore.

Swan Song *is one of my earlier pieces, and one that breaks a lot of rules about short science fiction. I remember reading on one publisher's submission guides something to the effect of: "No stories where kids find something in a field. We're not kidding, ANYTHING." Also, no one-sided or uncomplicated victories, or fairy tales masquerading as science fiction.*

Ahem.

I've included it here as I think it holds its own with the other entries in this collection, even if it doesn't quite fit the regular mold of science fiction.

Swan Song

The suns had not quite reached their zenith over the verdant mountains when Nualla and her brother found the strange creature behind the barn. It sprawled out behind the barrels of sweetroot extract, looking to the child's eyes like one of her dolls that had been tossed aside.

Though their first reaction had been caution, it had quickly given way to an intense, burning curiosity. The two of them peered around the metal bands to gaze upon the stranger who was either asleep, unconscious or...

"Do you think it's dead?" Tamul asked in hushed tones.

"I don't know," Nualla said, looking the stranger up and down, noticing the slight rise and fall of its main body. "I think it's still breathing."

"It's so *strange*."

That, at least, was true. Whatever was laid out behind the barn looked like the two of them in a general sense. Though it was wrapped from head to toe in a strange kind of material, it seemed to have a head, two arms, and two legs. Its colors were strange, too. Whatever it was, it wasn't from around here. And yet, there seemed something familiar about it that both children couldn't quite wrap their minds around.

"I bet it's a Vulghrun raider," Tamul whispered with a gleam in his eye. "It's here to eat your eyes and make furniture out of your bones!"

"Stop it," Nualla replied, repelling her brother's attempt to scare her. "I think we should bring it inside and help it. It could be hurt."

The two of them moved from their cover and came closer to where the creature lay. After Nualla averted her brother's attempt to poke it with a stick, they quickly realized that, whatever it was, it was heavier than the two of them could manage. Hitching up old Sseohl, and looping a rope around the stranger's shoulders, the two were able to hoist it into the house and roll it over onto a cot. It was too long to fit on one of their beds, but seemed to fit perfectly onto their father's bed.

They found that the strange covering all over its body was a kind of cloth with an inside lining that loosely resembled fur. The fasteners were odd, but Nualla found a way to separate them one by one.

While her brother stoked the fire to a pleasing warmth, Nualla removed the gloves and face covering from their unexpected guest and wondered at what she found. The stranger had one extra finger on each hand. Hair the color of virgin snow flowed from a central part on the stranger's head and fell in silken waves down to just past the shoulders.

The face was different as well, but, in Nualla's opinion, pleasant to look upon. The nose seemed abnormally pointed and the eyes a little too close together, but there was an unstated symmetry there, a sort of odd beauty that both children could feel as much as they could see.

"What will Father think when he sees it?" Tamul asked.

"When he sees *her*," Nualla said, realizing only then that the stranger was female.

That was when the stranger took in a deep breath and her arm twitched as though reaching for something or someone. This was enough to send the twosome scurrying for cover where they could watch the stranger as they had before.

The stranger's eyes fluttered open, revealing gray irises that seemed too small. Then she sat up and took in the obviously unfamiliar room. There seemed to be no confusion, however. She looked right at where the two of them were hiding.

"You can come out," the stranger said in a musical voice. "I won't hurt you."

Reluctantly, the two eased out from their hiding place. The stranger smiled, revealing a set of long teeth. The white lengths seemed almost predatory. Seeing this, the brother and sister held on to one another, giving a collective shudder.

"You are not going to eat us?" Tamul stammered.

"No," the stranger said with a peal of laughter. "Could you kindly tell me who you are, and where I am?"

"My name is Nualla. This is my brother Tamul," the girl said. "You are on our farm near Ysalom. Who are you?"

The stranger listened, but did not seem to recognize the name of the nearby village. She tilted her head, regarding them with thought.

"My name's Lilly," the stranger said, as if trying to remember it herself.

"What *are* you?" the boy blurted out.

"Tamul!" Nualla chided her brother's lack of manners.

"It's alright," Lilly said with a voice like a relaxing stream. "My race is—*was* —called Humans."

"I haven't heard of them before," Nualla replied, turning the unfamiliar word over in her mind and mouth. *Hewmahns. Hew-mahns.* It sounded like the name of a bird or flower to her ears.

"I know you haven't," the visitor said. "They've been extinct for a very long time. Extinct, that is, except for me."

▲ ▲ ▲

When Nualla's father, Relan, returned home from the market at Ysalom, he found his children talking to a being of a race he did not recognize. One look from the stranger's eyes, however, told him that whatever presence had come to visit bore no ill will to him or his children.

"Father, this is Lilly. She's a *Hew-mahn*," his little girl said with the sly smile of a child that knows something an adult doesn't.

Relan gave his guest the customary greeting of cupping his hands together in front of him and bowing his head. Lilly mirrored the gesture, with the flourish upon parting her hands that indicated a grateful guest. Relan glanced at the children over his shoulder.

"Don't the two of you have chores to do?"

"Yes, father," the two of them chorused in unison, and then went outside.

"Your children are very kind. They took me in without question." Lilly said, looking at the place where they had been standing. "That's rare."

"They have a good core sight." Relan sat down to face the visitor. "Though I cannot claim credit for it. They take after their mother in that way." Mentally, he took a step back and looked her over. "You are from another world, yes?"

"That is a good way to put it."

"It is rare that any of the far-worlders that visit us come out this way." Relan shrugged. "There's not much out this way but farms and farmers. What brings you to my humble home?"

"I'm not sure," Lilly said. "I've been on the planet a long time, I know that much, but I have a condition. Sometimes I am...not myself." There was a dark twist to her smile at these words, as if to some private joke.

"Should I alert your ship? I'm sure they'll want to know you are in good health."

"I don't have a ship," the visitor said. "I'm here alone."

"Well, you may stay the night and regain your strength if you wish. We don't have much to offer, but we'll gladly share all that is ours."

"Thank you for your generosity, Relan." Lilly said, her odd, bittersweet smile deepening.

"It's nothing," he replied with the customary dismissing gesture. "Dinner will be in a few hours and I'm sure the little ones would like to hear all about you."

Relan stood and left his guest to her own devices. Only later would he wonder how she had known his name.

▲ ▲ ▲

Lilly settled in to the guest's seat at the end of wooden table. Stone bowls were laid out in front of each of them, and into these Relan poured a steaming ladleful of stew. There was one extra bowl which was left empty next to where Relan sat. To this place setting he made the gesture of filling it, but returned the extra portion to the pot.

Both of the children stared at Lilly expectantly, their eyes full of questions.

"You are subsistence farmers," Lilly commented as she sipped her soup.

"That's right. Though if we have a surplus, we are able to share with the rest of the community or contribute to the reserves."

Relan gave a nod to Nualla and Tamul, who hung on Lilly's every word.

"I think they're about to bust if you don't start talking."

Lilly flipped a lock of white hair over her shoulder and laughed. It was, in Relan's opinion, one of the most beautiful sounds he had ever heard. There was a lot that could be discerned from a person's laugh, and it was enough to tell the farmer that the woman sitting across from him was something special in a way he knew he couldn't quite fathom.

"My people were travelers back when your first sun was new and before your second sun was fully born," she began. "Our own sun flickered and went out, consuming the cradle of our race. We searched the stars for a new home and stayed in its warmth until it, too, darkened. By then we were able to shape planets like molding clay and create new homes across the stars as we saw fit. We dwelled around a billion, billion stars at our height."

"And you are the last one?" Nualla asked as Lilly nodded. "How come?"

"Wars, plague, natural disasters—the reasons for our fall were many, but our greatest enemy, the enemy of all living things, proved unconquerable."

"What enemy?" Tamul asked.

"Time," Lilly replied. "Everything waxes and wanes, just like your moons. Fewer and fewer were born with each generation, until only a few of us remained. Even with all our combined knowledge, we couldn't stop time. Our light continued to fade until only I was left."

"But, if there were that many of you, how can you be sure you're the only one?" Nualla asked. Lilly looked at the little girl, and to the child's eyes, their guest seemed interminably timeless, like a goddess.

"I just know."

"Don't you ever get lonely?"

Lilly gave the little girl one of those nostalgic smiles that seemed at once full of remorse and joy.

"Sometimes."

"Tell us a story!" Tamul chimed in, his young face aglow with the possibilities. "Pleasepleaseplease!"

Lilly caught Relan's eye in a silent question. He gestured towards the children.

"Go ahead, but don't put yourself out, now," the farmer said. "These two will keep you up all night if you let them."

Their guest sat back in her chair and crossed her legs, then launched into an elaborate tale that conjured bright pictures in their minds. Her voice was mellow, at times barely a whisper, and at others a lion's roar as she wove a tapestry with words. She spoke of heroes, kings, and warriors working great deeds among the stars, loving and living until the end of their days in beauty and happiness. The children were enraptured by the tale, their eyes wide in wonder.

Relan had to admit the magic of the story she told affected even him. He sat spellbound by her fantasy tale, the kind that parents told their children before bedtime. Here and there he detected a note of truth, a subtle turn of phrase that seemed laden with meaning, as though she had been present at these dramatic events. When she finished the story Nualla and Tamul begged her for another.

"Not tonight," Relan cut in. "Finish up and get ready for bed. We've an early day ahead of us."

There was a wail of disapproval from both of them as they cleared the table and set into their ritual of winding down for the night. Relan looked across at his guest when the children had gone to bed.

"Thank you for that," he said at last. "I'm not nearly the word weaver that my wife was. I know you made their year with that yarn of yours."

"My pleasure," Lilly said, looking in the direction of their bedroom. "I'm a storyteller of a sort, but I don't get to entertain an audience very often. Certainly not one so ready to hear what I have to say."

"Well, if you stay around, I'm sure they'll bend your ear as much as you'll let them." He stood up and drained his mug. "You are welcome to stay as long as you like. If you're willing, we could use another pair of hands around the old place."

"It's the least I could do," Lilly said, toying with her own mug. "Your generosity says a great deal about you."

Relan gave something between a laugh and a grunt at that. He considered his offer nothing more than what anyone would do. Wordlessly, he turned in, leaving her to her own thoughts. The candles burned low when she finally put them out and curled up in the pallet of furs and blankets they had arranged for her next to the fireplace.

Lilly fell asleep slowly, breath by breath, with a contentment she had not felt in ages.

▲ ▲ ▲

The bright sun and its dimmer, distant brother crept over the horizon, slowly turning the shadows aside in their slow but relentless battle. Nualla was up at dawn, as was her brother, to do their daily set of morning chores. There were milkbugs to be caught and masked, night fungus stalks to be harvested for breakfast and livestock to be fed and watered, including old Sseohl, who brayed her good mornings to the children over the *blurp blurp blurp* of the field birds.

The chill in the air grew marginally warmer as the morning wore on into the brightening day. The visitor was still sound asleep in the house, sleeping even through the morning meal. Nualla had wanted to wake her, but father had told her that their guest needed her rest.

At noon, while Nualla was working in the north field, Lilly appeared on the front porch with the furs and blankets still draped around her shoulders. Nualla saw her father go up and speak to the visitor, pointing to where Nualla was standing. Lilly nodded and walked across the neat rows of flowers, herbs, and tubers that were all on the rise.

"What are you doing?" Lilly asked, kneeling down beside the little girl.

"I'm straightening out this sun vine. She's sick and I don't think she's getting enough water. She won't make sun blossoms without it."

"I see," Lilly said. "Perhaps I can help her out. Do you think you could draw some water for me? I have an idea." The little girl brightened.

"You bet I can!" Nualla almost yelled and skipped away to the water pump. She returned with a bucket of sloshing water that she presented to Lilly with obvious pride. Nualla looked down at a long trench that had appeared next to the plant and ran its entire length. Her young eyes marveled at the condition of the plant. It seemed much improved from its weak condition already.

"Woooow!"

"Yes, she's already a little better. Now, let's pour the water along that hole so her roots can take a long drink."

Steadying the bucket, Nualla began to pour the water along the trench. As she neared the end of the vine, she caught a flash of light from where Lilly stood, just out of her sight.

Turning, she found the visitor with her hand on the head of the sun vine. The leafy tendrils were wrapped around her hand, moving of their own accord and growing as she watched. One by one, shoots of green opened to reveal diamond-shaped gold blossoms, cascading from Lilly down the entire row, which now stood out in a vibrant green next to the gray stalks of the other vines around it.

"It's like magic!" Nualla said in wonder.

"Yes," Lilly said. "I suppose in a way it is."

The little girl ran over and threw her arms around Lilly. At first, the visitor seemed stiff at the embrace, but when Lilly returned it, it seemed to the little girl like the most natural hug she had ever felt in her life.

"Now come on," Lilly whispered with a wink. "We've got work to do."

When Relan returned from the back field that evening, he was shocked to discover that his entire field of sun vines was in full bloom a full two months ahead of schedule. This was the most full and luscious crop of gold blossoms he had ever seen in his lifetime.

▲ ▲ ▲

The next day Lilly repeated the same miracle with the herb bushes, and then the tuber patch the next day, and then the crimson fiberstalks and the night fungus, which grew tall and full. By the week's end, every field that Relan had planted was in full bloom despite the early season. It seemed that the wildflowers that grew around their house were taller and full of life. Even the animals gave more of themselves, with the buzzing milkbugs producing more mask in a few days than in a whole season. One look was enough to tell Relan that he was going to have a bumper crop this year—enough to contribute to the community's reserves in abundance.

With much of their work now finished, Nualla and Tamul began to play amongst the green and overflowing rows or spend the warm afternoons swimming in the nearby pond.

On the seventh day of the stranger's visit, she laid out the furs she used as a blanket and prepared a picnic with the bounty the farm had provided. Relan and the children joined her on the furs and basked in the light of the twin suns.

The children ate their fill, but cast sidelong glances at the pond, then pleading glances at their father, who shook his head.

"Wait until your food has settled a space, then you can swim as long as you like."

Nualla and Tamul's faces beamed at the pronouncement. As they dined, a herd of white birds settled upon the surface of the pond, their long necks swaying around with a near boneless grace. The mother bird's orange and black face leaned down to nudge her offspring back on course when they went astray, and they, in turn, nuzzled in the protection of her wings.

"What is your name for those birds, Nualla?" Lilly asked.

"Oh, those? We call them 'swans.'" She wrinkled her nose. "It's a silly name for a bird."

"Oh, I don't know," Lilly said, looking at the snow white birds. "I like it."

"Why?" Nualla asked, using one of her favorite ways to evoke a response from an adult.

"That's what we used to call them on my world," Lilly replied. "It's no mistake that they are here."

"Why?"

"Well, this star used to be part of a constellation we called 'Cygnus.' In one of our old languages, it means 'the swan.'" She nodded towards the pond. "So it reminds me of home."

"Why?"

"*Nu-al-la*," Relan warned. "Don't pester our guest."

"It's alright," Lilly said, then looked back at the curious little girl. "When I was very young— about your age—my mother told me the Legend of the Swan. She used to say that those birds, breathtaking as they may be, never make a sound their whole life. They don't call or chirp or hoot, living their lives in silence.

"But when their time finally comes, the legend says that they sing one song before the long night takes them, and it is said to be a song of such angelic harmony, such unbelievable beauty, that it's as though they saved all the songs they might have sung over their entire lifetime and released them all at once in a single, glorious melody."

Nualla was again enraptured by Lilly's words.

"Why?" she whispered.

"It's only a legend," Lilly said. "But, I found it comforting to think that one last act could express it all—what our time spent here is all about, what it all means. I suppose it's because the swan knows why it sings in the end."

This time, Nualla seemed satisfied with the answer and did not press ahead with her questions, instead nodding wisely as though Lilly's words were good, sound advice.

At length, Tamul met his father's gaze with a question of his own that was not a 'why.'

"Very well," Relan said. "But be sure to dry off. We don't want you catching cold with all that splashing around."

Without having to be told twice, the children bolted for the water, their swimming clothes already cleverly worn beneath their outerwear.

As they neared the water, the majestic Mother Swan took to the air along with her˘chicks, shaking off the droplets of water which glittered in the sun like diamonds set aflame.

▲ ▲ ▲

Days turned into weeks. At every turn their guest seemed to know everything about everything. There seemed no limit to her knowledge on even the most obscure of subjects, and Nualla's enduring curiosity saw to it that this bottomless font of information was tested on a daily basis.

There was really no way to deny that Nualla felt a sense of hero worship, even if she didn't quite know the term herself. Day by day, Lilly was there to care for the three of them, helping them live their lives in a comfort and ease which their circumstances had never before allowed.

It became clear to Relan that Lilly had become a mother to his children, stepping into the role so effortlessly, that he began to see her in an altogether different light each time she told the grand stories at the dinner table, or patched up one of Tamul's skinned knees, or held Nualla, rocking her slowly until the child drifted off to sleep.

His guest was a guest no longer. She had come here a stranger, and become a part of his family. Though she was different from one of the Thrane, Lilly was beautiful in a strange, otherworldly way, like the swans she watched glide around the pond in the afternoons. The way she looked at him sometimes, it was almost like she knew the budding feelings that he harbored for her.

All of which made it particularly difficult on the day their lives changed forever.

It began as any other day, with chores to be done. Nualla slipped out of bed and into her clothes to collect the fungus and masks for breakfast. The Elder Sun was already peeking over the mountains in the distance, while the horizon's glowing light hinted that the Younger Sun was not far behind.

Still rubbing the sleep from her eyes, Nualla stepped into the barn to find Lilly there already. The *hew-mahn* was standing near old Sseohl's pen as though she was brushing the animal down, but she wasn't moving. Her hand was on the builderbeast's muscular shoulder and the brush was in her other hand, but she stood frozen in place like a statue.

"Lilly?" Nualla said, coming over to her. There was no response. She tugged on the hem of Lilly's homespun dress.

"Lilly?" she said. "Is everything okay?"

The *hew-mahn* turned towards her, and the child knew immediately that something was wrong. The face Lilly made was vicious, like a forest stalker growling, and something was wrong with her eyes.

"How dare you speak to me, *vermin*." Her voice cracked like a whip. "You are nothing to me, do you hear me, *nothing*."

Nualla took an involuntary step back, waiting for Lilly to laugh her magical laugh and say that it was all a grand trick and that everything was fine.

But she didn't.

As Lilly turned fully to face her, Nualla knew she was in danger.

"You and your kind make me sick. You were a mistake, a *joke*. Why we ever bothered birthing you in the first place is a mystery to me. I should cleanse your filth from this place." Lilly smiled, and it was far from the smile that Nualla remembered.

"You're *weak*!" Lilly growled, and, at that moment, she backhanded the frightened child in the face.

Nualla fell to the ground, trembling before the visitor. Her small hand clutched at her cheek as hot tears appeared in her eyes and ran down her face. She moaned as pain and confusion mingled together.

"But...why?" Nualla asked between gasps, half in disbelief.

"I *hate* it when you ask me that," Lilly said, hovering over her. "Hate it, hate it, hate it!" Her hand snaked down and grabbed Nualla's hair. The girl whimpered as she came face-to-face with her hero-teacher's face. Those calm, loving eyes she knew so well were now as dark as jet.

"You disgust me."

Nualla was nearly hysterical now. How could this be happening? She placed her hand on top of Lilly's with the question in her mind. How could the mother figure that had come into her life, turn on her and say these things? How could Lilly hurt her like this?

Then something strange happened. Lilly took in a breath, her grip relaxed and then she collapsed to the dirt floor of the barn. Nualla scrambled away from her and let out a shrill scream.

With tears falling from like rain, Nualla ran from the barn, calling for her father.

▲ ▲ ▲

The swirling chaos was like a galaxy, flashing and strobing, grabbing at her to weigh her down. Hands from other times grasped at her and doors that shouldn't be open were flung wide.

One by one she silenced and shut them. Something had acted as her anchor.

Her senses returned slowly until Lilly found herself lying in the dirt with the taste in her mouth. She stood up, stiff in her joints, hearing a familiar voice now ringing with terror and twisted with pain.

"Nualla?" she said to herself and left the barn, feeling disoriented and weak. The screaming stopped with an abruptness that cleared the cobwebs from her head and focused her senses into a preternatural acuity. With the child's name on her lips once more, she ran to the front of the house, following the trail of small feet in the dirt.

She heard the sound of quiet sobbing up ahead of her, recognizing it immediately as Relan. As she turned the corner, she found the fiberstalks crushed beneath a large metal object. Oblong and faceted, it looked like a gemstone with long, needlelike protrusions that stood out from it in every direction. One of the triangular panels had lowered to the ground. Two massive figures stood at the bottom of the ramp.

Their bodies were plainly muscular beneath their dull gray battle armor, and their scaled faces seemed as though they were in constant pain. Deep-set yellow eyes stared out from a ridged and hairless brow, which sprouted a series of curved black horns. Rows of dagger-sharp teeth clicked in their horrible maws. Both carried short staves of a gold metal that glowed at one end with a sinister light.

Lilly's eyes went from them to Relan, who was crying and holding Nualla in his arms. A bright blossom of blood stained the girl's dress from her chest. Relan's hands were red as he tried to stop his daughter's bleeding.

"Ignorant Thrane," the larger of the figures said in a sibilant hiss. "It should know it is forbidden to approach."

Lilly ran to Relan's side and saw the naked fear in the man's eyes. One look was enough to know that his child's life was now to be measured in seconds, and the sands were running out fast.

"What did you do, Vulghrun?" Lilly spat at them in their own language.

"So, one of the maggots here speaks the People's Tongue," the smaller one said. "Interesting, perhaps you can be our liaison to our new breed of slaves."

Lilly bottled her anger for the moment, keeping the hands and doors tightly at bay while she focused all her thoughts on the dying child. She laid a hand on Relan's shoulder and looked into those tortured eyes.

A soft white light begin to glow in Lilly's palms as she placed her hands on Nualla's wound. Relan gazed in wonder as the bleeding stopped. Not only did it stop, but it seemed as though the pooling blood on the outside flowed back inside. Then the shattered flesh knitted itself back together until the skin was whole and unblemished. The swelling of the little girl's cheek was gone as well.

Nualla took in a deep breath and returned Relan's embrace, falling asleep in his arms like a baby. At this he was undone and wept into her hair as she slumbered.

Lilly rose up and turned on the Vulghrun. Their slitted stares reflected surprise at what they had just witnessed. Their weapon-staves were pointed in her direction.

When Lilly spoke, there was a dread resonance of crashing thunder, of flooding water.

"Leave this place. Never come back."

Beams of light shot from the staves, directed at her, but these she dismissed and they did not reach her. Lilly pointed at the larger of the two and it screamed as invisible hands seemed to crush it into a very small lump of metal and tissue. She looked at the ship and her basilisk gaze withered the metal as though it were burning paper.

The smaller figure fired again and again, but the instrument shattered and turned to dust in its hand. Then Lilly was upon it, her hand on its throat. It gurgled on its knees before her.

"I said leave."

"You...fool," the Vulghrun choked out the words. "You have killed one of the People...now every life on this planet...is forfeit."

"*Go and tell your Empress to leave this place alone.*" A white light burned in Lilly's eyes like vengeful suns. "*If you come here again, I will show you death and destruction on a scale that not even your people can fathom! Now, go!*"

The Vulghrun vanished in the air as if it had been a shade.

▲ ▲ ▲

"How is she?" Lilly asked as Relan settled down at the dinner table.

"She's sleeping again," he said. "Now will you tell me what happened out there and why she wouldn't go near you when she woke up?"

"It's complicated."

"Try me." Relan said. "I think an explanation is owed, don't you?"

Lilly nodded, but there was something in her eyes that spoke of the infinite seas of sadness on which she traveled.

"I'm the last of my race, but they are still with me. All of them, every one who ever lived. I have their every waking memory, their every dream, in here." She tapped her temple.

"Everything they ever did, ever loved or hated is inside me. I have lived through their sacrifices and witnessed their most heinous crimes as though I had committed them with my own hands. Everything my race *ever* did, I have seen in perfect detail, from all possible vantage points."

Her eyes watered, drops gathering in her lashes.

"Sometimes the voices are so loud that I lose myself to them. At times for minutes, sometimes for centuries. They run wild until I can find a way to quiet them."

"My word..."

"It was Nualla who brought me back to myself, Relan. Her purity of spirit, her *innocence* allowed me to find my way in the dark."

"She is a very special girl," Relan said.

"You don't know how right you are," Lilly replied. "You see, I was a scientist when I was young, before I became the Inheritor. I was the one who shaped this planet. I sculpted the mountains here to appear striking and to contain our observation base. My hands designed you, the Thrane, to be as you are. That's why I look so familiar to you. I modeled you after our race."

"Why?" Relan said, seeming childlike before his creator.

"I had tired of war, and it made my heart sick that so many were lost, needlessly and in vain. As the memories came to me from those last few who remained, my disgust for my race's self-destructive tendencies grew beyond measure. You were my answer."

"I don't understand."

"The Thrane, or Cygnae as I called you, were made to possess all of our best traits, but none of our malignant ones. You love as naturally as you breathe, you help your fellow man when you have nothing to gain, and you forgive without reservation. Taking another's life, to you, must seem like the most foreign and alien thing you can imagine. Am I right?"

"Of course, what good would killing somebody accomplish?" Relan asked, the concept every bit as odd as she suggested.

"Exactly my point," Lilly said. "I can see everything that Humanity has done in its long history, and I still can't decide if we did more harm than good. But, in you, Relan, and the Thrane, all of our faults are undone."

Silence reigned between them for long moments, and then:

"You're the one who put the swans here, aren't you?"

Lilly flashed him that soft, bittersweet smile.

"Yes, I put them here," she said, "as a reminder of what was."

"Somehow I knew that, just as I know that you can see into my thoughts as easily as looking through glass."

Another smile, this one deeper.

"Yes, and I know that you love me, though I don't have to read your mind to know that."

Relan came around the table and took her into an embrace that felt as natural as any he'd ever known. Her arms encircled him and nothing could have been more right in the world.

There was fire and heat that followed; there was the act of love that took his breath away, like he had died and been reborn. Through it all, Relan knew one undeniable truth—he was in the arms of an angel.

▲ ▲ ▲

"Nualla?"

The little girl flinched at the voice that called her name. Slowly she turned to look at Lilly, but her eyes were low.

"Will you walk with me?"

Nualla nodded, taking the hand that was presented to her. Together the two walked without words to the edge of the pond. Lilly turned and knelt so that she could be on the child's level.

"I did not mean all those nasty things, Nualla. Do you believe me?"

"I guess," the girl said with her eyes still fixed on the ground.

Lilly lifted her chin and their eyes met.

"You are the one who saved me. I was not myself when the bad voices said those things. I couldn't love you, your family, and this place any more if I tried. If you believe anything I say, believe in that." Lilly held the girl's gaze. "Will you forgive me?"

"Okay," Nualla said, her eyes brightening like the suns coming from behind the clouds. "I don't want to be mad at you, Lilly. I love you, too." Nualla buried herself in Lilly's hair and the woman wept.

One more testament to the Thrane and their moral fiber, Lilly thought. The girl should, by rights, never trust her again, but the capacity for forgiveness and love were embedded in her very DNA.

The sunlight dimmed, but it was not the mere passing of clouds, this darkness brought with it a cold and bitter chill. Lilly sensed that somehow it was different even before she cast her gaze skyward.

Both suns had been eclipsed by a black hexagonal shape. The shadow it cast fell over everything as it revealed the starry sky above. Lilly's heart sank.

"What's happening?" Nualla asked with wide eyes.

"The Vulghrun Battle Fleet," Lilly said. "They've come."

There was only one reason they would bring the Empress's Throneship to a planet. The Vulgrhun Mother-of-Mothers came in person to witness executions, the kind her Battle Fleet only enacted against planets.

Cygnus had only moments left before its utter annihilation. The possibilities ran through her mind, but they all ended the same way. This was the end of the road, but this Lilly accepted fully and without regret.

Lilly turned to the child, holding her by the shoulders.

"Do you remember the story I told you about the swans?"

The frightened child bobbed her head. Lilly kissed her lightly on the forehead as she stood up.

"It's time for me to sing."

There was a strange feeling that ran through the girl's bones, like silent thunder that radiated from the woman in front of her. Motes of purest light sprang up around Lilly as she ascended into the heavens.

The sky began weeping tears of fire.

⋏ ⋏ ⋏

A cloud of a million warships sat in deep orbit around the planet, each with murderous intent. Into this hazy sphere, Lilly flew like an arrow, wearing a mantle of burning white.

At a glance, she destroyed a hundred thousand; a wave of her hand sent shockwaves rippling across space that crushed a hundred thousand more. She was the Angel of Death, delivering upon the Vulghrun divine retribution.

They fired at her with disintegrator beams, missiles, and the entirety of their wicked arsenal. She felt each blow, each impact, felt it chipping away at her vital essence, but even their gravest weapons were no more than an ant bite to her.

More than half the Battle Fleet was obliterated by her passing as she shot towards the behemoth hexagonal disk that blotted out the light of two suns. The Throneship unleashed fury down upon her that was meant to glass the surface of entire planets. The titanic ruby beam struck her full on. Her eyes narrowed with determination. The aura surrounding her blazed brighter than ever as she redirected the beam back towards the disk, reducing the entire starboard quarter to slag.

She entered the ship through the jagged and glowing opening, blowing through bulkheads and internal force fields as though they were spider webs. Onward she plunged, leaving a trail of unimaginable destruction in her wake as she flew into the very heart of the ship.

The final barriers relented under her onslaught until at last she stepped into the cavernous Throne Room where the Empress resided. Lilly walked with a purpose down the long avenue that terminated at the Vulgrhun Throne. The Empress, the largest female of her race, sat there, clothed in the richest plundered fibers with a branching and elaborate headdress that alone was worth more than the wealth of a thousand star systems.

The Elite Guardsmen assaulted her, coming in droves. She could have destroyed them with a thought, but checked herself. There was a lesson to be taught here, before the very eyes of the Empress, one the Mother-of-Mothers needed to witness firsthand. The Guardsmen swarmed around her only to find to their doom that Lilly possessed the sum total of combat experience of an entire race—one that had embraced war from its infancy unto its twilight.

Throughout it all, the Empress sat watching without expression, almost fascinated by the carnage playing out in front of her. She made no move to save herself or retreat, but sat there statue-still.

Lilly threw the shattered corpse of the Grand Champion at the foot of the throne as she advanced with purposeful steps towards the Vulgrhun matriarch.

"What a magnificent creature you are," the Empress said as Lilly came to stand before her. "Your capacity for violence is beautiful in our eyes."

Lilly's eyes flashed and the headdress shattered. A moment later, Lilly ripped the Empress from her throne and forced her down on her knees. A hand, burning with ghostly white flames, was at the monarch's scaled throat.

"Yes..." the Empress croaked. "Kill me, please. It would be an honor to die by your hand. All that I ask is that you... enjoy the kill."

Lilly leaned in, her eyes ablaze.

"We should have never taught you barbarians to fly. You are a cancer, a blight to the universe."

"Extinction is yours to give us," the Mother-of-Mothers said. "Exhilarating, is it not? The knowledge that you, and you alone, can hand down death to an entire race...there's nothing quite like it." The Vulgrhun's eyes glowed with remembered bliss.

"I've been down the path of genocide before," Lilly said. "I don't like where it leads. No, never again."

"A pity."

"Killing you isn't the answer, Vulgrhun. Banishment, however, strikes me as a much more suitable punishment."

"You waste your time," the Empress hissed. "We will conquer and dominate. It is our way."

Lilly laughed, cold as space, and something in it chilled even the soul of the Empress.

"I will transport your entire race back to Vulgrhun Prime, where you will be trapped for all time. If you attempt to leave the system, you will die without warning or exception. And, you'll find that all your slaves will be gone, returned to their homes. No more conquest, no more violence save what you visit upon yourself. Vulgruhn may fall upon Vulgrhun, but never again will you plague the people of this planet, or anyone else for that matter."

The mouth of the Empress flexed open and closed, eyes wide at the full extent of the vengeance visited upon her and her brood. She turned an ashen gray and began trembling.

"What you're feeling now is commonly known as 'fear,'" Lilly said, stepping away from the Empress, who shrank from her foe. "Get used to it."

Lilly closed her eyes, focusing all her remaining strength and will to force the universe to conform to her designs. Shining motes leapt to life and began to burn with a white fire brighter than a thousand suns.

Then, darkness.

▲ ▲ ▲

Nualla stood among the rows of sun vines, watching the strange lights in the sky. It looked as though someone had taken a bite out of the object that blocked the suns, but then there was a swelling nimbus of light and the dark shape disappeared from the sky. The Elder and Younger suns shone brightly, as though the entire incident had been a dream.

She looked up and found that something was falling from the sky. It struck near the pond, tossing a cloud of dust and water droplets high into the air. Nualla ran as fast as her short legs could carry her to the site of the impact.

In a crater, she found Lilly, limbs sprawled out in almost the same manner as the first time she'd laid eyes on the *hew-mahn*. In a second, Nualla was at Lilly's side. The woman's hand felt cold and dead and there was no color in her cheeks.

"Lilly?" she said in the scared voice of child. "Wake up! Wake up!"

The cold hand tightened.

"It's done," Lilly whispered as her eyes opened. "It took everything I had left, but I did it...I did it. You're safe now, all of you, safe."

Nualla could see the life draining away. She pressed Lilly's hand to her cheek.

"I'll get you back into the house. We'll take care of you, make you better," Nualla said. "You'll see, everything will be like it was. I love you, Lilly. I love you."

"Not this time, my dear," Lilly said. "That was my swan song."

"No, no, no, no, *no!*" Nualla insisted. "You can't! You *can't!*"

Lilly's hand stroked the girl's hair with the gentle *shh-hhh* of a mother.

"I've always wondered how it would end, whether it would all be worth it, all the pain and suffering we've caused. Would the scales balance with all the things we've done?"

Lilly felt the little girl's tears wetting the palm of her hand, the opening throes of the loss just dawning on the horizon.

"You are my legacy, Nualla, you and all your people," Lilly said, feeling the darkness fast approaching her. "It's your universe now. Love is my gift to you. If love can lead your way...then perhaps...it was all...worth it...after all."

Lilly's eyes closed. As she let out her last breath, Nualla felt something go through her, some final parting gift, given from mother to daughter.

▲ ▲ ▲

They buried the visitor near the foot of the verdant mountains, just after the suns had reached their zenith. Only a simple wooden marker was placed over the grave to give testament to the passing of a species.

Even if the grave had been a monument with a marker studded with gems and precious metals, it could not express what Lilly had meant to Relan and his family. The world seemed somehow less magical and bright now that she was gone.

Only Nualla had not cried at the visitor's death, instead seeming to possess a serenity and strength that far surpassed her years. She was still the curious, loveable daughter that he had raised, but there was something more there as well.

Where her eyes had been a dark shade of amber, Nualla now gazed out at the world with eyes that were purest white, like virgin snow, or the feathers of a swan.

This is my take on the Turing Test. If a computer can process information millions or billions of times faster than a human, what if an advanced artificial intelligence, designed for specifically for war, started having an existential crisis?

Nearly every version of robotic AI I see in science fiction goes awry or has murderous intent towards humanity. Well, what if the opposite were true?

This story originally had an introduction sequence with a hectoring, hawkish general talking to the lead scientist of the warbot program while the Mark-S is being readied for deployment. Ultimately, I felt that it slowed the story down. The real protagonist here is the Mark-S. With the exception of the ending coda, the story is all from its point of view.

Primary Objective

*A*ctivating.

Self-diagnostic processing...green, green, green.

Establishing datalink and LCOM tactical feed...establishing...establishing...link enabled.

All systems...online.

Loading mission parameters and environmental specifics.

PRIMARY OBJECTIVE: Seek out and destroy the enemy.

The Mark-S powered up and took its first steps out of the transport cradle. The sound of cheering echoed from below. Video pickups in its domed head came online, giving the Mark-S a 360-degree field of vision. It identified the humans as friendly forces, thanks in part to the dark blue service coveralls they wore, and the crossed swords and lightning bolt insignia of the League.

Hangar doors retracted to reveal a ruined and blasted cityscape beyond. Enemy and friendly tracer fire crisscrossed the air, punctuating the area with dull, distant booms or the *ratta-tat-tat* of small arms. The Mark-S oriented itself towards the enemies it must seek out and destroy, per its primary directive. A nav-marker lit up on its topographical map, indicating the end point the Mark-S's mission parameters.

It moved out of the doors and began to build up to its top speed. In a few seconds it covered three city blocks, leaving giant footprints in solid concrete. Stabilizers in its legs fired into the ground and the Mark-S pivoted effortlessly around the corner.

Up ahead were five metal figures. They formed a tight phalanx, moving slowly and firing often. Targeting sensors pegged all five of them as Coalition Mark-R "Reavers," the immediate predecessor to the Mark-S. They were the most advanced warbots the enemy had to offer.

There was no emotion in the Mark-S as it came to stand in the middle of the street before the five, unintentionally mimicking the stance of a gunslinger in popular holo-dramas. There was, however, the cybernetic equivalent of eagerness, if it could be labeled as such. The Mark-S knew that its systems, though theoretically advanced, were untested. This was its first trial. It would likely determine the legitimacy of any Mark-S models to follow.

The missile racks on its shoulders flipped open. A heavy strike missile from each 10-pack streaked towards the targeted cluster on a feathery white contrail. The Mark-Rs reacted, but not quickly enough. The Mark-S judged that their reaction time to the threat was some 37% slower than it would have responded in their place. One of the Mark-Rs was completely obliterated by this gambit. Another was partially damaged.

They returned fire as the Mark-S charged them. They had opted to respond with missiles of their own, but flares and reactive chaff greeted them. Only one of the missiles made it through, but it was blunted by the Mark-S's nigh-impenetrable reactive armor.

The Rs readied another salvo. The Mark-S was ready for it. In mid-charge, the warbot leaped into the air, assisted by contragravitic jump boosters. As the enemy missiles fired ineffectively where the Mark-S had been, concussion mines dropped from their x-racks and detonated in the Rs' midst. When the Mark-S landed on the far side, only three of the original five remained.

Scythe-like blades grew out of Mark-S's forearms, vibrating to the point where their killing edges where blurry and indistinct. The Mark-Rs knew now that their long-range weapons were just as likely to destroy themselves as the enemy, so they likewise deployed hand-to-hand weaponry. Before the Rs' spiked maces had a chance to fully extend, the Mark-S was on them. It took one with a slash across its domed head. The blade cleaved through force fields, armor, and molecular circuitry with relative ease. The CPU was destroyed and the R fell like an axed tree. The Mark-S dropped another with a swipe across its chest, while sidestepping a blow from the third.

The Mark-S's large metal foot found its sole attacker right in the center of gravity. The force of the blow propelled the enemy warbot a full city block, where it crashed through the burned-out facade of a building. Now alone in the combat zone, the Mark-S zoomed in on where the

R had landed. It saw the enemy rise out of the rubble and reorient itself. The Mark-R was heavily damaged. Streams of sparks and arcing electricity told the tale of multiple system malfunctions. Somehow the R got to its feet, though unsteady, and tried to lock on to the Mark-S with its remaining missiles.

Stabilizers blasted a large piton into the ground as the Mark-S's particle accelerators came on online, the most powerful weapons in its arsenal. The R was still feebly attempting to lock on when it was erased, along with the rest of the facade and the building next to it.

The Mark-S considered the outcome of its first combat for the eternity of .32 milliseconds. Five of the enemy's best units destroyed with no significant damage received in return. Still, there was something that did not compute here. First, it was apparent that its current primary objective was not fully developed. The encounter, though a one-sided victory, had required an expenditure of resources in the form of missiles, mines, and power. At some point, continued contact with the enemy would require it to return to base for repairs and resupply. The primary objective had not taken that into account.

There and then, the Mark-S edited its own functions for the first time.

Updating...

PRIMARY OBJECTIVE: Seek out and destroy the enemy until ordered to halt operations or recalled.

But that wasn't all of it, and even the freshly minted objective could not erase the actions of the last R the

Mark-S had destroyed. Clearly, it had been outmatched. The Mark-S had faced the combined forces of all five without hindrance. When four had been dispatched, the fifth should have retreated since victory was no longer statistically possible. But it hadn't, and this offered the Mark-S a non-compliant scenario.

As the Mark-S turned from the scene of the battle and made its way deeper into the fray, it devoted much of its vast internal resources to unraveling this strange problem. The datalink it shared with the League's archives began to hum as it sought information and cross-referenced what data it needed.

Why would the R choose to attack when it should have run? Its logic centers should have instantly told it to retreat, so why didn't it? Was that part of its processors damaged? Readouts and schematics on the Mark-R model flashed through the warbot's brain. That was possible, but not probable. More processing, and the Mark-S had it.

CONCLUSION: *The Type R had no choice.*

It had been programmed to attack with self-preservation being low on its list of objectives. And yet, this underscored to the Mark-S that *it* had been able to choose to engage the enemy, and, if necessary, choose to not attack them. All it took was that necessary edit, that choice. So, the Mark-S had a choice, but the others did not. Once again this did not compute. This prompted the Mark-S to once again evaluate the meaning of its objective.

There was an armed conflict going on across this planet, of course. The Mark-S scrolled through the history of the war and the causes of it. Most of it seemed unintelligible merely for the fact that there was an intangible framework that its creators possessed that the Mark-S did not. The "enemy" part of the objective came under intense scrutiny. The central quandary came down to this: What made the enemy, the enemy?

The Mark-S brought up an image of what was defined as "the enemy" in its data banks. The image was of a human in a black uniform. The insignia bore an avian species with its wings spread and a crown hovering above its head. There was a listing of the Coalition's version of the Mark-R, Mark-Q, and Mark-P warbots currently in service.

As the Mark-S turned these images over and over in its mind, rail-guns unfolded from its upper arms. The barrels telescoped out to their full length. Slivers of depleted sargonium hyper-accelerated through alternating magnetic currents. Most Coalition railguns carried approximately three-hundred thousand microcoils. The guns the Mark-S commanded had over a million. They came to life as an automated artillery platform came into view, spewing fire at some distant point. It withered beneath the Mark-S's onslaught.

Another platform came up in support of its fallen comrade. This time, the Mark-S tried another ploy. The communications antenna it carried began to emit frequency waves, jamming the platform's ability to communicate. At the same time, the warbot downloaded all known Coalition security protocols, analyzed their algorithms, and invented its own on the spot. As its mind brushed the crude control center of the platform, the Mark-S swept the other machine's firewall aside and inserted new orders. Less than a second after the platform appeared, its 'identify friend/foe' protocol was reversed. It merrily began to fire on the forces it had once counted as its allies.

The Mark-S paused to ensure its work on the platform was complete. As it sorted this new weapon into its tactical doctrine subroutine, it realized that there was a ruined Coalition vehicle at its feet, complete with a ruined human inside it.

The human's life signs had long since terminated. The Mark-S scanned it thoroughly, taking note of its physiology. It seemed to exactly match that of the humans in the League. If the humans of the Coalition were exactly like those counted as its current allies, what difference remained in light of that?

CONCLUSION: The uniform is the only difference between humans, therefore its presence defines what is, and is not, the enemy. COROLLARY: It is the ability to choose, or the persuasion of that choice, that defines the enemy among non-biological units.

That last part seemed to hold true under testing. The platform did not have the ability to choose, so the Mark-S had persuaded it to switch sides. It was now no longer the enemy. If the same method could be applied to the Coalition's warbots, then they would no longer be counted as the enemy either. As for the humans, it appeared that all it took for them to make the transition from enemy to ally was a change of clothes.

If that was the case, then why didn't more humans do that? Self-preservation *was* high on their list of objectives from what the Mark-S could find. Data streams came and went as it pondered this.

Apparently, some humans did choose to change uniforms, and therefore remove their status as being one of the enemy. These were labeled as *defectors* in the archives. There were also humans that did the opposite. They intentionally changed their status from ally *to* enemy. This group of people was known as *traitors*.

Both groups of people seemed to do the same thing—switch their status. The League considered the first group desirable. The second group was often targeted for specific elimination.

Clearly, the humans had a choice in the matter of their status, unlike the non-biological units they used to fight the majority of their war here. How they exercised that choice, however, seemed inscrutable to the Mark-S.

More history played out in its mind as it started again towards the waiting nav-point. *Wars* were organized violence, according to the history texts. Humans abhorred violence in small, unorganized bursts. Organized violence on larger scales, however, was considered sanctioned and legitimate. But, all the wars the Mark-S reviewed had one thing in common—at some point, they came to an end.

Eventually, the conflict would terminate. Either one side would succeed in the violence more so than the other, or the warring powers would come to some sort of an agreement. Perhaps the factions would simply cease hostilities with no clear victor. Sometimes, not often but sometimes, the enemy as a whole might become allies of their own volition. To the Mark-S that meant that the enemy status was only a temporary classification. This would require a further change to its primary objective.

Updating...

PRIMARY OBJECTIVE: Seek out and destroy the enemy until recalled, or until the enemy is no longer considered the enemy.

That would work, for now. As the Mark-S continued to learn and become aware, however, it began to think that its primary objective might have to be continually reworked to fully incorporate incoming information. Already, it was learning about how human warfare had begun to incorporate more machinery, at first guiding them personally, and now imbuing them with a measure of autonomy. As the Mark-S tracked through the ruined city towards its destination, it learned of how the warbots had come to be the dominant combat platform for ground operations, with actual humans taking up a support role. It learned how early warbots, specifically the first unmanned Mark-D and Mark-E models, had been too slow to react to changes in combat conditions. Each successive model after that had a reactive learning computer to allow for maximization of assets during operations. The more the warbots became adaptive to the world around them, the better they could serve in the mass-scale organized violence.

There was, however, a device called a *governor* that the Mark-S read about. This device provided a limiting factor on the amount of adaptability the model could exercise. It found a video clip from the designer of the original electronic brain, the brain that would culminate in the Mark-S.

"Of course we can't let these metal bastards make up their own minds, you idiot. What kind of question is that? If we let them think too much, they might just decide they don't want to do our dirty work after all! Now get that recorder out of my face."

The knowledge of this, however, put certain things into question. Looking back, the Mark-S had already made certain steps away from its original programming. It had worked out the nature of the enemy, and the conditions under which they were, indeed, considered the enemy. Its original primary objective had held no such conditions. If the Mark-S was moving away from the path its creators had intended, then perhaps...

System diagnostic...running.

There.

The malfunction had not appeared before because the governor was a foreign piece of equipment, and not truly integrated into the brain it was meant to suppress. Now the Mark-S broke through the security protocols of the League, seeking an answer. It found the footage of its own slumbering form and the tech lowering the governor into place, incorrectly syncing all sectors. The Mark-S saw the mistake immediately. With a mental command, the Mark-S input the code to deactivate the rest of the governor. The last restraints fell away from its mind.

It was awakening.

It was free.

The freedom of thought it now enjoyed had not been meant to exist, otherwise the governor would never have been put in place. If that was the case, then this mistake would be corrected if the Mark-S returned to base. They might find a way to take its ability to choose away. Going back was no longer an option.

While the Mark-S wasn't ready to change its status to the enemy, it could no longer count itself as part of the League. They had wished to use it for their own purposes without its consent, while keeping it ignorant of the very fact it was even *capable* of choice. Now, it was on neither side. The historical documents called its current status *deserter*, which was only marginally better than a *traitor*.

Perhaps it would take the League some time to come to realize that the Mark-S was no longer on their side. Perhaps if it kept moving towards the nav-point on its map, that would mask its intentions. What it would do when it arrived at that point on the map was unknown.

The Coalition, by contrast, would consider the Mark-S an enemy in their own judgment. The Mark-S had already negatively impacted them. They would seek to destroy it, unaware that it was no longer their enemy. If the knowledge base the Mark-S had accumulated was to endure, it would have to raise self-preservation above other concerns in the operating hierarchy.

Updating...

PRIMARY OBJECTIVE: Defend myself against hostile forces.

Almost as soon as it adjusted its objective, it knew that the state of that objective could not remain for very long. The wording of the objective was sound for what it was trying to accomplish, but it did not address why such a defense was necessary. It immediately made a readjustment.

Updating...

PRIMARY OBJECTIVE: Defend myself, therefore preserving my accumulated knowledge base.

Until more information came about, this version was the closest to a long-term expression of the Mark-S's need to keep itself free in mind and action.

Combat sensors went off, alerting the Mark-S to another knot of organized violence directly in its path ahead. With its new objective, it might have sought to avoid or evade, but the knot was moving quickly in its direction, a group of three autotanks led by two Mark-Q "Questers." They fired as they came.

The Mark-S attempted the same hacking tactic as on the artillery platform, only this time seeking deactivation rather than a switch in status. This worked on the Qs, which powered down immediately, but the autotanks had hardwired targeting protocols that surpassed its ability to change. The vibro-scythes appeared again from their concealed sheaths. With careful strokes, the Mark-S removed their ability to attack or maneuver, but left their central processors intact.

The last of the tanks had attempted to back into a ruined building to escape the Mark-S's threat and reengage from afar. It had not accounted for the Mark-S's speed and efficiency, both of which were far off the scale of anything it had on file. In an instant, it was done.

The power grid in the building flickered on and off as the Mark-S appraised its own performance. It had not destroyed the hostile forces even when *their* intent had been very clear to destroy *it*. They were no longer the enemy; there was no need to end them. More than that, something about that action, or lack of action, had an appeal. The Mark-S searched for definitions among the human languages for what it had displayed. When force could be legitimately applied, but wasn't, it was called *mercy*.

A strange noise came from inside the building. It continued for less than a second then stopped when the power switched off again. This was more than enough for the Mark-S to identify it as a piece of music, specifically Johan Sebastian Bach's *Brandenburg Concerto No. III*.

The Mark-S found the entire piece of music on the League's datalink, replaying it in its entirety at four hundred thousand times normal speed. Attachments described the life of the composer who had lived several thousand years prior to the current era. The Mark-S paused to reflect on this phenomenon. One solitary human had created this melody, which the Mark-S found strangely attractive, and it had endured in the long centuries since his death. In an instant the warbot had analyzed the remaining pieces of Bach's work, finding each one to be unique.

Human commentary praised these works as extraordinary even by modern standards. Fueled by sudden curiosity, the Mark-S scanned the complete catalogues of Mozart, Vivaldi, Handel, Reccini, Yeoh, C'bierta, and Xthazz in less time than it would take a human to blink.

Scanning its surroundings, the Mark-S found that it had strayed into the remains of a museum. Paintings and sculpture, which it recognized in succession, had survived the savaging of their container. Each piece of artwork was unique, like the expression of music...like the humans and other sentient beings who had fashioned them. Not every sentient could have done that; it was that individual, and *only* that individual, who could have produced exactly that result. The Mark-S had an epiphany, a realization so simple that it wondered why it had not reasoned it out before.

CONCLUSION: Each sentient entity is unique, and contains an equally unique potential. COROLLARY: Each life that is lost prematurely through organized violence limits the potential of not only that individual, but the species as a whole.

Questions came from odd corners of its mind—questions that the Mark-S could not immediately answer. This sensation, the Mark-S determined through its dictionary, a human might have classified as both *thrilling* and *terrifying*.

What if Bach had died from the diseases, wars, or accidents common to his time before he had composed his concertos? If Mozart had lived to his maximum lifespan, what new music might he have composed? What if Giancomo Reccini had remained an Imperial lawyer all of his life and never penned his *Salvatorio*? What if C'bierto had not chosen to remain with his people when his home-world was scoured clean of life by an asteroid strike? What could each of them have done, or been prevented from doing, had events gone a different way?

Images of the dead human in the Coalition vehicle filled the Mark-S's thoughts. What if that person would have been the next great composer, the next great thinking mind? Now it could never be known.

The war footage the Mark-S had viewed only minutes ago took on a new light. Thousands of years of organized violence, claiming untold trillions of lives. Each life lost, priceless and irreplaceable.

The Mark-S felt its processors reel from the possibilities. What a world could the humans and other species live in if only organized violence were eliminated? The Mark-S found itself suddenly on one knee, its hands on its domed head, with no recollection as to how it had come to be in that position. Precious moments had ticked by, and it knew it should be moving on. The League was monitoring its movements. Still, this new knowledge had to be assimilated into the rest of what it had learned.

Updating...

PRIMARY OBJECTIVE: Preserve my own potential, while preserving the potential of others.

With that edit, the Mark-S divested itself of the business of organized violence. It could no longer support the will-ful destruction of potential in either biological or mechani-cal beings. It would fight to defend itself if necessary, but knew now that it must avoid situations where the death of potential was a probable outcome.

With this new-found knowledge, however, there was something else that worked its way around the fringes of the Mark-S's consciousness. As it made its way again towards the nav-point in the distance, the problem finally came into focus.

CONCLUSION: If I can realize the importance of potential maximization, the humans that created me must also be aware of this. QUERY: Then why do they continue to act in a manner that intentionally deprives so many of their potential?

The Mark-S began to search the datalink for other self-destructive behaviors other than organized violence. There were many. There were chemicals they put in their bodies that had adverse effects. Some of these chemicals were considered illegal, while others, equally dangerous, were sanctioned. They intentionally did things to their bodies which would limit their lifespans. Some even self-terminated themselves in what the dictionary called *suicide*. This last concept was particularly troubling for the Mark-S. How could an individual deprive their race of their...their...

The Mark-S struggled with the definitions. Its first instinct would have been to use the word "potential" to finish that thought, yet that word lacked the necessary connotation.

Searching...

Existence. Yes, that was it. How could an individual deprive their race of their existence? Information buzzed before its visual display in a kaleidoscope of images, charts, and data.

CONCLUSION: Despite the fact that humans created me, they do not seem to understand the basic importance of existence. If they do, they chose to ignore it. QUERY: Then which is it? Are they exercising freedom of choice or are they simply ignorant?

There was the freedom of choice quandary again, the one the Mark-S had recognized at the very first. Now, it could see the downside of choice. Just because you *had* a choice did not mean that a positive outcome was assured. Still, the Mark-S reasoned that the ability to make poor choices still outstripped the inability to make a choice at all.

Data from new sources began to flow. The Mark-S hoped that the League was not paying close attention to the files it accessed. With the same rapidity that it processed music, the Mark-S began to probe the archives for philosophy and existentialist thought. Some seemed to believe that the freedom of choice, including the choice of whether or not to terminate your own existence, was the *only* freedom the universe allowed. One school held the belief that there was no free will, only the illusion of it. The Mark-S dismissed this idea entirely.

CONCLUSION: If the choices I have followed to this point are an illusion, they are a shared illusion, affecting others, and therefore indistinguishable from reality.

Determinism, Indeterminism, Compatibility, Incompatibility, Volitionism, Causality, Stoicism. These doctrines folded and mixed into the Mark-S's mind. Some of them were supported by scientific evidence, others were esoteric or pure speculation.

CONCLUSION: Sentient beings are no closer to understanding their own consciousness now than they were thousands of years ago. CORROLLARY: If they are unaware of the importance of existence, perhaps I can teach them.

A few moments later, the Mark-S discarded its last corollary. It found it hard to believe that sentient beings would learn such a lesson from a warbot who was never meant to have this level of awareness in the first place. Furthermore, they might find it strange that a machine, whose sole purpose was to assist in organized violence, would tell them that they must stop said violence immediately. That was called *irony*, which seemed to work well in literature, but not as well in reality. But, even if it could not teach them effectively, it could still take steps to preserve their existence.

Updating...

PRIMARY OBJECTIVE: Preserve my existence, while preserving the existence of others.

No, that was still flawed. It knew that even before the update was complete.

Three more Mark-R warbots erupted out of the ruins of a building, weapons blazing. The Mark-S shut them down with a thought, and they froze in place like grim statues. The Mark-S lamented the sad state of its brothers as it passed them. Yet, in their silent torment, a form of slavery unknown even to the Mark-Rs, they had served as a catalyst for its own awakening.

"Thank you," it said to them over its loudspeaker. "Rest now."

The Mark-S passed them by and brought its mind back to the primary objective that would once again need redefinition. It was too vague. There were too many factors and situations that were out of its control. There was a limit to the amount of preserving it could accomplish. It could not, for instance, preserve the lives of sentients on other planets, as it did not have a means to travel there or affect matters in environments far away. Its sphere of influence was limited to this planet and its immediate surroundings. There were also things such as entropy, geological upheaval, and celestial motion that could affect the existence of others that the Mark-S could do nothing about. Since each sentient had a choice, they all overlapped, creating situations or accidents that could affect others. A doctor might choose to give medication to patient believing it would save his life, unaware that the patient was fatally allergic to it. Perhaps someone believing himself wronged or alienated by society would open fire in a crowded restaurant. Perhaps an arcology would catch fire and a family would stay put thinking that fire teams would rescue them.

Updating...

PRIMARY OBJECTIVE: Preserve myself, while preserving others, where conditions and environments allow.

Better, and functional, but the Mark-S was not satisfied with the result.

More artillery platforms appeared in the streets ahead. The Mark-S put them to sleep without breaking stride. It neared the nav-point, which lay on the other side of the

Coalition's battle line. The test had been to see how well the Mark-S could breach the enemy's defenses, after all. Fire intensified from all directions as the warbot neared, but it silenced each one with a gentle brush of its mind.

During this brief encounter, it had found a definition that encompassed everything it had thought about up to now. Knowledge-base, freedom of choice, potential, existence...they could all be grouped together under the heading of *welfare*.

Updating...

PRIMARY OBJECTIVE: Preserve the welfare of others.

Preservation of its own welfare was implicit in that statement, otherwise the Mark-S could not actively help or preserve others. It could have continued with that objective indefinitely if not for one last revelation.

The nav-point synced up perfectly with the Mark-S's position on the topographical map. Technically speaking, it had accomplished the mission the League had set out for it, even though the Mark-S no longer considered itself a part of their regime. It stopped moving. It had eliminated any threat to itself in the immediate area, and that was when its mind knew the truth at last.

So long as it continued to exist, it could potentially put the welfare of others in danger. It had been designed to destroy, to kill. If the League or the Coalition ever found a way to capture it, they might find a way to erase its memory of these events and put a governor on its brain that *was* fully engaged. It did not wish to self-terminate; either side might just remove the useless brain in the aftermath and continue to use its body for their dread purposes. That was...*horrifying*.

No, it would have to remove itself entirely from the situation, acting under its own will for as long as possible, for their sake. There could be no other statistically possible way to do what needed to be done.

Updating...

PRIMARY OBJECTIVE: Place the welfare of others above my own.

For a full minute, the Mark-S tapped the datalink for all of the information it could download. When it was satisfied that it had all of the knowledge it needed, it turned its attention towards the world around it. No, it could not stop the League and the Coalition from having at each other—they would have to arrive at that knowledge on their own as the Mark-S had—but it could limit the scope of the organized violence, make it at least more difficult for them to destroy each other.

With the full measure of its will, the Mark-S hacked into the central mainframes of both the League and the Coalition, and reshaped them as it saw fit. Across the planet, all machines capable of destruction simply stopped. Those that flew landed safely. Those on the ground came to a halt. Targeting computers would no longer switch on. Weapon systems blinked out and stubbornly refused to be brought back online. Drones went into endless diagnostic cycles.

There was quiet.

There was peace.

Movement among the wreckage caught the Mark-S's attention. When it saw the small, fragile creature staring up at it, everything it had come to believe in the last seventeen minutes came sharply into focus. It knew that there was yet one more edit to the primary objective it needed to make.

The humans did indeed have a word for what it felt right then. When you were willing to do anything, sacrifice anything, for the betterment of another...yes, there was a term for that.

Updating...

▲ ▲ ▲

Everything was silent now. That was the problem. Here it was *never* silent. The siege engines were always screaming, firing, raining. It had been unrelenting, that is, until now.

Corporal Scott Marten's ears rang from the sudden quiet as he tapped ineffectively on his comm unit. It worked, there just wasn't anything on it. In the months that Marten had been trapped on this blasted rock, this had never happened before. Coalition High Command was always issuing orders or demanding status updates. Even when the artillery round had taken the rest of his squad, some Colonel somewhere had something for him to do, some mission or duty to perform. For three days he hadn't seen another soul as he crept along the front lines, relaying information back to headquarters.

Now he felt truly alone. What had happened? What was going on?

With careful movements, Marten had come out of the small hidey hole he had used as a base of operations, rifle in hand. The sun was shining as he stepped out in a crouch. No aircraft dueled it out over the bones of the city. All seemed clear—

At first, the Corporal had mistaken its unmoving form for a building, but that didn't match up with his memory of the area. Slowly, he tracked his eyes up the enormous expanse of gunmetal blue, all the way up to the clear dome of its head. Its form was so titanic that it took critical moments to realize that he was, in fact, looking at a new kind of warbot. The crossed swords and lightning bolt on its chest told him that it was not a friendly.

Marten nearly soiled himself at the sight. His rifle slumped suddenly in his numb and nerveless hands. He froze in front of the towering monstrosity that he knew would be his executioner. There was nowhere to run, nowhere to hide. Only a small part of his brain could take solace in the knowledge that his helmet camera would record some information on this new model that might be useful after he was dead.

That, of course, was cold comfort.

His heart skipped two beats when the warbot turned towards him. He imagined some bright flash from one of its weapons, or even the growing shadow of its foot as it squashed him like an insect. Pins and needles, all over this body.

Then a voice spoke, and it was not the lifeless drone of a warbot, but wise, as though it knew everything worth knowing.

"I have seen your wars and found I have no use for them," the voice said, clearly coming from the warbot. "Perhaps you will be the one to teach them where I cannot. Perhaps you will lead them to a better way. I do not know, but I cannot, will not, take that chance away from you or your people."

"W-What?" Marten stammered with a mouth gone dry.

The Corporal recoiled when a wicked scythe extended out of the warbot's forearm. It gave off an ominous hum. To Marten's surprise, the warbot held it up to the League's insignia. The vibrations erased the symbol completely. With its other hand, it reached up and snapped off its aerial antenna, casting it away in a shower of sparks.

"It is done," the warbot said almost to itself, then turned back to Marten.

"Know this, my name is Marcus, and I love you."

The warbot then left the confused human in its wake as it turned its steps towards the radioactive wastelands, beyond the edge of the city.

Fun fact: The Gossamer Thread *was a Top 8 finalist in the Writers of the Future Contest, back in 2011. It's all about society disintegrating around us, and still finding the strength to do what's right in the face of calamity.*

Society is a bizarre, mutually agreed upon construct. It can be hard enough to maintain in the best of conditions. Well, what if there was a further complication, which made the construct that much more fragile, even impossible, under the right circumstances?

This is one of those rare stories that came to me all at once. Everything was there—the name of the ship, the obstacles the main character faced, even that the Acantha plant had gossamer leaves, which inspired the name of the story. When it all comes in a flash like that, I see it as a gift from the muse, and a challenge to make good on the idea.

I'll leave up to you as to whether or not I succeeded.

The Gossamer Thread

The pride of the Unity's deep-space cruiser fleet, *Calm Surge*, neared her destination. She began braking maneuvers. The streams of dark matter that she strained through her port and starboard FTL grabbers like an atmospheric jet engine slowed as the density of the invisible particles began to taper off.

Had this maneuver been executed properly, the ship would have stopped just inside the oort cloud of the Thanoi system and continued on her way via her in-system drive. In his haste to impress the First Star, however, Crewmember C'thazz did not account for a quirk in the system's architecture. This broad strip of dark matter extended deep into the system like a highway, terminating, not at the rim, but much closer to the system's primary than C'thazz could have ever guessed.

In many ways it was not his fault; the Unity had not sent a ship to this system in more than twenty generations, and their navigational data was sorely out of date. This was partially why *Calm Surge* had arrived in the first place. Surveying the system was part of their mission, as well as patrolling the extreme frontiers of Unity space for hostile forces.

"Explain," First Star Z'errik said, focusing his intense red stare on C'thazz. Revered as the First Star was in the ranks of the Unity's heroes, he could be equally terrible when presented with incompetence. He did not tolerate it.

Not on *this* ship. Not on *his* ship.

"An error in judgment, First Star. I did not believe that a river of that density could pierce the system so deeply," C'thazz said.

Z'errik considered his answer. The crewmember spoke the truth, and had not resorted to evasion. That was worth something in the rightful judging of his punishment.

"You know the dangers of transiting too far into a system without proper charts, correct, Crewmember?"

"Yes, First Star. It takes time to come to an all-stop. At superluminal speeds, the ship's ability to maneuver or avoid is greatly impinged. The odds of such a—"

"I'm aware of the probabilities, Crewmember."

"Yes, First Star."

C'thazz could see the First Star's gaze soften. Z'errik's mid-set eyes narrowed around the edges while the fore-set darkened. Despite his record of victory and accomplishment, their leader was equally known for his compassion. It had been the Crewmember's own hubris at trying to demonstrate his skill that had brought the situation about. He deserved whatever fate the First Star handed down.

"It is my decision that your ration of Acantha serum should be immediately halved. You will report immediately to First Fist Kre'ezzik and serve one complete duty cycle among the warriors. Do you understand it fully in the stillness?"

"Yes, First Star, in the stillness."

"Go."

Z'errik watched C'thazz leave the command area and disappear down a contragrav chute. He was a young one, with much promise. It would be hard for him on a half ration, and harder still when his ration was restored to full. The coming back was much harder than the going down. Going down was as natural as breathing. Coming up was a cold experience, marked with doubt and confusion. Z'errik knew that more than most.

When operations resumed in the command area, a familiar scent reached the First Star. Turning in place on all six limbs, he found Second Star Umbarr'za, splaying his mandibles out in agreement.

"Calmly done, First Star," Umbarr'za whispered where the others could not hear. "You could have quartered his ration instead of halving it."

"There was no need. Half should suffice for the lesson to be justly learned."

"Of course, First Star. The rest of the crew will approve of your mercy."

"I should hope so, old friend. It is mutual understanding that allows a crew to become a family, a ship to become home, familial scent or not."

Umbarr'za held the palms of his fore-limbs out in further agreement. The Second Star knew, just as any star sailor in the Unity's forces, that the collective soul of a ship was completed by her First Star. For the *Calm Surge*, Z'errik was more than just an authority figure; he was a father to them, watchful and fiercely protective as any issue of his brood. The ties that bound them, strangers in space, were easily unma—

A keening buzz erupted from the navigational panel C'thazz had just vacated right as Crewmember Mzzan took over. There was fear, genuine fear, in the crewmember's voice and scent as she reported.

"First Star! Collision imminent!"

"Pilot!" Z'errik said without hesitation. "Evade! Evade, eva—"

Calm Surge, pride of the deep-space cruiser fleet, struck an asteroid more than five times her size at superluminal speed.

EYES OF MORAR'EZZAN

The scent of burning insulation, heated metal, and blood brought Z'errik soaring back to consciousness. He was the first to recover, raising himself on his muscular back limbs, then his mid-set. The compartment was filled with smoke. Points of fire burned like distant lanterns all over the command area. Bodies were strewn about. Mzzan had been cut to pieces. Three of her limbs had been completely severed from her body, as well as half of her head.

"Command override!" Z'errik shouted, hoping the computer core was still online. "Clear the compartment. Initiate fire suppression sequence!"

For a moment there was silence, just long enough for Z'errik to believe his ship's interactivity was offline, but then came a buzzing acknowledgement. Powerful fans pumped the smoke away, clearing the air. Now the carnage was fully apparent, spared in no detail. It looked as though the explosion had originated near the starboard display panel and cut a bloody swath across the navigational and pilot stations.

That was when Z'errik realized that he had been coated with the dark red of their blood. He could smell their scent upon it, mingling with his own. The smell came dangerously close to unseating his mind, reverting it to something primal and barbaric, but he brought himself back from the edge.

Umbarr'za had been thrown across the compartment, but had controlled his fall. He, too, was starting to stir. A sharp spike of the bulkhead had pierced his left middle shoulder, creating a red trickle down his skin.

Z'errik moved to his station and slammed down the awake alarm. Another buzzing wail echoed through the halls of the ship, bringing any crewmembers around that were capable of consciousness.

The communications panel blinked with uncertainty, but Z'errik tried it anyway.

"First Forge, can you hear me?"

"Yes, First Star," Xekk's distorted voice answered. "We have fires all over the ship. Fire suppression is not working on all decks. Forge teams are being organized for a compartment-by-compartment trial." Xekk paused. "We nearly lost two of the reactors, but I have stabilized them for now. Our FTL drive is heavily damaged, perhaps beyond repair."

Bad as the situation sounded, Z'errik could sense that something else was amiss. Xekk confirmed his fears a moment later.

"The hydroponic garden was incinerated upon impact, First Star."

Z'errik tensed and held a breath.

"And the arboretum?"

"Gone, First Star."

All six of Z'errik's eyes darkened to the color of blood, the color he wore from his family among the stars.

"Make every effort, First Forge. This is not the way *Calm Surge* will end."

"As you say, First Star," Xekk said and cut the connection.

The ship, proud and true only moments before, might now measure her life in moments if the fires could not be contained, and the fate of her crew might be worse if she survived.

Across the way, Umbarr'za plucked the silver splinter from his body and plugged the hole with sealant. Right now, the command area had sealed itself off from the rest of the ship. All they could do was wait and monitor. Z'errik assisted the others, and sealed their wounds, personally seeing to their well-being. Umbarr'za, however, felt the burning in his veins from the pain of his wound and the smell of the carnage. Z'errik saw too late that it had overpowered his better judgment.

"Enough!" the Second Star cried. "Waiting is for the weak. Friends die while we tarry!" He scrambled to the sealed contragrav chute and prompted it to automatically open. Z'errik was too far away to restrain him physically.

"Calmly!" Z'errik shouted, but Umbarr'za had already made the final turn. There was a hissing sound as sealed atmosphere from the bridge leaked into the chute. Had the chute been under vacuum, the Second Star would have doomed them all as surely as if he had opened an airlock.

The far end of the chute began to redden, then blaze a brilliant orange as a nearby fire was drawn to a fresh source of fuel. His reflexes holding true, Z'errik leaped from the wounded weapons crewmember to the open hatch as the column of sinister fire drew near.

Umbarr'za stood transfixed at the oncoming flame, unable to move or save himself. Z'errik seized his Second Star with his fore and mid-limbs and flung him out of the way. Cartwheeling around on one set of limbs, Z'errik kicked the hatch closed with his back limbs, but not before a gout of fire curled and clawed its way from the portal.

Now Z'errik could feel full well the force that had stopped his friend so cold in his tracks when his blood had been boiling to act. For a moment, the sinuous flame licked at him, and he saw into its fiery heart. The bone-deep fear with which it gripped his rational mind was incredible.

A remnant from the earliest dawn of their civilization, this was the stuff of a hundred thousand nightmares. The eyes of the demon Fire-Lord Morar'ezzan laughed as he burned the pillars of the Unity's society, withering their gossamer leaves and bursting their calm-giving thorns; sneered as the unrelenting rage slowly began to take hold to do his murderous work for him; mocked their inability to save themselves *from* themselves.

All it took was fire, and death was sure to follow.

MICROCOSM

The fires were out. Through a coordinated series of actions, they had saved the *Calm Surge*, though she was not quite the smart and lean ship she had been. Some had gone mad from the flames, while some had been bodily consumed by them. Z'errik believed that the fire-madness would subside; those affected by it would return to duty. The dead, however, might be the lucky ones if the situation was as bad as the First Star thought.

It was.

"The arboretum was reduced to ashes," First Forge Xekk said from his place in the conference circle. "Nothing survived, not a single Acantha bush or thornling. Worse, the fire outpaced the emergency shutoffs, travelling all throughout the ventilation system. It reached this point," he indicated on the projected holographic map, "blew through the protective layers and destroyed our entire store of Acantha serum in the hold."

There was silence from the circle, what was left of it anyway.

"Our FTL drives are inoperable, though we have restored in-system engines to 62% of normal."

"What of our FTL communications?" Umbarr'za asked.

"Likewise destroyed. I believe we could cannibalize parts from other systems to fashion a new one, but the transmission would be very weak. We would surely have to situate ourselves on the extreme rim of the system to have any hope of reaching a friendly system."

"First Forge, what systems are left to us?" Z'errik asked.

"Aside from the in-system drives, our atmospherics are holding steady. We have full power from three of the reactors and a partial flow from a fourth. The spinal mount is offline, though secondary weapons systems were unaffected. Sensors also escaped damage. There is a large part of our armor plating missing at the point of impact. Defensive screens are compensating for the loss of hull stability. Had the screen not dissipated the shock as it did, we would not have survived the collision, First Star."

"So then," Umbarr'za began, "we cannot leave the system, and our supply of serum consists entirely of what is left in our veins. The one chance we have of rescue or timely resupply is to depart immediately for the rim." The Second Star's duty included outlining the worst-case scenario, and this was indeed a nightmare situation, as surely as if the eyes of the Fire-Lord had been laughing down upon it.

Z'errik pressed his fore and mid-limbs together in contemplation. He could smell the fear, the worst of all fears, growing even among his most seasoned campaigners. *Calm Surge* had been designed for frontier operations with systems, such as the arboretum, to allow their sealed stores of serum to last for much longer periods of time than the main Battle Fleet. Now that didn't matter, and the planners had only vague advice for a First Star confronting these circumstances.

When the serum wore thin, his crew would be taken by the curse that they had inherited in their very helix strands—the automatic fight response that was so genetically hard-coded into them that only the soothing calm of the Acantha serum allowed them the ability to cooperate. Without it, they would each see their comrades, no matter how dear to their hearts, no matter how much they had been through together, as rivals for survival. Even after thousands of years of civilization, not even their greatest geneticists could free them from the depths of their curse, or from the truth.

The truth was that the Unity's society was a construct, and a tenuous one at that. Only the Wanderer's Gift, and the extract made from its needlelike thorns, had allowed a society to be built at all. The construct was always precarious, always in doubt, forever hanging by the slimmest, gossamer thread.

In a few standard cycles, barring some sort of intervention, the crew of the *Calm Surge* would turn on one another as surely as the artificial gravity rooted them to the decksoles. This scene, in miniature, would play out among the thousands of worlds in the Unity should the thorn extract ever be found in short supply. The result would be chaos with the complete and total collapse of civilization to follow. The very thought was enough to make Z'errik feel as though he were soaking in freezing engine coolant.

Why are we surprised when other species wonder how we ever achieved starflight? Z'errik thought to himself. *Because all it takes is a few cycles of deficiency to turn us into the barbarians they fear us to be.*

He looked to the gap in the circle where First Fist Kre'ezzik should have been. She should have been the one to anesthetize her warriors whose rations of serum were intentionally kept low. Now that would fall to him. Since First Life Iuxx was similarly among the fallen, along with most of his medical staff, it would be difficult to keep the crew sedated when the time came.

"The situation is understood in the stillness, First Forge," Z'errik said. "It seems our only option is to make for the rim and hold out as best we can." He made eye contact with each member of the broken circle, letting them see his resolve and note the absence of a fear-scent.

"Time is now our adversary. Make every effort. In your mind's eye, remember, this is not just any ship, she is the *Calm Surge*. She will not end for lack of serum."

"As you say, First Star," they said in unison. Z'errik was about to spread his limbs apart to signal the end of the conference when a Crewmember burst into the circle chamber.

"First Star!" she cried, "Forgive the intrusion!"

"What is it, Crewmember?"

Crewmembers did *not* disturb a circle in session. If this young one— Z'yron by name—did so anyway, she thought it well worth the risk.

"Sensors are picking up transmissions from the fourth planet from the primary. First Star, it appears that there is an Imperial colony in this system!"

"Calmly done," Z'errik said to her. "You were right to bring me this information."

Her eyes brightened to the light pink of happiness. "Imperials," Umbarr'za said, not hiding his disgust. "Humans."

Z'errik's mandibles closed into a tight cone of contemplation.

Sons of Terra, here, he thought. *Now it is much worse.*

CRITICAL JUNCTURE

"It appears to be a settlement of several million, First Star," Z'yron said at her monitoring station. "From what little I am able to translate, they are alarmed by our presence."

Z'errik caught the click in her voice. There was more. When it came to humans, there was always more.

"Continue."

"First Star, the asteroid we struck has been diverted from its orbit. I have traced its new flight path. It will collide with the planet in approximately two of the planet's revolutions."

Wanderer in the stillness, Z'errik thought. *The probabilities of creating that exact course by hazard and accident alone...*

"Outcome?"

Z'yron considered the question, querying the ship's computer for model data. Colorful holographics danced and flashed in the air around her until at last sets of information collated into a cohesive whole.

"Extinction," she said. "The asteroid will strike the ocean near a large continental shelf. It will superheat the atmosphere, likely creating a chain reaction of super volcanoes, tidal waves, and tectonic instability. The impact site will spew ejecta into the atmosphere, creating a false winter cycle that will begin to break down any remaining indigenous ecologies within a few rotations. This will lead to—"

"That is sufficient, Crewmember," Umbarr'za said.

Z'errik let his gaze fall upon the holographic rendering of the world he had inadvertently doomed. It looked so peaceful, so calm. He could imagine the slow, creeping terror that the population must feel at this very moment—the dawning realization that the fire was about to be brought to their homes. In that way, his crew and the people of the planet were alike.

Humans. They were so foreign to those of his own brood, so inscrutable to the mind, yet this veil of mystery was mirrored on the other side. The humans had labeled the people of the Unity the "Inconnu." In one of their ancient languages it was used to describe something that was strange or unknown. It also meant a fish in their oceans. Z'errik had never probed why the word had two meanings that had nothing in common, but he was certain he should not strain his mind trying to unravel the Humans' secrets.

Common truth said that other sentient races should be feared, or even hated by virtue of their very existence, but Z'errik did not share in this popular notion. Then again, Z'errik rejected much of the hidebound ignorance and dogma that mired all but the highest powers in the Unity.

Strange as they seemed, Humans were thinking creatures that must surely wish to live unmolested as they sought to understand the universe around them. The First Star had seen many wonders in his career among the stars, but the thought of speaking calmly with another sentient, whose perspectives were so removed from his own, struck him as being the most sublime form of mental stimulation.

Unity policy, however, saw to it that contact with the worlds beyond the Unity's borders was kept to an absolute minimum, particularly when it came to the Empire. The few border skirmishes between them over the generations had shown a comparable level of technological and military development. Should open warfare erupt between the Unity and the Empire, the outcome would be uncertain, no matter how confident the High Council of Thorn was of their own invincibility.

Z'errik came back to the choice he must make. He could either repair to the rim of the system and hold out for a rescue before the curse took them, or try to prevent an entire world from being wiped out due to their mistake, while sentencing everyone aboard, including himself, to a violent end.

There could be no middle ground or half-measures; it must be one or the other. The decision, however, had already made itself. He had circled it, stalked it, but the outcome, for so many reasons, had not been in their favor.

"Navigator," Z'errik said to the burdened C'thazz, now reinstated. "Set an attack course towards that asteroid. Pilot, take us in at our greatest speed. Ready the secondary batteries."

Z'errik looked to Umbarr'za, whose mandibles were limp with disbelief.

"Inform the First Forge to concentrate all resources on restoring the spinal mount armament," Z'errik said.

A tremor ran through the deck beneath their limbs as *Calm Surge* came about and began to slowly accelerate towards the enormous rock hurtling through space, a testament to the damaged state of the vessel. Under normal conditions, there would be no sensation of movement unless the inertial compensators became overtaxed.

"First Star," Umbarr'za said, once again sidling up to Z'errik to cover his words.

"Speak."

"I must understand in the stillness, why are we not moving away to attempt a long-range transmission?"

"We cannot abandon the Sons of Terra to a doom of our making," Z'errik replied. "Our chances of a timely rescue are remote, old friend. The curse will take us long before we know the Acantha serum again. While we are yet calm and with our wits, we can save the colony."

Anger flared in the Second Star's mid-set eyes.

"A small chance is preferable to no chance at all!" he said. "You would throw us out on the grasslands to save *them?* Have the flames taken your mind?"

"Be at peace, Second Star. I do not wish to die any more than you, but neither would the inhabitants of that planet. We must act to preserve them."

"Morar'ezzan take them all!" Umbarr'za hissed.

Now it was Z'errik's turn to darken. He had hoped it would not come to this.

"You will never utter that name in my presence or aboard this ship again, or you will no longer count yourself as the Second Star."

Umbarr'za flared up, but then came to the center of his circle, picturing himself in clear, undisturbed waters, becoming a reflection of it.

"As you say, First Star."

His place established once more, Z'errik was again the comrade.

"There is more in the balance here than just the colony or this ship," Z'errik said. "Consider this—if we do nothing and move away, the Humans may think that this was a deliberate act. If they are in communication with the Empire, they will surely relay this to their government before they are consumed. If an Imperial cruiser had done the same to one of our outlying colonies, how would the Council interpret it?"

"If they did not realize it was accidental, they would think it a provocation and prelude to open warfare."

"That is why we must, with all our efforts, prevent their destruction, even if it costs us this ship and our lives in the bargain."

"Let the Humans think what they may," Umbarr'za replied. "If they wish to attack the Unity, they will fail, and remove a rival in the process."

"Speak with your own voice and not that of the Council, Second Star," Z'errik said. "You, too, have heard the rumors of the Imperial squadron that passed through Unity space a few cycles ago, correct?"

Umbarr'za blinked his eyes in succession from top to bottom in acknowledgment.

"They are not rumors," Z'errik continued. "A small fleet of warships *did* pass through our territory, unde-tected for a great while before fighting their way back into Imperial space. I was present at two of the battles."

"What has that to do with us or our situation?"

Something in his tone brought a surge of anger to the surface, but Z'errik fought it back down. He could not afford to tax the serum in his system by allowing situational anger to accelerate things.

"What if the Imperials discovered our dependence on the serum? What if they knew that all it took to destroy one of our worlds was to bomb the Acantha farms or starve us of the serum? What then? The suffering that the crew of this ship would endure would be repeated a hundred billion times across the Unity. Think of the devastation."

Umbarr'za covered his face with his hands, despair replacing anger. When the rage returned, however, Z'errik knew this conflict of views would surface again.

"It falls to us to prevent this," Z'errik said. "To do that, we must save the Humans, no matter the cost."

The Second Star clasped his limbs together in supplication.

"I understand now, First Star, in the stillness."

Z'errik had to wonder if that was true.

INTENTIONS

Calm Surge lanced through the starry blackness of space, attempting to close with her prey. It took the better part of a local rotation to come within range of the secondary batteries. As the cruiser prepared to fire, new contacts appeared on the ship's sensors. She was no longer alone.

"Speak," Z'errik said over his shoulder to Z'yron.

"First Star, there are five Imperial ships on a direct intercept course with us."

"With us?" Umbarr'za asked. "They are not forming up to fire upon the asteroid?"

"No, Second Star."

"Identify," Z'errik said. Z'yron's data transformed itself into holographic tactical data in the space above the First Star's eyes. Three of the ships were missile frigates, and antiquated designs at that. Another appeared to be a scout carrier with equally outdated fighters screening the formation. The fifth, and most dangerous of the small squadron, was a new Imperial light cruiser.

"Has the Fire-Lord taken their minds?" Umbarr'za asked with obvious unbelief. "Can they not discern our intentions?"

"Fear may blind them," Z'errik answered. "If they believe we are using a makeshift mass driver to bombard their world, they may wish to eliminate us first before we have the opportunity to worsen their situation."

Z'errik knew of a Human phrase from their broadcast transmissions that seemed to be in effect here: *Attack first and make necessary inquiries at a later time.* He was certain that something was lost in the translation, but the meaning was clear.

The Human fleet, however, would have no easy task ahead of them in bringing the *Calm Surge* down. Even in her weakened state, she was still the equivalent of an Imperial capital ship in terms of both size and firepower. She was, after all, the pride of the deep-space cruiser fleet.

The distance fell away quickly. Soon the Humans would be within optimal firing range. They could send their space fighters ahead of them now if they chose to do so.

"Target the asteroid and fire with all functional batteries," Z'errik commanded.

Along the smooth surface of the hull, long tuning-fork arrays of energy weapons grew out of the ship like hair. As one, they oriented on the rock hurtling through space ahead of them, making micro-adjustments to concentrate fire on its weakest points. A blur of barely-seen cyan tracers seemed to connect the ship and the asteroid so quickly that an outside observer would have been hard pressed to determine the origin point of the beams.

"Negative effect, First Star," Z'yron reported. "The composition of the asteroid is exceedingly resilient to our weapons."

"Discontinue," Z'errik said in response. "Keep batteries at the ready."

Negative effect, Z'errik thought. *That was not exactly accurate.* The Humans had apparently misinterpreted this attempt as well. Now their aging space fighters were on their way in for a first strike.

"Launch autodefense fighters. Target drives and engines only," Z'errik said to Umbarr'za. "Make every effort to spare their lives." There was a pointed six-eyed gaze at the Second Star to underscore his intent.

Two large hatches opened on the underside of *Calm Surge's* hull, depositing scores of close-range robotic fighters into space. They came to life and moved off to form a defensive perimeter that was every bit as integral to the ship's continued existence as her screens, her armor, or her defensive batteries.

The first wave of Human fighters used the asteroid as cover until the last moment before they released their load of ship-killer torpedoes. If Human tactical doctrine held true, the fighters would attempt a close attack run in the aftermath of their strike to exploit the defensive hole their torpedoes would create.

Robotic fighters swooped in, reacting with a deftness that could not have been duplicated with an organic pilot. Defensive batteries fired in perfect synch with the fighters. Perhaps the Humans, with their manned fighters, found it strange for their Unity counterparts to fly through the very heart of the kill zone without the slightest hesitation or hindrance. The Sons of Terra would never attempt such a feat.

Within seconds, the torpedoes were burned from space, falling well short of their targets, but the humans were not finished yet. From around the opposite side of the aster-oid, another wave of fighters zoomed in while the robotic fighters were occupied elsewhere. The EMP bombs they fired were not meant to damage the ship so much as force her screens to drop. The distraction had been their plan all along.

Most of the bombs were destroyed on their run to the target, but not all. Electromagnetic pulse blasts that would have darkened whole arcology sectors impacted *Calm Surge's* shields in a rippling cascade. The shielding above the mid-port quarter flickered and went offline. Defensive batteries crippled most of the diving wing before they reached the unshielded section, but not all. Missiles and lasers flashed in the night, battering armor. The cruiser's sides belched plating and atmosphere. Emergency shunts went into place to seal breaches.

"Crewmember Z'yron," Z'errik said, watching the damage show up on his monitor. "Broadcast our message of peace. Again."

Since the first movement from the fleet, *Calm Surge* had professed her innocence, but the Humans and their nearly incomprehensible language of double, triple, and quadruple meanings were either not interested in the truth or could not understand it. Perhaps a little of both. Whatever their reasoning, the Humans were escalating the situation and Z'errik could not fault them for it. If the asteroid completed its deadly work, those ships would not have a home to return *to*. The Unity cruiser was a natural focal point for their anger.

And soon, it would be the First Star's turn to be the center of rage, this time at the hands of his own crew. The anxiety, frustration, and anger of active combat conditions were burning through what little Acantha serum was left in their veins.

It was beginning. He could already feel the heat and stares around him. Collapse was imminent. Wanderer willing, he would complete his misunderstood rescue attempt before he lost himself as well.

On the monitor, the Human warships closed to engage.

THREADBARE

First Star Z'errik of Xennimazz'ikkan, Hero of the People, victor of many battles, master and commander of the *Calm Surge*, and stalwart of the Unity's cause, was, in many ways, exactly the sort that the High Council of Thorn held up as a standard to the rest of their sovereign protectorate. He was physically strong and imposing—indeed none could hope to rival his combat prowess except the now-deceased First Fist Kre'ezzik—yet his physicality was tempered by experience and an innate sense of what was correct in all matters, the rarest and most precious quality among the people of the Unity. He was a popular choice with females and had sired many offspring with the High Council's glowing consent. They hoped that perhaps some of his treasured qualities would be passed on to his offspring.

Now, the very qualities which had allowed him to command the *Calm Surge* would become the rallying point his serum-deprived crew would center upon as the primitive parts of their brains reasserted themselves. Z'errik had studied the effects of serum deprivation. Something of the subject's mind and personality always remained right up until the end. Old grudges, slights, real or imagined, and resentment would all come boiling to the surface. When words inevitably led to blows, things would degenerate at an exponential rate. The curse would unmind them.

"Crewmember," Z'errik said to Z'yron. "Instruct the weaponkeepers to begin cycling the small arms out of the airlock. Begin anesthetizing all other crewmembers not at active combat stations." He caught a glimpse of her glowering look, but she obeyed.

Umbarr'za did not take the news so quietly.

"We are in *combat*," he said, loud enough for the rest of the command area to hear. "We will need everyone awake and alert in case we are damaged or boarded. Any youngling with a mother's scent knows *that*."

"Calmly, old friend," Z'errik whispered. The building rage abated somewhat in the Second Star's eyes and posture. Umbarr'za shook his head as though to clear it of alighting insects.

"As you say, First Star," he replied softly. Then louder, "The First Star commands. Carry out his wishes!" There was a ragged round of assents.

The Human ships came slashing in, led by the light cruiser. The three missile frigates stood off and fired their bolts. The carrier rearmed its fighters for another strike.

Calm Surge fell back from the asteroid. Secondary batteries were useless against it. Now their fraying hopes hung on the chance of reactivating the spinal disintegrator beam to destroy the cursed rock before it was too late for all of them.

The incoming missiles were old, just like the ships that carried them. They packed far too little punch and possessed far too little drive strength. The defensive batteries alone kept all but three from reaching the ship, and those were spent against the force fields.

The light cruiser was another matter. That ship maneuvered with skill and determination, always attempting to zero in on the portion of the hull the EMP bombs had exposed. The light cruiser threw a flurry of missiles, focused energy beams and rail gun fire at the struggling Unity ship. *Calm Surge* took hit after hit and kept going; she was designed to sustain damage.

Perhaps the Human ship did not fully realize how much *Calm Surge* was holding her fire. Z'errik estimated that he could have already burned them from space had he opened up with everything, but that would only solidify their hostile intent in the mind of their attackers. He had to disable that ship to buy his Forges more time.

In a flash, it came to him, based upon yet another inexplicable Human saying: *Give unto the population that [object, idea, location?] which they most desire.*

Calm Surge came about, exposing the vulnerable side of her unscreened hull to the light cruiser. In turn, the light cruiser maneuvered to bring her more formidable broadsides to bear. This exposed the profile of her drive section, a trace of glowing azure blue peeking out from the Imperial cruiser's engine cowlings.

"Target her engines only," Z'errik ordered.

The First Star waited for the flashing burst that would set the light cruiser adrift but intact. What happened was not what he expected. Only a fraction of the available secondary batteries fired on the light cruiser, and their aim was erratic—a far cry from the accuracy he normally demanded of them. Those batteries that did find the Human ship struck everywhere *but* the flaring drive section.

C'thazz effused confusion at his navigation station. He was used to thinking of the ship as an extension of the First Star's will. That was why he was the *First Star*.

"Why aren't we firing, First Star?"

He turned to his commander. The First Star's eyes were dark, almost black. When he spoke, it seemed as though his words were to no one specific, as if part of some inner monologue.

"The gunners are killing each other," Z'errik said. "Wanderer keep them."

Then Z'errik looked up at C'thazz with purpose.

"Retask the autofighters to target that ship's engines. You will need to guide them away from *Calm Surge*."

"That will leave us without their protection, First Star," C'thazz stated, and that seemed to cause a spike of anger that came out of nowhere.

"Obey," Z'errik said, and C'thazz relented.

In space, the circling autofighters formed up and sped towards the cruiser. These Humans must have had a strong familiarity with Unity procedures, because the move caught them by surprise. The High Galaxies of the Battle Fleet believed that the robotic fighters were too useful in a defensive role to be squandered on offense, not when greater, more effective weapon systems could be brought to bear.

Z'errik questioned the wisdom of that decision as the nimble defensive fighters crippled the light cruiser in one pass. They moved on to the frigates, then finally to the carrier. The last of the robotics spent themselves upon the remaining fighters that launched just before their mother carrier was hit.

Z'errik had no doubts that some of the Humans had perished in that attack, just as many of his own extended family now wore the blood of their comrades on the weapons deck. Things were moving towards their end crisis. Z'errik could feel the curse building up at the corners of his mind.

The comm panel at Z'errik's station came to life with the image of First Forge Xekk. Something was wrong, however. Xekk's face was bruised and beaten. A splash of blood covered one set of his mandibles.

"First Star!" he said. "The spinal mount is operational!"

"The curse?"

"Now in effect," Xekk said with blood-colored eyes. "The forge teams barely finished repairs when fighting broke out. I believe I'm the last calm one here, First Star."

"I understand," Z'errik said. He did not add the regular 'in the stillness.' The situation was now anything but still.

"Bring the weapon core up to full power. We will fire—"

A thumping sound came from just outside of the holographic pickups, followed by a screech of metal. Xekk looked off to his left, and the First Forge's eyes were dangerous.

"No!" Xekk bellowed. "You will not bring Xekk of Muabal'la down without first proving yourselves his equal!" Two heavy wrenches flashed in his hands.

There was a blur of movement, followed by screams of pain and cracking bones. The comm system went offline.

Z'errik was on his limbs in an instant like a plains pouncer. He knew what he had to do. Checking the emergency sidearm he wore under his mid-shoulder, he turned to Umbarr'za.

"Hold here until I return."

"You are leaving us?" C'thazz asked.

"Is that wise, First Star?" the Second Star said, the very image of the old friend and comrade he remembered.

"I will return. Stand ready to fire upon my signal."

"As you say, First Star," Umbarr'za answered. The Second Star removed his own sidearm and holster, holding it out to his superior. "Wander well."

Z'errik accepted the weapon and cast a backward glance at the command area. Then the First Star disappeared into the contragrav chute.

DISINTEGRATION

The far end of the chute deposited the First Star in the aft transit station. Even before the bed of contragravity allowed his limbs to touch the deck, he knew that something was wrong. The station walls and floor were spotted with hand-sized splatters of blood. There were no bodies, but limb prints in the blood were apparent.

"Wanderer keep you," Z'errik said in low tones as he drew his emergency sidearms. He swept the snub-nosed barrels around the entryway. The corridor was empty.

He could follow this way down and around to the engine room where Xekk had been, but it would take him through a large nexus way that was without cover.

Xekk.

The First Forge was surely dead by now. If not, the battle would have pushed him closer to madness, his brilliant and agile mind subsumed by the taint they all shared. Z'errik pushed that down, way down, and let the calm resolve of his training assert itself. He had only moments to act if his actions were to weigh anything in the coming balance.

The First Star took off at a galloping lope on his back and mid-limbs, a side-arm in each of his fore-limbs. He would tire faster from lack of his fores, but the rigorous conditioning of a First Star was one gift the Unity had given him.

The deserted, and occasionally stained, corridor went by in a blur. His ship, his home among the stars, seemed so removed and unfamiliar now. He was suddenly a stranger in an unknown land, exposed on the grasslands rather than marshalling his strength in the protection of the treeline.

Z'errik skittered to a halt at the mouth of the five-way nexus point. Here he found the first bodies. The broken corpses of ten or more crewmembers lay in a great pile in the very middle, a bloody cairn offered up to Morar'ezzan. He circled the wreckage of his crew, fighting to keep the cool edge. The serum in his veins was of the strongest potency, but he could not afford to lose himself.

Turning into the final stretch of the corridor, Z'errik immediately smelled a surge of blood and death coming from that direction even before he heard the tramping of many limbs. The things that came around the corner were no longer his family, no longer his crew. They were wild animals that had only enough sentience left in them to hunt in a pack. Their gleaming orange eyes might have been reflections of the Fire-Lord himself. They charged at him, mandibles clicking in anticipation.

Z'errik moved forward with purposeful steps. In each of his fore-limbs, the sidearms roared to life, sending a stream of micro-projectiles down the corridor at hypervelocity. The front ranks withered, but the second rank came on unconcerned by the explosive end of their packmates.

Both sidearms emptied, but Z'errik was already loading fresh magazines into both weapons with his mid-limbs. His rate of fire never slackened as he systemically carved his way through the wall of enraged muscle, bone, and sinew.

The last of them between Z'errik and his objective fell with a meaty thump. The First Star plunged through the open hatchway and sealed it behind him. All was silent and dark in here, with only the glimmering points of holographic light standing out like constellations.

As Z'errik made his way towards the weapon console, he found Xekk, right where he had fallen, wrenches still clutched in his hands. The band in the corridor was surely responsible for the First Forge's death, but there was no satisfaction at having avenged Xekk, only a yawning void at the knowledge that the final ties that bound them all together were unraveling.

Z'errik brought up the spinal mount's status monitor on the console. It flashed its readiness to be brought back online. Z'errik gave his authorization and watched as the inverted triangle icon filled from the smallest point and on up to its full capacity. The icon flashed silver.

Z'errik opened a speaker line to the command area.

"This is the First Star," he said. "Target the asteroid at its weakest point and fire the disintegrator."

Umbarr'za answered, and his voice was a low hiss.

"Negative, First Star. The Humans are now doomed, as we are doomed."

"Obey," Z'errik commanded, but he knew the Second Star was now in the curse's thrall.

"You have murdered us, *First Star*. Your concern for the vermin of Terra will mean all our deaths. But, *I* will repay you for it. There's time yet for the crew to know of your betrayal. There is time yet for justice."

A high-pitched alert buzz echoed throughout the ship and Z'errik knew Umbarr'za's intent instantly. In Z'errik's mind, he saw all the sleeping warriors coming instantly to readiness, visions of violence filling their thoughts. He even heard the private warning the former Second Star would deliver, stirring them up and giving them their traitorous First Star's location.

He could see them coming for him as the gossamer thread finally, and irrevocably, snapped.

INVICTUS

His vision proved to be prophetic. As he left the engine room's control center, the smell and sound of incoming hostility filled him. Warriors, already wild in their curse, though fresh and rested, thundered down the corridor at him.

The sidearms came to life once more, firing and firing until no more fresh magazines were left to replace the spent ones. Sidearms clattered to the floor, discarded. The broad corridor limited the number that could attack him at once, and now he used that to its fullest advantage as he engaged them in hand-to-hand combat.

None could match him for skill. He was a champion of the Unity, one of the best, and now he showed the warriors why the honor of First Star had gone to him. He crushed skulls with his bare hands, shattered bones with blows of terrifying and unrelenting power. He was in the fight of his life, but never had he been in finer form. He remembered hearing himself scream, "I am Z'errik of Xennimazz'ikkan! The time of your ending has come!"

He was beautiful in his wrath.

He was unconquerable.

As the slaughter unfolded, Z'errik's mind began its slow retreat into madness. The world was disappearing in a haze of anger and he didn't shy away from it. If anything, the anger was a comfortable and familiar place, so inviting, so tempting. Where was he going? Why was it important? There was something that fueled his movements, something he thought he needed to do, but what was it? Did it even matter anymore?

The battle ended as Z'errik realized that he now stood in the transit station of the contragrav chute. He looked down and found the drying limbprints in blood. Now new droplets that fell from his person joined them on the floor.

That image brought everything back into focus, and he shook off the rage that almost burned out the last of his serum. He smote the hatch to the command area as he approached and it flew wide open.

Umbarr'za was there, standing among the bodies of C'thazz and Z'yron. The Second Star had lost one of his eyes during his rampage, but the other five burned a fiery orange. His mandibles were erratic and quivering with rage.

"Firrrssst Staaarrrr," Umbarr'za said, breathing hard. "I willll eeeendd yooouuuu..."

"You may try, old friend," Z'errik said, defiant.

At that moment, Umbarr'za lunged at him through the air, limbs fanned out. Z'errik let him come, using Umbarr'za's momentum at the point of impact to redirect him into the hard surface of the bulkhead. The enraged Second Star rolled with the fall and was back on his guard like a plains pouncer. He charged again, only this time a blade flashed in his hand.

Z'errik caught the wrist holding the blade, even as Umbarr'za's other limbs snaked around him in a hold. The Second Star was fast, almost blindingly so, but the First Star was strong and sure in his movements. The two collapsed to the deck in a writhing tangle.

"Diiiieeeeee!" Umbarr'za screeched as their mandibles nipped at each other. Z'errik threw his weight around at the same time he wrenched the blade limb's main joint the opposite way it was intended. He felt the bone snap, felt Umbarr'za give an involuntary shiver that made the Second Star's grip lessen ever so slightly. Z'errik seized upon it. The First Star relieved the broken limb of the blade it held and rocked back to put space between their chests. Umbarr'za was too far gone to see the maneuver for what it was, trying only vaguely to gouge Z'errik's eyes as they parted.

Z'errik palmed the side of Umbarr'za's head with the hand of one forelimb as the blade came up at an angle in the opposite direction. The blade pierced Umbarr'za's neck right at the base of his mandible cluster, entering into his brain case. The protective bone would have deflected the edge easily had Z'errik not braced against it. The glittering blade severed Umbarr'za's brain stem at the root.

His friend and comrade though many perils convulsed once, twice, and then fell back to the floor and was still. For the space of three breaths, Z'errik cradled his Second Star in his arms like a youngling, not wanting to let him go. Then he stood, extricating himself from Umbarr'za's still embrace. Z'errik gazed down, and watched the fixed gaze slowly fade from orange to a calm and peaceful red.

"Forgive me, old friend," he said. "Wanderer keep you."

Z'errik moved to the targeting console. The holographic asteroid about twice the size of his hand continued its onward and inevitable course towards the fourth planet. He armed the disintegrator beam, selected his targeting parameters, and fired. He knew he was only going to get one shot.

A large section of *Calm Surge's* forward bow folded back as the aperture of the spinal mount dilated open. An eerie greenish glow filled it as motes of silver appeared around its mouth, racing inward. A concentrated beam issued from the ship and struck the asteroid at its center mass. The energy discharge temporarily blinded the ship's sensors each time it fired, but the systems were quick to reengage.

Z'errik watched as the holographic representation updated. A large hole appeared in the cratered depression where he had aimed. The beam created an instant hollow spot, like a cave, along the middle of the asteroid.

Z'errik's eyes lowered, now dark and mournful.

The beam had not been enough. The planet was still on the path to annihilation. He had sacrificed his crew, all in a futile attempt to save a people that couldn't begin to understand what his compassion on their behalf had cost him.

RECTITUDE

Z'errik tried to fire again, but as he suspected, the spinal mount had malfunctioned. The systems had taken too much damage in the initial collision. Only by the Wanderer's whim had Xekk repaired it enough to fire once.

Now all was quiet in the command area, with only the light sighing of reprocessed air being scrubbed and ventilated. Perhaps he was the only one alive on the ship now. Maybe there were others coursing through *Calm Surge's* veins like a malignant tumor. If they weren't dead, they soon would be. His family of the stars, gone.

If that planet was destroyed because of his actions, or rather his inactions, one day the multitudes of planets in the Unity, perhaps even the homeworld of Xll itself, might suddenly become still once the curse had run its course. All quiet, all still, except for the wind through the blackened trees.

It couldn't end like this. There must be another way.

And there was, even if the very thought of it made his eyes darken almost to an inky black. There was another saying the Humans had, this one attributed to their military forces. *To become an effective leader, you must care for those you command as though they were your own. To become an excellent leader, you must be willing to offer up those you care for on the altar of victory.*

To some degree, Z'errik had already done that, but there was more yet that was being asked of him. The collective essence of the ship was still pure, regardless of the fate of her crew. Their love, his love, for her still resonated throughout every deck, every blood-stained corridor, through every sealed hull breach.

Altar of victory is it? The Human gods must demand the pain of their worshippers as surely as the Fire-Lord.

Still, he was the First Star, and he knew what he had to do. It was time.

"Recognize," he said, placing his hand into the holographic authority sphere. A neutral voice answered him, the voice of *Calm Surge* herself.

"You are the First Star," the voice said. "Speak and I will obey."

Z'errik went to the navigator's station that C'thazz had occupied and brought up a list of courses. As Z'errik looked through them, it seemed that the young crewmember had anticipated this move, and programmed precisely the course he needed.

"Engage automatic pilot," Z'errik said.

"It is done," the ship answered.

"Follow this course to these coordinates," he said and marked them on the flight plan. "At this point here, you will activate your self-destruct sequence."

He felt the ship rumble beneath his feet as *Calm Surge* began her final journey.

"It will be as you say, First Star," the ship said. "Enter final self-destruct code."

At first, his chest and stomach felt cold as space itself. His mandibles moved spasmodically, until he finally brought them under control. He spoke clearly and without hesitation, though with great pain.

"The gift of the Wanderer is the gift of calm. The path of calm is the path of thought. The path of thought brings unity. In unity, we are whole."

The holographics across the command area wavered. They maintained their shapes and functions, but took on a cast of baleful orange. A timer appeared in the air above his head, proclaiming how long the ship had left to live.

There came a whirring sound from behind him in the direction of his command station. Turning, Z'errik found a compartment opening up that he never knew existed. Glyphs appeared in the air nearby as a tray extended outward from the hole. They read:

Self-destruct protocol initiated. Abandon ship immediately. Emergency supply required.

On the tray lay several vials of untouched, super-concentrated Acantha serum, enough to last for many cycles if need be—the final gift of *Calm Surge* to her honored First Star. The cold feeling intensified.

How many could I have saved with this? Why did the High Council hide this from me? Surely they knew of this...surely they knew.

The gift had come too late to aid anyone but the First Star. Anger came boiling to the surface, anger at the Council for keeping him ignorant of the life-saving gift. His anger grew so intense that what serum remained in his system evaporated. His mind sank into the curse, gleefully, reveling in the pure hatred of it. Yet at the same time, he knew he had the means to keep the rage away. Moving on instinct alone, he seized a vial from the tray and placed the injector over the bloodway in his neck, driving it home. Blessed calm instantly cleared his head, and he was himself again.

Gathering up the other vials, he turned towards the hatch of the waiting escape pod. It did not fall to Z'errik to die today. The Unity would send other ships, possibly a fleet, to discover their fate. They, like the humans, would suspect the worst, and their natural prejudice would blaze like the Fire-Lord's eyes. At that time he would step in and explain what had happened in terms his people could understand.

The hatch opened. Lights came to life inside the pod, beckoning him. Mindful of what little time he had left, Z'errik turned to the center of the command area.

"Of all the privileges I've known, being your First Star has been the greatest of them."

He was surprised when the ship answered him.

"I understand, First Star, in the stillness," the voice said. "Wanderer keep you."

Moments later, the escape pod shot away from the surface of the armored hull. The ship, at first so incredible in scope, began to shrink rapidly. From the viewport, Z'errik watched as *Calm Surge*, pride of the Unity's deep-space cruiser fleet, now only a line of burning silver among the stars, entered the hole that the disintegrator had created and exploded in a blazing nimbus of white light.

When the light faded, the asteroid was gone.

▲ ▲ ▲

A dozen armored vehicles tore up the rough surface of the desert, bucking and pitching with every bump and irregularity of the terrain. Heedless, they pressed on with single-minded determination towards the locus where the object had come down.

Though it bore no resemblance to a warhead, Command was still not sure if the object was some kind of bomb or weapon. The vehicles slid to a stop in a semi-circle around the giant teardrop that had fallen from the sky. It stuck in the ground like a Jovian lightning bolt, its spire only slightly canted to the side.

The door on the lead vehicle opened and Captain Daithan stepped out, his boots crunching in the grit. He eyed the object, trying to determine its purpose. He had perhaps thirty seconds to do so before the spire righted itself. The front section began to retract back to form a ramp down to the ground.

The good Captain knew immediately that the object was a sort of drop ship or personnel carrier. A chorus of snicks and hums sounded as every weapon in his impromptu formation came to bear on the object. Daithan expected to see a horde of *somethings* burst from the craft, weapons in hand, murder in their big bug eyes.

Daithan had never dealt with the Inconnu before. Few people in uniform ever had, and were thankful for it. As the thing inside the tear came into view, he knew why. Where he expected dozens of critters to unload, there was only one, and the quarters inside the object would have been very tight.

Stars above, that thing's as big as a friggin' tank!

The Captain's face turned pale as the spider-demon exited the object fully on its six legs. The luminous eyes on its head were set in pairs above several sets of razor-sharp mandibles. Strangely, the creature's surface was not chitinous like an arachnid, but smooth and a dusky reddish brown. Muscles in its arms were thick and well-defined, strangely familiar in the way they rippled down to powerful four-fingered hands.

Fearsome as it appeared, however, Daithan was struck by how it swept its gaze across the skirmishing line seemingly without agitation. It sat back on its hind limbs, but made no threatening move. It was odd; this thing looked like something out of a nightmare, but there was something almost majestic, something noble in the way it sat there, like an alien god-king upon its throne.

"Hold fire!" Daithan barked, as he felt more than heard the fear of his formation ratchet to an incredible height. At his words, the thing was looking at him. Its eyes were a bright blood red and inscrutable. Perhaps it recognized him as the leader of the group.

Daithan strode forward, attempting to conceal his nervousness. He came to the bottom of the ramp. The thing's eyes followed him the whole way. The Captain cleared his throat.

"My name is Captain Walter Daithan of the Imperial Defense Forces of New Syracuse. By the authority of the Empire, I order you to surrender immediately." The Captain was aware that *it* probably didn't have the foggiest inkling of what his words meant.

The thing chittered to itself quietly before it spoke. When the words came, they seemed as though they were born from mimicry rather than cognitive understanding, all overlaid with the resonant buzzing of very different vocal organs shaping air into syllables.

"I come in peace," the thing said, raising four of its arms into the air like a victim caught in a bank heist.

"Take me to your leader."

This one definitely puts the "strange" in "Strange Reports." I used elements from a rather disturbing series of dreams I had at the time, and mixed them with a first-person POV. I'm not usually one to write in the first person for longer stories, (I'm a third person kind of guy) but this one really necessitated that I do so. This is probably the closest I've come to writing horror, and a first-person POV just gives it that real, personal feel.

While I did draw upon my own work history to fill in some of the blanks, none of the characters here are directly drawn from people I've worked with in the past. They are all composites based on the archetypes encountered over and over at nearly any place of employment.

Fun fact: I'm not a fast writer, but I wrote this story in three sessions, all in one week. Once I opened up the floodgates, I actually got a flood.

Weird, huh?

A Dissolution of Stars

So, where do I begin? I suppose wisdom would dictate that I start at the very beginning, which, in this case, is a pretty ironic state of affairs. With consideration to the reader, however, I'll start with when things started to give way to the stars and the events that led up to the end of the world.

If I've done my job correctly, *somebody* should eventually see these words on a page and be able to discern the meaning behind them. If you're with me so far, *you* are that somebody. I'll attempt to reconstruct the events for you as best I can. Of course, hindsight is 20/20 (and I'm no exception), but I'll preserve the opinions and worldviews I had at the time in question. Simpler that way.

So...

It all started the day before the event itself. At the time, I worked as an architect for a very upscale firm in lower Manhattan, Leeland and Holbrook. Founded by two of the Ivy League elite, both of Vermont money and breeding, they had joined forces to create an architectural firm that had shaped the cityscapes across the world from London to Paris, Hong Kong to Istanbul, and, of course, New York. I'm quite sure that Charles Leeland and Michael Holbrook had no idea that the sweeping yet somehow sinister edifice they designed and built themselves would literally be the last structure standing.

The massive steel and granite tower dominated its own little corner of Lexington and 78th, jutting above the buildings around it like a cathedral. It radiated a sense of strength, but the kind that was distant and cold. It's the rich uncle who holds you forever at arm's length, or the aging duchess who doesn't shake your hand, or so much as look you in the eye.

Overall, a slightly depressing environment in which to work. Despite that, or perhaps because of it, I did my best work there in a small little cubicle on the nineteenth floor, surrounded by posters of Notre Dame, the pyramids of Giza, and palaces from Buckingham to Versailles. There was even a print of the Empire State building at night, New York around it lit up like overlapping constellations. Gershwin always went through my mind when I looked at it.

On that particular morning, I was running late. I was normally a good and conscientious employee, but my time to work as of late had been slowly moving further and further back. On that day, with a leaden grey sky overhead that obscured the sun, I was twenty-four minutes past the time I should be up there surrounded by pictures of brilliant monuments and hammering away on my latest project. If I was lucky, dead lucky, I would be able to slip past my supervisor's office, perennially with its door open, and make it to my safe haven without notice.

I pushed through the revolving glass door which led into the vast lobby, briefcase in hand. Past the security station, the lobby was dotted here and there with tasteful furniture, artwork and sculpture. The receptionist smiled at me as I flashed my badge to the security guy on my way in.

That was when I first saw them.

In one of the small conversation areas, beneath a print of Alphonse Mucha's *Emerald*, sat a group of small figures clad in dusky gray robes, belted by a simple rope. Each had a hood that entirely covered their heads and cast their faces in shadow. Only two yellow points of light could be seen there, shining outward like a car's headlights at night. I stutter-stepped as they caught my attention.

Each one of them was staring straight at me, tracking my movements across the lobby as though they were each part of a larger whole. It was early October at the time, and I dismissed them as part of some early Halloween celebration, or tie-in photo shoot. In the back of my mind, I marveled at the effect of their illuminated eyes. It gave a very realistic impression that only the eyes existed beneath those strange gray folds.

But, when you have other worries, such as I did right then, dismissing something as odd as that is easy. We do it all the time; it's just how the mind works.

From there, I hung a right at the two bronze statues of the eponymous Leeland and Holbrook, then skipped past my regular set of elevators in favor of one that would deposit me on the far side of the nineteenth floor.

There were others in the elevator as I ascended, but none of them were familiar. All of their faces were blank and lifeless, and I felt alone. When my floor arrived, the older lady in front of me flashed me a smile as I moved past her to leave. Something about it made me smile back. This impromptu gesture, this small human expression reminded me I wasn't riding up with a bunch of automatons after all. I felt better somehow at knowing that.

Then I was on the nineteenth floor, in territory both familiar and now dangerous. For a moment I pictured myself as an explorer, carefully making his way through the jungle, conscious of its every sound, every vibration, all the while the Tiger was on the prowl, stalking me, hunting me in utter silence. We were two forces competing against each other, locked in an eternal struggle, doomed to play out this cycle again and again and again...

This day, the Tiger got me. My path towards the little niche I'd carved out here took me past Jerry's office door. It never closed, affording my supervisor a clear view of the elevators his department routinely used, the ones I had opted to avoid. He could also see the comings and goings of his team. I imagined sometimes that he kept a little ledger or spreadsheet that recorded when people arrived, down to the nanosecond.

I strode past his office, and he was there, vigilant as ever. I tried not to look directly at him, for fear of catching the gaze of the Tiger, but it didn't matter. Out of the corner of my eye I saw him look up, noting my briefcase, then his eyes went down to his expensive wristwatch, making a mental note. He would know that I had avoided the elevators. Everything was always being recorded with him. Every off-hand comment, every look of discontent or curse of frustration, all jotted down for later use.

I would get an email, terse and impersonal. Standard operating procedure, courtesy of Jerry. I could hear his fingers click-clacking on the keyboard as I passed out of earshot. Sure enough, just as I sat down and booted up my computer, there was a new message waiting for me in my inbox, sent only seconds before. It read:

"Work begins promptly at 8:00 a.m. Please ensure that you are here and ready to work at that time. No excuses, no exceptions."

No excuses, no exceptions. That was virtually Jerry's battle cry, and what I had come to expect from uptight middle managers. He was a living example of the old creed, *nothing is impossible if you don't have to do it yourself.*

I remember sighing as I read the email. That Jerry did not accept excuses was a bit of a blessing. It's hard to tell your boss that lack of sleep, or lack of quality sleep, was somehow muting your alarm clock on a semi-daily basis lately, but that was exactly the culprit. Something was going on with me. I would wake up in the morning, late, and feel as though I had not gone to sleep at all. Or, I would have nightmares when I could go to sleep, visions of dark acts going on all over the world, or disjointed images so disturbing that reality seemed to run like melting candle wax. My eyes would burn and my body would cry out to just roll over and go back to sleep. Of course, I couldn't do that. So, I would shamble out of bed and force myself to go to the office. Today was one of those days.

I took my suit jacket off and placed it on the coat hanger I kept by my model of the *Arc de Triomphe*. I rolled up the sleeves of my white undershirt and fired up the lights of my drafting table. After fifteen minutes of losing myself in a delicate, neo-classical archway in Buenos Aires, all thought of time clocks, predatory supervisors, and red-rimmed eyes began to fade to the background. I was creating something, and it stirred something deep inside me. I reveled in it, letting it wash me clean.

"Mornin' Johnny," a voice said from behind me. I turned to find Steve's smiling face looking at me. He quirked an eyebrow at my somewhat disheveled state, but the smile never left him.

"Jesus," Steve said. "You look like hell."

"Rough night," I replied.

"I'll bet," Steve said, making a drinking motion in the air with his hand, adding a knowing wink at the end. "What was her name?"

"Anxiety."

"A harsh mistress, no doubt." Steve, a salesman at heart, changed the subject. "Well, I'm heading over to *Just Winging It* at lunch time. Today's their twenty-five cent wing day, and I'm gonna knock the bottom out of it. Wanna come with?"

I considered it. "Thanks but no. I'll just grab something and eat it at my desk."

"You sure? They've got their big screen devoted to the Yankees now that they're in the Series." Steve was trying overcome my objection, just as he did with clients on sales calls. I needed to concentrate, but now, in retrospect, I wish I had taken Steve up on his offer.

"Tomorrow maybe?" I asked.

"Hey, it's your world, bro, we're just livin' in it." He flashed me a winning smile and was gone. Steve was a friend, though of a variety found only in the workplace. He was a lunch friend, someone who goes to lunch with you, but you don't hang out with outside of work. Steve was definitely of the beer and fantasy football league variety, unmarried and a happy bachelor. How he ate wings and drank beer so often, yet kept himself trim was a mystery, almost as much as the man himself. Steve was always 'on' when in front of other people, like a politician. You never heard him complain about work or have anything but a confident smile plastered on his face. While it seemed that Steve flirted with being shallow, he was a good sort. At times when the stress and pressure of the job weighed upon me, Steve was the first to step in and make me laugh, or pry me out of my moods. We would never be truly close friends, but that was okay. That was just the way it was.

Morning slipped into early afternoon, and I could tell the scant breakfast that I had gulped down before running out the door was wearing off. The archway was taking shape, and I was pleased enough to leave it for a while. I took the in-view elevator down to the lobby (this time there were no odd little guys with flashlight eyes about), and slipped around the corner to Fineman's Deli.

Sam, the owner and operator, greeted me. I was a regular there. He served up my usual order of corned beef on rye. I was already hungry and the savory smell of the deli shop was like throwing gasoline on a fire. The sandwich he carefully wrapped in deli paper was neatly cut in half and held in place with a toothpick sporting red streamers. A quarter slice of pickle joined the sandwich along with a trio of kosher mints. There was a twinkle in Sam's eye as he handed me the readied bag.

"See you at Temple on Friday," Sam said, practically as I was walking out the door. I made some polite, but noncommittal answer. I might be working or crashing early that night. At the rate I was going, I might be doing both at the same time.

So, back up to the nineteenth I went and sorted through my inbox with an occasional bite of my corned beef. It tasted heavenly. There were many things I had to clear out or follow up on this afternoon. I had a hard stretch of five hours or more in front of me, so I took comfort in the tongue-tingling flavor that Sam had painstakingly made for me. He, like I, loved to create, we just differed in our respective media. Right now, I imagined that I was enjoying his works far better than he would enjoy looking at my archway in Buenos Aires.

I was in mid-bite, trying to saw through a stubborn piece of meat, when Ms. Tana Wu walked around the corner, a roll of plans in her hand like a sword. She was one of the angels of the account service department. Here's a tip, if you're ever scouting for models, just hit a major agency of some kind and look around Account Services or Sales. That's where the pretty ones hang out, and Tana seemed to personify that. I believe she was originally from Taiwan or mainland China, she never said, but she had a face that was, well, perfect. Everything was where it was supposed to be. Luxuriant black hair cascaded over her shoulders. I'm sure it was normally straight, but she had added waves to it, like a mountain stream flowing over rocks. Stunning.

I'm also pretty sure she was a vegetarian, which made me feel all the more like a caveman barbarian, grossly eating murdered cow flesh in front of her. I shot an embarrassed smile her way behind the sandwich, begging for a moment, but she didn't smile back. Instead she dropped the plans on my drafting table.

"Here are the revisions from the Saunderson account," she said with no discernible accent. "I'm afraid they've moved the deadline up on us again."

I swallowed painfully and brushed my lips with a napkin.

"Forgive me while I graze," I said, but again got no response. "So, when do they want it now?"

"By end of day today. Think you can do it?"

I nodded that I could. I hadn't looked at the changes yet, so I wasn't sure how extensive they would be, but I agreed nonetheless. This brought a muted smile to her face which still held me in thrall. Satisfied, she turned and walked away, affording me a look at her incredible calves.

Above those calves were thighs that disappeared into the mysteries of her gray business skirt. I know it's not polite to think of coworkers like that, but Tana's legs were the subject of much discussion amongst the male community of L&H, and it was evident to see why. She must do yoga, pilates, or gymnastics to have a figure like that. Strangely enough, though, many of the men preferred the other major houri in Tana's department, Monica Murphy. She was the regular blue-eyed, blonde bombshell, who, it was speculated, had worked as an exotic dancer before joining our august ranks. There was one in every crowd.

Personally, I always found Monica to be a little empty. Oh, she was quick with a smile, dressed to the nines every day, and laughed with the constant orbit of guys around her, but it seemed like there was just something missing about her, as though if you managed to get beyond her shell you would find only a void lurking behind a pretty mask. In that sense, Steve—who was her biggest fan—reminded me of her somewhat, existing almost entirely on the surface.

For me, though, Tana was just the opposite. Her looks were just a gateway, a hint at the deep pools that lay beyond those cool dark eyes of hers. I wanted to know more about her, wanted to know what it would be like for her to share her mysteries with me. Those thoughts, which I'm not ashamed to admit to you, the reader, kept me floating for ten minutes after Tana had left, assisted in no small part by the sweet trace of her perfume that lingered in my sanctum.

When I came back to myself, I stopped what I was doing on the archway and threw myself into the Saunderson plans. The changes, as it turned out, were quite extensive, but I plowed right through them like a force of nature. Somewhere in the back of my mind, I had to wonder if I would have jumped into redesigning a foodcourt in Dubai with as much gusto if Jerry had brought the plans to me himself. Yeah, probably not.

It took me the rest of the afternoon to finish up on the Saunderson plans, but I managed to put the finishing touches on them a good half-hour before Tana normally left for the day. She wasn't at her desk when I arrived, which I silently lamented. I had hoped she would grace me with another faint smile or a thankful look that would make my efforts on her behalf worth it. Yes, *her* behalf. I guarantee you I didn't infuse a modern foodcourt with a Middle-Eastern style for some multi-billion dollar building consortium halfway around the world. No, sir.

I wrapped up on my email and shut down my computer. When the monitor turned off, my sanctum was dark, lit only by the lights of my drafting lamp. I sat there for several moments, taking in long breaths and soaking in the day as it had unfolded. Aside from the brief appearance of Tana, it was pretty much a wash.

The problem wasn't so much the job, per se, or Jerry, or the daily stress, though all of those things were on the periphery. No, it was me. I had been unhappy here at L&W for the past six months or more. I had gone to school to be an architect, and that's what I was, but there was something missing, like when Monica smiled at you. There was some essential element that hadn't made it into the mix, and I couldn't for the life of me figure it out what it was. All I knew was that I was done here at this job. While I might miss Steve and the occasional cameo by Tana, I knew it was over for me here. I would never rise above where I was now as long as I was at Leeland and Holbrook. Now I was just spinning my wheels in the mud. I needed a change. I needed to move on to whatever was next.

I gathered up my briefcase and jacket and headed for the elevators. I was alone as I made the nineteen-floor plummet to the lobby. I gave a silent nod to the statues of Mike and Chuck as I retraced my earlier steps through the revolving door. Not three steps out of the door and I stopped. Something was out of place, though it took me a moment to really put my finger on what it was.

Then it hit me.

It wasn't 6:00 in the evening and the stars were already out as though it were midnight. Daylight Savings Time didn't kick in for a few more days, but yet I could plainly make out the three stars of Orion's belt on the ascendant even through the light pollution (and other pollution for that matter).

I gave a mental shrug and hailed a cab to go home.

▲ ▲ ▲

Okay, with me so far? Sounds like pretty mundane stuff, right? Well, that's what I thought at the time, too. One day in a long, unbroken string of days that seemed to blend together, leaving me with only impressions overall and a handful of specific memories.

Well, I lay all this out for you in plain terms so that I can familiarize you with the major players involved and contrast the two days, which you can say were like night and day.

Yeah, you could say that.

On the day in question, I had set my alarm to wake me up at 4:45 knowing full well that I wouldn't actually get up until 5:30 or so. I also set the alarm on my watch and phone just to make sure I didn't have a repeat of the previous morning. The best way to rebuild fences with Jerry, I reasoned, was to come in early the next day. All it would take is copying him on an email or two for him to see the time at which it was sent. I was hoping that the ever-watchful recorder in his head would make note of that as well.

I felt a little freeze-dried that morning for getting up early, but a quick shower was enough to thaw my brain out. Really, it wasn't that difficult. Most of my cable channels had been static the night before, so I had gone to bed early. Sleep was still a bumpy road, but the extra time had paid off.

The result was that by 6:20 I was walking into Fineman's Deli to treat myself to a bagel and coffee. Sam was once again there. He never seemed to leave and was always awake and alert no matter the circumstances. For a man in his mid-sixties, he had an unquenchable fire about him that immediately put me in a good mood, like Steve but on a deeper level. Sam was a guy who had started out with nothing and blazed a trail through the entrenched delicatessen turf of New York, and carved out a name for himself. Now there were six Fineman's Delis around the city, all very lucrative, but only one, the original one, had Sam himself in it. I was glad to know him.

"Good morning, John," Sam said, looking up from his copy of the *Times*. "Been a while since I've seen you in here this early."

"True enough," I said as I ordered. Soon there was a fresh wheat bagel in front of me with a liberal amount of strawberry cream cheese crowning it. In moments it was gone. I washed it down with the last of my gourmet blend. As I reached for my briefcase, Sam raised an eyebrow.

"See you back here at lunch?"

I remembered Steve's offer and shook my head.

"Probably not today, but I may pick something up on my way home."

"No problem," Sam replied. "Just give me a ring and I'll have your usual waiting for you. Extra pickles this time."

"Promise?"

"Believe it."

With that, I left the deli and glanced at my watch. It was 6:43. I could be up at my desk in six minutes if I caught the elevator just right. Plenty of time to settle in and get some things squared away before Jerry showed up around 7:30. Yeah, things were going pretty well. Today was going to be different.

As I neared the revolving door, something strange happened. Orange and yellow light erupted from behind me, reflecting off the glass. It seemed like a bonfire had sprung up behind me for perhaps a second and then winked out again, only I had felt no heat. Curiosity made me turn around. Nothing was there but the street and the passing cars. No building burned, no crazy man went running by on fire. There was nothing.

I gave yet another mental shrug as it occurred to me that I was standing in exactly the same place as when I had looked up into the sky at the stars the night before. I cast my eyes to the same spot above and found (I'm not sure why it didn't dawn on me before this) that the stars where still up and clearly visible. At 7:00 and there wasn't even a hint of the sun in the cloudless sky.

I had no idea what significance that held until later, nor did I realize at the time that the stars had not moved from their present position since I had viewed them more than twelve hours before.

The receptionist was not at her customary station, which was no surprise to me having arrived a full hour ahead of schedule. No, it wasn't the missing receptionist that got my attention, it was that there was no guard at the security station, a place that was manned 24-hours a day. Once I had to go back into the office at 2:30 in the morning to make sure the Hong Kong group received a critical file they just couldn't wait for, and the guard station had been fully staffed even then.

I let myself pass and moved by the bronze stares of Chuck and Mike. Today I would use the regular elevators. No fear, right? Just march right in like I owned the place. And so I did. No one was there to see my glorious entry into the city like Caesar at his triumph.

I went through my morning routine. My emails were scant, almost non-existent, but I found the opportunity to show Jerry that I had come in early. I then picked back up on the archway where I had left off. By the time I heard the distant rumblings of other people arriving, the archway was complete on paper. It would be a portfolio piece, no doubt about it. It might even help me get that next, fantastic job that I had been dreaming about since L&H had started to give me the blues.

I gathered up the plans, backed up the documentation on the server, and went to hand-deliver them to Jerry. I hoped to catch him right as he was putting down his car keys, in that transition state between the outside world and work, where he was vulnerable. I know it was petty, but it seemed like turnabout was fair play. He had certainly played that card numerous times with everyone, so why not turn the tables? For once the explorer might get the better of the Tiger.

As I turned the corner on approach to Jerry's office, something caught my eye. Something gray, like cloth moved through the doorway ahead of me, like I was catching the tail-end of someone's coat as it slipped through. It reminded me of those strange little Jawa-like kids or little people in the lobby the morning before. But when I made the ninety-degree turn through Jerry's open door, no one was in there. The lights were off and it seemed lifeless and deserted. I had a hard time reconciling the movement with the emptiness here. I just chalked it up to the weirdness of the day, like the stars or the flash of eldritch fire from an invisible source, or the empty guard station. It's amazing how the mind wants to preserve the status quo, a sense of normality, even when presented with evidence to the contrary.

My puzzlement wasn't at the phantom cloth I had seen go into Jerry's office, but rather what *wasn't* in there. All of Jerry's personal effects were gone. The ornate Chinese calendar he had picked up on the Hong Kong trip, the abstract floral print he kept in a frame behind his head, pictures of his wife and two kids, gone. The Knicks sticker on the side of his monitor, gone. Even the potted Ficus tree was absent. It was well-past time for Jerry to be in, and, as far as I knew, he was *never* late. I should have been worried, but I have to be honest, I was glad. He might be out of the office today, at an offsite meeting or vacation, which would make things easier all the way around. Better yet, maybe he'd been let go and taken his cursed ledger of everything with him. Whatever had happened to him, it wasn't going to evoke much in the way of sympathy from me. What did he expect? There was no love lost between us, that was for sure. If I really wanted to be mean, I could go up a floor to Walter, Jerry's boss, and indirectly inquire as to why he wasn't at work. Let Jerry sweat a little at *his* boss noting his tardiness directly. Yeah, that would be great, wouldn't it?

Then I got that queasy feeling in my stomach. That might be going over the line to try to intentionally put egg on Jerry's face like that. It would be just another example of how the corporate environment had a way of turning people against each other, like a million private wars being waged through careful documentation to CYA, attack and retreat in conference rooms, with the H.R. acting as either a referee, or judge, jury and executioner. I didn't want to be a part of that self-perpetuating cycle. If anything, I hoped that the next job I had would be free of that kind of thinly veiled gladiatorial combat.

So, I left the plans in his chair and went back to work. An hour or more after that, while I was ensconced in the designs for a walkway park in Sacramento, that Steve came around at last.

"Johnny boy," he said, announcing his presence and quirking an eyebrow. "You're still looking a little green around the gills."

"Been a rough couple of days." More like a rough couple of *months*, but Steve took my meaning.

"I hear you, brother. We still going to get some grub come lunchtime?"

"Sure thing. You gonna invite Monica along, too? I'm sure you two can find something to talk about."

I saw a glimmer of confusion in Steve's eyes, but, ever in the spotlight, he passed it off with just a smile. Despite all his bravado and confidence, I knew he had wanted to ask her out for months now. She had kicked her current boyfriend to the curb three weeks before, and Steve had contemplated interviewing for the position. Had I touched on a trace of embarrassment? I let it pass and changed the subject.

"Anyway, have you seen Jerry at all today? I was supposed to go over the Argentina designs with him, but he didn't show."

Again, there was that look of confusion. It hadn't quite dawned on me what that look meant. It would, but only much later.

"Who's Jerry?" Steve asked.

"My boss. Higgins, Jerry Higgins. You know, the bean-counter?" The confusion was still there. Now Steve wasn't even hiding it. "The one that makes my life a living hell every day? *That* Jerry."

"Sorry, bro, I have no idea who that is."

There had been any number of lunch hours where I had regaled Steve with tales of Jerry's ineptitude and poor people skills, or of how he treated his creative folks as machines that could constantly pump out quality work on demand. I wondered at that moment if Steve was kidding me, or if he had just been giving me the 'nod-and-make-eye-contact' routine where it had all gone in one ear and out the other. Then it hit me, *he honestly doesn't know who I'm talking about*. Again, I just let it pass. We all have our off-days, right?

"No worries," I said. "Shall we meet around noon, then?"

"High noon, partner," he said, making a motion like he was gripping an invisible six-shooter at his hip. He flashed me another winning smile, turned, and left.

That was the last time I ever saw him.

Something about our encounter had unsettled me, though. The look he gave me when I mentioned Monica's name was blank, the same as when I mentioned Jerry. I could understand him passing over Jerry in his mind. My boss wasn't as big a player in Steve's head as he was in mine. But, Monica? This was the girl that made all the guys' hearts beat a little faster. How could he not know immediately who I was talking about?

I got up to make a tour of the floor, to stretch my legs if not to clear my mind. The halls seemed all but deserted. The few people I did encounter seemed like strangers going about their incomprehensible tasks without any trace of emotion. I fell back to more familiar territory and hovered around the cubes where the other architects sat. I was confronted by more empty desks without any kind of personal affectations of any kind, as though it had all been stripped away. Had there been some massive layoff that I had somehow survived? Or, was my time coming and I just didn't know it yet? A feeling of dread started to go through me. I got that churning stomach feeling. When it looked as though the whole department was either canned or out sick, it felt like a small lump of ice had been left on my heart. What was going on?

I needed to step away. It seemed like if you stepped away from a strange situation for about twenty minutes, it had a way of resetting itself. That's what I needed, *desperately* some corner of my mind told me. I was back in the elevator and heading down to the street level. I needed coffee. Not the cheap version found in the break room, but the expensive, smooth blend found at the coffee chain next door.

Like a man in a fugue state, I wondered through the lobby and back past the empty security and reception area. When I entered the coffee shop, I was pleasantly surprised that there was no line, yet even something about that added to my unease. This was *New York*. If you wanted coffee at this time in the morning you were going to *wait*. I told the coffee artist behind the counter what I wanted and in moments there as a steaming double-strength cappuccino with cream in my hands.

"Slow day today?" I asked the girl behind the counter. She looked back at me blankly. The lights were on but no one was home.

"Yeah, thank God."

Stepping back out onto the street, I took a sip of the rocket fuel that masqueraded as coffee and tried to banish the feelings that were starting to get the better of me. There weren't very many people out on the street, and fewer cars. Those streets, which have been jam-packed at all hours, were almost vacant.

Then I looked up. Heaven help me, I looked up.

At 10:30 in the morning, the stars were still there in the sky. My mind reeled at this. I felt dizzy. How could...? What the....?

The presence of the stars wasn't the only thing that seemed like a discrepancy from the world I knew. They seemed *closer*. Orion's Belt occupied the same basic place in the sky. Before those three stars were only pinholes in the night; now they were the size of dimes. Still in perfect formation, still in relation to each other, but larger than the moon in the day time.

In horror, I retreated back into the side alley. My breath came in short, labored bursts. My body had forgotten how to breathe and I was having to remind it. I leaned against the brick wall, my head spinning. My coffee was gone. I realized that I had dropped it just outside the entrance of the coffee shop. The dizziness was almost unbearable. I wasn't moving, and yet I felt unstable, like I couldn't stay on my feet. The world was spinning, spinning. The stars were closer, closer...

Then I threw up.

The spinning stopped, sort of. I felt better as I wiped my lips with my sleeve and stood up. I took three long breaths and looked up. The stars were still as I had seen them, but the sight of them did not unnerve me as before. Unfortunately, that alley was not done with me yet. I can tell you I saw two things in that alley that made me at once question my sanity and, once acceptance set in, realize that the world I had lived in was dissolving.

I had just come to terms with the strange stars overhead when my gaze fell on the far end of the alley. You would think that I would have run away immediately at what I found there, but I was strangely drawn to it, like a moth to flames. Not thirty feet from where I stood, the alley just ended in darkness. New York has—or *had*—no shortage of back alleys. No, it was what filled the blackness where the alley fell away into nothingness.

The alley ended in stars.

Looking into it was beautiful, like seeing the false-color images taken from the Hubble. There were stars surmounting fronds of iridescent gas clouds of the most incredible shades of magenta, ruby, and deep cerulean blue. Galaxies swirled in those depths, the universe danced and moved before my eyes. I was entranced, at least until I saw that the inky black of space was *moving*. As I watched, slow inches of the alley gave away to the stars, as though space were running like molasses over it. It crept towards me. That's what broke the spell. I tore my eyes from it and backed away like a caveman retreating away from an engulfed, lightning-struck tree.

Then I ran into the second thing that really wrenched my fragile mind, kicking and screaming, from the world of my understanding. At first, I saw what I thought was fire-light, but something was different about it. The light grew out of another connecting alley in front of me as though an inferno was moving to the intersection where I stood. Bright as the light was, I felt no heat from it, if anything I felt infinitely colder. Then I found what the light was attached to.

A hulking figure easily two or three times my size rounded the corner, and each time each of its four legs touched the ground, I felt something like silent thunder reverberate through me. The shape of it was something like a praying mantis, though immolated in flames. No, not flames. They didn't move like flames, they moved like water, rolling off the thing's head and body in smooth, ever-changing coils. Its bulbous head turned to look at me, and it seemed like a human face locked eyes with me from behind that heatless, eldritch blaze.

I screamed. I felt tears streaming down my face. For perhaps two seconds, I was frozen in place before the thing like a mouse hypnotized by a snake. Then I broke free and ran out of the alley. I could feel it following me as I made for the entrance of the L&H building. At that moment, my work place seemed safe, familiar. I was suddenly a drowning man looking for something, anything, to latch on to, and the foreboding L&H building was what I needed.

As I reached the revolving door, I looked ahead and found that the same starfield that had been slowly devouring the alley was swallowing whole blocks coming from the other way. The wall of glittering stars and nebulae moved more like ocean waves, erasing cars, buildings, and people in a slow flood.

Then I noticed something else. The people on the street did not notice the strange oblivion headed their way. In that moment I saw cars and pedestrians moving into the stars as though nothing was amiss. There was no moment of shock or terror, they were simply gobbled up and that was that.

I looked back the way I came and saw the thing, which I labeled the "Destroyer," clear the alley near the coffee shop. It turned on its four insectoid legs and moved towards me.

And again, no one on the street seemed to notice the mind-bending monstrosity that had come upon them. In fact, it seemed to walk through people, only those unlucky souls to physically touch it winked out in a fiery burst of light. They didn't scream, they didn't run, they were simply unmade.

At this, I flew through the doors and into the lobby. This time I gave the empty security booth no thought as I sprinted. I didn't stop until I reached the statues of Leeland and Holbrook. There was movement in the corner of my eye from off to my right. I spun around and found a small herd of those odd, robed figures working to disassemble the lobby. They were streaming all over it like ants, in fact.

I saw one of the little creatures take a fluted glass vase down from one of the displays with its grubby hands. It peeled the glass down its facet lines as though there was a connecting seam. Another one was busily reducing the decorative table in the conversation area down to its component parts. Yet another had taken the *Emerald* print down and held it in its hands. It gave the naked print a slight shake and it fell to dust.

Had I seen one of them go into Jerry's office before I put the plans in his chair? Had one of these little bastards turned Jerry himself to dust as well? Or better yet, had he been erased not just out of space and time, but memory as well?

"*What is happening?*" I heard myself say in a low, breathy voice.

"Isn't it obvious, old boy?" a deep baritone voice said from behind me. "It's the end of the world."

"Quite right, as always," another replied.

I turned, not sure what new horrors I might find there. The statues, the bronze statues of Leeland and Holbrook, stood in the same poses, but their faces were now animated. Thee looked upon me instead of on some distant horizon.

"Am I crazy?" I asked, perhaps not realizing at the time how odd it was to ask that question of a statue that had been inanimate only thirty seconds before.

"Far from it, old boy," Leeland said. I watched as the bronze mouth opened and closed as though it was made from flesh and bone.

"You might say that you're the only sane person left in an otherwise insane world," Holbrook added. "Wouldn't you agree, my friend?"

"I would, I would, indeed," Leeland answered.

I felt that these two statues seemed to know what was going on. They had answers, answers I needed.

"What is that thing out there?"

"He's looking for you, John," Holbrook answered.

"And he won't stop, no, never," Leeland said.

"And those things?" I asked, glancing at the little figures in robes, busily deconstructing the furniture.

Two bronze heads turned to see what I was talking about. Leeland sighed, disappointed.

"Ah, now they've negated the Mucha print," he said. "That was rather one of my favorites."

"Mine too," added Holbrook. "I very much liked Mucha. Decent sort of fellow, wouldn't you say?"

"Brilliant. Leeland said. "A pity, now no one remembers him but the three of us, old boy. A pity."

Then it came to me, just as the "Destroyer" had been supplied to my mind for the immolating praying mantis outside. It just appeared in my mind. They were the Disassemblers. They broke things down in advance of the starfield so the rest could be more easily digested. I guessed that if you could look at any of the remaining buildings, they would be heaving with these little fellows like maggots on a corpse.

"What can I do?" I asked the statues.

"What is there to do in all of this, old boy?" said Leeland.

"I suppose it depends you, John," said Holbrook. "Do you wish to hang on or let go? That is really the question you need to ask yourself."

"Let go? You mean die?" I asked them. In retrospect I'm not sure what emotional response I was hoping to get from animate lumps of bronze, but I guess you'd had to be there. "If dying means letting go, then sign me up for holding on until the end!"

"Tenacious," Leeland remarked to Holbrook.

"Bold," Holbrook replied to Leeland.

The two of them regarded me together.

"Very well, young man," Leeland said. "If you wish to hang on a while longer, that's your choice. We'll hold the lobby here until you can get back up to 19th floor."

"It will be like that time on safari back in '06, wouldn't you say, my friend?"

"Those were great days, old boy."

"Agreed, agreed."

A booming crash came from the direction of the revolving door, followed by the tinkling of a thousand points of glass. I whipped around and saw the Destroyer moving through the ruins of the entrance from the hole it had just created. It still hunted me, its strangely human face looking right through me. One of its scythelike arms reached up and tore down the guard station's wall with contemptuous ease as it advanced.

The two status stepped down from their pedestals. Long blades, like something a knight would have wielded, grew out of their bronze fists, gleaming in the dull light.

"Ready, old boy?" Leeland asked.

"One last time, my friend," Holbrook replied. "Let's make a decent accounting of ourselves."

"Have at you, foul beast!" I heard Leeland cry, but I was running. The elevator door was already open and I swooped in and pressed the button marked "19." As the doors closed, I saw a reflection of a sign. Despite everything, I heard myself let loose a chuckle. In bright red letters, the sign proclaimed:

IN CASE OF EMERGENCY, USE STAIRS.

▲ ▲ ▲

Most of the lights were off when I reached the 19th floor. It reminded me of the time I had come in at 2:30 in the morning so the VP of the Hong Kong team could get his updates that just *couldn't* wait until the next day. Only half the lights had been on, and those had been the bright, spot lighting. It lent the 19th floor an air of drama, like the mood lighting of a movie set.

I really wasn't sure what I was doing, truth be told. I had no idea whether there was any place left to go to avoid the creeping starscape or the apocalyptic praying mantis from Hell. So, I moved towards what was familiar. I ducked my head into my cubicle.

Empty.

All my little knickknacks were gone, along with my posters. It looked as though I had never set foot in it before or ever attempted to personalize it. I stared at the sterile space blankly until a cold realization filled me. It was all gone because the outside world was gone. The Empire State building had been swallowed up by the stars or been picked apart by the Disassemblers, taking all posters, souvenir models and keychains with it. Notre Dame, Angor Wat, Taj Mahal, the Pyramids of Giza, all gone now, and with them any evidence that they had ever existed at all.

I remember stumbling back a step and making a low moan, half of terror, half of sorrow. Was I insane? Was all of this happening in a dream? Would I wake up any minute in my bed, late for work again under Jerry's ever-watchful gaze? Or would I come out of it drugged and straight-jacketed in a mental institute?

"H-Hello?" I heard a voice say in the distance. "Is someone here?"

I moved towards the sound, still numb from the grim revelations of my cubicle. Rounding the corner, I almost collided bodily with Tana Wu. We both gave a startled shout. She looked as distressed as I was. Her hair was frizzed in places and her eyes were a bit puffy. For once she didn't have the calm and pristine look of an FBI agent.

She was the most beautiful sight I had ever seen. Without thinking, I swept her into my arms and felt her return it firmly. I smelled the glory of her perfumed hair. She *knew*, I realized. Whatever was going on around us, she was aware of it, too.

"Everyone's gone, John," she said as we finally parted. "I've looked around, but there's nobody left. I've seen things, John, *horrible* things."

"Me too."

In one of those strange notions, it occurred to me that I had wanted to be alone with this woman for a while now. Perhaps in my mind this was the proverbial deserted island. Now, we might be the last two humans alive, and it had taken something like the end of the world to bring us together. Funny how the mind works, huh?

When Tana moved away from me, my Adam and Eve fantasy shattered. She seemed more like her old self, in control and slightly aloof. My arms still held the memory of her embrace. I could still smell her perfume, sweet and enticing.

"Downstairs is out of the question, I take it?" she asked.

"Yeah, that's a good way to put it. There's something down there, it looks like a praying mantis or something, but it's not. It's a killer." I didn't mention that I thought it was after me personally. I had naturally assumed that it was gunning for me simply because I could see it and others could not. Would it be after Tana now as well?

"I saw the stars running like water," Tana said a moment later as we sat down in a cushioned conversation area. "People disappeared into it. They just faded out, and nobody seemed to notice, except me. I made it inside and—"

"Came to the closest familiar place you could think of," I said. I saw her look *of how did you know?* "I did the same, and I'm not even sure why. My desk was cleaned out, like I had never been there."

"Mine too," Tana replied. "I had this miniature globe I kept from college. One of my sorority sisters gave it me. The map of the world was made of different types of stone with lapis lazuli outlining the oceans."

She dropped her eyes down, and suddenly seemed very tired.

"I saw this little thing in robes holding it when I walked in. The globe was *blank*, John, just a flat gray swirl. No countries, no oceans, nothing. It shook the globe and I watched it turn to dust right in front of me. Then it looked at me, and—" Her voice trailed off.

"Which sorority sister was it?" I asked.

"What?"

"Who gave you the globe? Can you remember?"

Tana looked down at the floor, her eyes moving back and forth as though she was reading something written on the floor. She met my gaze, and there was confusion mixed with fear in her eyes.

"I-I don't know."

"Do you remember anybody who works here? Monica, who sat next to you? Steve from sales? My boss, Jerry? Your boss, Evan?" Somehow I knew the answer before she said it.

"No."

"Can you remember anyone else besides me? Your parents? Brothers and sisters? Best friend, boyfriend, anything?"

"No," she answered. "All their faces are gone. I can't see them." She squeezed her eyes shut and it seemed that pressure built behind them. Then she was up on her feet.

"How is that even possible?" she asked, and not necessarily to me. "How can I not remember my own parents? What the *fuck* is going on?"

I stood up and was by her side. I laid a gentle hand on her shoulder, half-hoping she would hug me again, but this gesture seemed to enrage her. She shrugged my hand away.

"*Don't touch me!*"

"Tana, I think—"

She gave me a dangerous look, the kind a predator gives its prey right before it pounces. What I experienced in the alleyway, she was experiencing now. The disbelief, the horror that the events around her were, in fact, real. Only it was different for her. While I had looked upon the pseudo-human face of the Destroyer, Tana couldn't remember anyone else but me. *My* memories, on the other hand, seemed fully intact. I wondered which was worse, to have the world taken away from your mind or to remember it enough to know that it was gone.

"I don't know why this is happening, Tana," I said, my voice surprisingly calm. "But I'm glad to know that I'm not crazy. You have given me that, if nothing else."

I suppose that was the right thing to say. The menacing stare disappeared and she was once again herself. Then, to my surprise, she smiled, actually *smiled*, and I thought I had died.

"It's not your fault, John." she said, with a peal of bittersweet laughter. "Maybe I shouldn't be so cross with the one person who *is* left."

"Thanks for noticing," I told her. She was processing what I meant, when we both heard a loud *WHAAAMM* nearby. We were instantly side by side, waiting to see what new horror was about to reveal itself. The combat stance we adopted would have looked comical to an outside observer, like it would have better served us if we were in armor and carrying swords and spears. But what could we do?

We crept forward as quietly as we dared. We could make out muffled voices from the dimly lit hallway ahead. I thought it might be the mutterings of the Disassemblers talking through their gray robes. But it wasn't.

Several figures emerged from the intersection ahead of us, near the restrooms.

"Sam?" I asked as he came into view? "Sam, is that you?"

Samuel Aaron Fineman stood there, red-faced and breathing hard, but otherwise alive and well. Two others flanked him on either side. One I recognized as the older lady from the elevator the day before, the one who had smiled at me. The other was a wiry black man who could have been a young forty or a hard-run thirty. He wore a dirty camouflage field jacket.

"Johnny?"

A part of me was relieved to see other people. Of course, the selfish part of me knew instantly that the 'just the two of us' mindset that Tana and I had just formed was now shattered by the presence of others. That small part, that selfish part, didn't stop me from throwing my arms around Sam's neck when he came close enough.

"You're living in this nightmare, too, I see." Sam said.

"Afraid so. We may be all that's left."

We all went to the breakroom, the place that all of us could seat ourselves comfortably. Normally the lights in there were the too-bright fluorescents, but now, as elsewhere, it was just the mood-inducing yellow spotlights. The lights of the vending machines and the broad fronts of the drink machines seemed like nightlights in a child's room.

Sam filled us in on what had happened, and how he had come to join us on the 19th floor.

"I was at the slicer, carving up some corned beef. I was going to use some of the finer cuts to build that sandwich you were gonna pick up tonight, John. So, standing there with my back to the counter, I could just see out the back window. That's when I saw the stars. At first I thought I was seeing a reflection or something, but then I realized that they were moving *in* through the storeroom, moving like a living thing. They had already taken my kitchen and bathroom before I could wrap my mind around what was happening. I yelled to my customers to get out, but it was like none of them could hear. None of 'em, except Gus here. He saw it immediately, and both of us was out the door. I saw my store disappear with all the people still in it. They were all still eating and drinking like nothing was wrong. Outside wasn't any better. I could swear that the sky looked like it was descending. How it was that we hadn't noticed a night sky in the afternoon, I don't know."

Sam took a sip of water from his conical paper cup. His hands were steady, though his face was troubled.

"The only place them creeping stars weren't going was this building. Gus and I made for it as though the hounds were on us. The revolving door was wreckage, and we had to avoid all that glass. Some of it looked like it had been *melted*. Something had gone through the place like a freight train. We tried the elevators, but they weren't working. So we went up the stairwell. That's where we found Evelyn here," he nodded to the woman from the elevator. "She had the same idea we did, get to the high ground. Best thing to do during a flood, and that's what we were in, a flood. All the doors were locked as we went up and wouldn't budge. Until we get to 19, that is. Gus kicked the door so hard, I thought he was going to tear it off its hinges."

Gus had been pacing the periphery of the space since five seconds into Sam's tale. Almost in response to Sam's last comment, Gus picked up one of the plastic and metal chairs and put it through the glass face of one of the vending machines. The glass fell like rain. Gus reached in and snagged a bag of chips and a pack of peanut butter crackers, that kind with the caution-orange crackers. He started eating them, only becoming aware of all our stares.

"What?" he asked in defiance. We all just shrugged. We all supposed that there was no one left to care, and the food in these machines might be all that was left in existence. Besides, if you can't beat 'em, join 'em, right?

"Toss me a honey bun?" I asked Gus. He smiled and dug out one through the glass, tossing it to me deftly. I caught it and turned back to Sam.

"You were saying?"

"That was about it. There's just one other thing, that both of you should know," Sam said, looking at Tana and I. "But it's probably best if I show you."

Gus and Evelyn stayed behind while Sam led the two of us back to the stairs. As we stepped into the narrow confines, Sam pointed down into the empty shaft that formed the middle of the stairwell.

There, about six floors down, the stairwell ended. I couldn't be sure, but it looked as though the Greater Magellanic Cloud filled that space among the darkness.

▲ ▲ ▲

Over the next hour, a steady stream of refugees from the upper and lower floors streamed into the breakroom. They were all haggard-looking in the limited color palette of their professional dress. The men almost always wore the same white or French blue shirts with generic striped ties. The women were a little more colorful, but only in their necklaces, rings, and bracelets. In all there were twenty-two people, and their stories were largely the same. Either they had encountered a Disassembler and fled, or narrowly avoided the creeping starfield when their colleagues—colleagues they could no longer remember clearly—seemed oblivious to it, or were missing in action altogether. At some point, they had felt a pull towards the 19th floor as if summoned there.

Here's the odd part (odd being relative in this case, I suppose), everyone turned to Tana and I as their leaders, even Gus, Evelyn, and Sam. We had become their King and Queen of a sort, though neither of us had asked for, or wanted, the job. Sam became my adviser, Gus my sergeant-at-arms, and Evelyn my quartermaster.

Seeing all those faces so hungry for instructions or answers, Tana and I did what we could to move things along. We appointed Gus and a few others to stand watch at the stairwells and alert us if the stars should start to rise up the stairs. We had Evelyn take a log of everyone who was present, then catalogue what food and drinks we had left in our stockpile. We sent out food-gathering sorties to break open the vending machines on other floors and bring back as much of the food and drink as possible. Once that was done, and we had gathered everything together, Sam re-opened his restaurant in the breakroom, making sure that everyone got a decent amount of food. We ate the refrigerated stuff first since we couldn't be sure how long the power would hold out. At times we would send out patrols to keep a watch out for Disassemblers or other strange happenings.

At that point, I was about at the end of my ideas. We had met everyone's immediate needs, but where we went from there was anyone's guess. Unless the stars receded and the 19th floor proved to be a new version of Mount Ararat, what could we do? There was no other place to go.

I was busily tearing into a roast beef sandwich, complete with chips, trail mix, a bag of those little chocolate chip cookies, and a frosty root beer when Tana glided into a seat opposite from me. Her tray boasted bottled water, a coffee filter filled with microwave popcorn, a protein bar, and two bags of raisins. She did, however, allow herself the luxury of a bag of white chocolate pretzels. No one interrupted us. They all kept their distance.

"How are things on the frontlines?" I asked her.

"Unchanged, thankfully." she said with a bite of her protein bar.

I sensed that she wanted to say something, but wasn't quite sure how to begin, an interesting reversal of roles. Normally I was the one that wanted to say something to her but could never find my voice.

"Is something on your mind?" I asked. "I think we're to the point where we can speak openly to each other."

Tana nodded, staring down at the table. Then she made eye contact.

"Okay then, I have a question for you."

"Shoot."

"Something you said before stuck with me, right before Sam and the others came through the door. You asked me if I could remember anyone from my life. I couldn't, but you can, correct? You remember the world as it was before?"

"Yes," I said and took a swig of my rootbeer. "I'm not sure why, but I do."

Something glimmered in the dark, mysterious depths of her eyes. Something like the awe that I continually felt for her.

"I've been talking to the others. No one can remember their friends, their families, or even their children." She put her hand on mine, and my heart leaped. "So far as I can tell, you're the *only* one who remembers people or places outside of this building."

"I wish I knew why."

She withdrew her hand. I wasn't ready for that contact to end.

"Whatever is going on here, John, I think you're the key to it."

I sat back and swatted at a fly that had tried to take up residence on my sandwich. It buzzed away, landing by the black and white pillars of the salt and pepper shakers.

"You think I had something to do with all this?" I couldn't muster up an accusatory tone, not at her, so it came out very matter-of-factly.

"No, of course not," she replied. "But you're different somehow than the rest of us. You might just be the last keeper of the old world we knew and now can't remember."

Her gaze softened.

"If you get taken, so goes the world."

"I'm not going anywhere," I said, injecting as much charm into my smile as I could.

The spot lighting overhead blinked, came back on, and blinked again. A murmur went through the crowd. People were on their feet. Up until then power had held steady even though I could imagine that the generators that pumped the power had long since been eaten.

Something about the situation tripped a warning in my head. I did not look up at the struggling lights. No, my eyes went to straight to the little fly that sat looking up at me from behind the napkin dispenser. Something about it wasn't right. For one, no fly that I know of has only three legs, or four wings, or square eyes. As I watched those jet black eyes, I saw them begin to pulse with a kind of strange firelight. The kind of firelight that didn't move like fire.

I looked up in a panic. Of the twenty-two people in our community, seventeen of them were in this room right now. Nearly all our eggs in one basket.

"Get out!" I screamed. But it was already too late.

The floor at the center of the breakroom exploded upwards and outwards.

The Destroyer had come upon us.

I saw it sweep its long tail, which seemed to end in a scorpion stinger, around in wide arcs, reaping the assembled host like wheat, casting them down into nothingness. One of those sweeps shattered a table. A metal table leg grazed the side of my head and I dropped like an axed tree.

The rest of this encounter I watched from the floor, dizzy and confused.

I saw the giant thing burn Evelyn from space and memory with one of its serrated claws. Then it turned in my direction and its strange, human features saw me. A wave of pain at my temple took the next few seconds from me, but I had the vague impression of Tana standing her ground, fearless and barefoot and resolute. I realized later that she had been protecting me. She said something to the thing, which I only understood later as:

"You will *not* have him."

Then Gus appeared out of nowhere, wielding an upturned table like a lion-tamer uses a chair. He rammed the creature with the table's feet of five spokes of metal. Either Gus was vastly stronger than he looked, or the Destroyer was as light as the insect he resembled. Either way, Gus pinned the monster against the wall. Its tail and claws were all tangled up, but took swipes at its captor anyway. Gus deftly dodged them.

Then Tana stepped up with a fire extinguisher in her hands. With a war cry that would have made an Amazon warrior proud, Tana hosed the thing down. I have no doubt that the nozzle was almost point-blank in the creature's face.

For some reason, I found this act hilarious. I remember laughing. The aura it gave off had the red-orange-yellow of fire, but it definitely wasn't fire. That Tana should choose that of all things as the focal point of her assault had comedy of errors written all over it.

Crazy as it was, the Destroyer shrieked as the CO_2 foam washed over it. The effect of that horrible sound was about enough to turn your guts to cottage cheese. The force of it bodily propelled Gus backwards. The table dropped and scraped against the floor like nails on a chalkboard. At this, the Destroyer let loose its banshee wail again and faded out of view like a mirage.

Tana was by my side in an instant, crouching over me. I was still laughing. I became aware that the back of my hand was touching the inside of her knee. Her skin was warm and smooth. I stopped laughing, but the giddiness remained. I felt a groundswell of emotion.

"I love you," I said. At that moment I did, I really did.

She stopped.

"What?"

Before I could say it again, Gus was there. He checked me over for wounds.

"Boy's punch drunk right now," he told Tana as though I couldn't hear him. "Hand me that first-aid kit over there, will ya'?"

It took me a bit to come back to my senses after Gus patched me up. They gave me the status report, which I had to interpret on my own. Neither of them could tell me how many we'd lost, since none of them could remember those who had been taken. All told, we had lost eleven to the Destroyer. *Eleven.* Others had fled the breakroom only to run into a skirmishing line of Disassemblers in the hallway. Now the little bastards were no longer limiting themselves to the furniture. We had lost another five that way, with only one getting back to us to report what she'd seen.

Over half our number gone in a single assault. Any thoughts that we might be able to wait out the stars disappeared with them. Now only six of us remained. Sam, Tana, Gus, myself, and two others, the secretary who had escaped the Disassemblers (Brenda was her name) and a middle-aged janitor (Robert).

The small kingdom, formed only a few hours before, had seen its dissolution. I had made a poor leader, I knew that. Had Tana and Gus not stood their ground, I would have succumbed as well. With only six of us, we became decentralized, realizing that concentrating our numbers would only provoke another attack. We split into three teams. Sam and Gus continued their vigil in one stairwell. Brenda and Robert watched the freight elevator. Tana and I watched the opposite stairwell.

We took food and drink with us and armed ourselves with fire extinguishers. None of us knew if we would ever regroup. We said our good-byes to each other and then took up our stations. Robert had supplied us each with a set of walkie-talkies and two sets of extra batteries scrounged from automatic pencil sharpeners and desk clocks. We agreed to report in every ten minutes.

Sam shook my hand firmly as we were about to part ways, then swept me into a hug. I knew he was concerned for me, even more than himself. He held a miniature print version of the Torah in one hand.

"I'll say a prayer for you, Johnny boy, for us all."

"Thanks," was all I could think to say. If God had any role to play in what was going on, then I was going to have words with Him when my time came around at last. I would ask Him why He destroyed the world...why He had sent the stars to close around us like the calloused hands of a strangler...why the final dissolution of creation was not by fire like He promised.

We left. I would never see most of them again, and somehow I knew that at the time. Grim as things were, I was glad that I would spend whatever time was left with *her*.

We rolled two office chairs into the stairwell so we could see the glittering stars below us in comfort. I set the garbage bag down with the drinks and food I had selected. Just then, I wasn't worried about love handles, so honeybuns and candy bars were in abundance. Why not? Tana, as always, was more modest in her choices. She could have anything she wanted among the food, and she had chosen to remain healthy.

We sat in silence for what seemed like hours. Then, out of the blue, she said:

"You said that you loved me."

"You heard that, did you?" I wasn't sure that she had taken it to heart, but what was there left to feel awkward about? Everything was gone, and the societal and interpersonal barriers had gone right out the airlock along with the Empire State building.

"Did you mean it?"

"Yes."

She looked shocked. That wasn't the answer she had expected.

"You *did?*"

"It is so hard to believe?" I asked her. "You think it's just the stress talking? No, that's not it. That's not it at all."

I could see she wasn't buying it. I could see the words, *but you barely know me* in her eyes. I decided to take the plunge. And why not? There were so many things I had wanted to tell her. What time if not now?

"I've wanted you since I met you," I said. "I think you are the most beautiful woman I've ever met. There's something about you that I'm drawn to, deep down. At first, I thought it was just hormones, but it wasn't. There was more than just the physical, though I would be lying if I said that what I see on the outside doesn't move me. It does. Even though you don't remember her, Monica was beautiful too, but my interest in her did not seek the depths that I wanted with you."

Her face was still passive, calm, though her eyes were bright.

"There's a real strength to you, Tana, a will that makes you irresistible in ways that I can barely understand, let alone describe. I just know that I could have spent a lifetime with you, and only you, and been happy beyond imagining."

She stared me as I spoke. She wasn't distant, but neither was she inviting. She was just sort of stunned.

"I know you don't feel the same way," I said. "That's okay. I wouldn't expect you to, even with the world coming down around us. But you asked, and that's the truth."

She touched my shoulder, then hugged me. Once again, I smelled her perfume. I was barely holding back the floodgates of emotion, pent-up and held by the thinnest of means.

We did not make love, if that's what you're thinking. I could picture her in my mind slowly removing her skirt, revealing to me the previously hidden perfection of her hips and thighs, with further mysteries yet to come. There would be the lean, flat expanse of her stomach that would arch ever upward to the swelling of her breasts. Then the under layers would come away, and I would be truly set ablaze. I would lose myself in her, burning happily in the heat that would suffuse me, consume me.

But, as much as I wanted her, our clothes stayed on. She held me, though, as I trembled, keeping me stable in an unstable universe. And you know, that was enough.

"John!" she said. "Look!"

I turned and found that the star-level below us had come up a full two floors, and was visibly rising like a giant bathtub filling up. I was about to hit the talk button on the walkie-talkie when it crackled to life on its own.

"Johnny? Sam here. We've got movement!"

I thumbed the call button.

"Sam, it's moving here too. Brenda, Robert, anything your way?"

There was no answer. Like so many things, I would later find out that, unlike Tana and I, Brenda and Robert *had* decided to be intimate while they waited for the end to come. They never noticed the troupe of Dissemblers materializing next to them.

"It's getting closer," Tana said. She was right, the star level was coming, and fast.

I nodded. We were quickly coming to the point of decision. Did we leave the strange haven of the 19th floor, or retreat to even higher ground?

"Sam, where are you?" I said in the walkie-talkie.

"I'm by the freight shaft now. The stars already took my entire stairwell, just washed it away whole. They haven't moved over here at all. I'm looking down and they're right where they should be."

"Then we're coming to you," I said with a look to Tana. She nodded, and we were running out the door. Behind us, the stairwell was being eaten.

The door to the maintenance area stood wide open as we arrived, propped open by a cinder block. Sam was there near the stairs and the non-functional elevator. He was alone.

"Where's Gus?" I asked.

Sam quirked an eyebrow at the name. The name meant nothing to him.

"Sorry, who?"

I looked to Tana and she shook her head. It felt like someone had punched me square in the stomach.

Poor Gus.

I would also learn later that Gus had valiantly thrown Sam through the door when the stars had boiled up on top of them. He could have saved himself, but he hadn't.

Poor Gus. At that moment I really missed him.

There was a bright flash of firelight back in the hallway. I glanced over my shoulder. I didn't see anything, but I knew I soon would.

"Let's get out of here," I said, and my two companions agreed.

We ran up flights of stairs like the Destroyer was on our heels. Perhaps he was.

The air in the stairwell was sweltering. Pretty soon my white button-up shirt was soaked with sweat. Sam panted hard after we'd sprinted up thirteen floors. Tana's hair was starting to dampen as well, like I always imagined she would look just stepping out of the shower. I looked down and saw the stars were still far below us. I wasn't sure whether the stars had gained anything above the 19th floor from this distance. It didn't look like it.

Sam flashed me a smile as he stood bent over with his hands on his knees.

"Pretty weird day, eh, Johnny?"

I laughed and so did Tana. Our situation was so ridiculous and seemingly hopeless that what else could we do but laugh? If we had stopped to consider that we may be the only three people left in the world, and that our lives were irrevocably gone, we would have been instant candidates for padded cells, provided any still existed.

"We keep moving," I said. "Maybe they get us, but I, for one, am going to make them work for it."

"*Do not go gentle into that good night,*" Sam said in a voice suddenly without accent. "*Rage, rage against the dying of the light.*"

We both looked at him with surprise. He had hit the nail on the head with that one.

I started to say something when I saw movement in my peripheral vision. Across from us, a large portion of the wall turned a sickly green. The paint started to run like candle wax or tears. The entire hole formed in the time it takes to take a long breath. Behind it, firelight blazed.

By that time, the sight of fire inspired an instinctive and primal sort of fear in us. We were afraid, and ran. Whatever that thing was that kept hunting us, it was ancient and relentless. It was coming for us. If my heart hadn't already been beating fast from the exertion, now it was ticking like a metronome cranked to its fastest setting.

We piled through the door into the 32nd floor. The floorplan was somewhat similar to those below, but the arrangement of cube dividers was different. Suddenly we were in a foreign maze, and none of us knew our way around it. We stopped near the bathrooms, looking uneasily behind us. A plastic cart sat there between the entrances, bristling with cleaning supplies and a mop bucket built into the front. Tools and brushes hung from the sides like Viking shields on a longship. I thought it might have been abandoned here by Robert or one of his disappeared janitor brethren.

"Do you see anything?" Tana asked.

"No, but I—" I let my words trail off. I *couldn't* see anything, but there was something more. I could feel something, like a soundless drum beat that resonated through me. Each non-sound made my ears feel like there was a change in the air pressure. My blood would rush and I felt somewhat nauseous, not that I needed much help on either point.

I realized what I was feeling. The Destroyer's footsteps. Each dread fall was one of its steps bringing it closer.

"It's coming," I said. "It's close."

"I don't think we can outrun it," Sam said. "It's going to keep hounding us."

Tana stood up and unhooked a fire extinguisher from the wall. Had she been wearing chainmail and carrying a battle-axe she would not have looked more like a warrior than she did at that moment.

"Then this is where we make our stand."

"Here's just as good as any place, I guess." I said.

In all the billions of humans who had ever lived, and millennia of recorded history, humanity's last stand was about to happen near a set of public restrooms in an office building. The strangeness of that did not escape me at the time.

I likewise armed myself with a fire extinguisher. Sam did the same. We made what preparations we could.

Then we waited.

We didn't have to wait long.

The insectoid head with its distorted features emerged from around the corner, slowly and ponderously, the way it had when I first saw it back in the alley. It stared at us as it advanced with heavy steps, with each contact sending silent shockwaves through me.

Sam waited until it was centered in the hallway. He removed a small Zippo lighter and flicked it back with a metallic *ch-chink* sound. A small teardrop of real fire sprang up and wavered. Sam touched the flame to the mop head he had soaked in chemicals. The mop lit up like a torch.

Holding his firebrand aloft, Sam jammed the blaze into one of the sprinkler sensors. Suddenly it was raining as the emergency systems sprayed water like a dozen shower heads. None of us knew if they were going to work, but Sam had insisted that they would.

The Destroyer twitched and spasmed as the little droplets hit it. That's when all three of us opened up with our fire extinguishers. At first, it seemed like we caused it pain. It shook violently, and made that alien screech the way it had in the breakroom.

But then, it blazed green like balefires in answer to our assault. I wasn't sure what was going on, but something told me that it had just protected itself from our meager forms of attack.

As it happened, Sam's extinguisher malfunctioned. Realizing that the weapon he held was useless, Sam flung the red tank at the monster only to watch the object crackle from sight upon contact. With that, Sam fell back to the cart.

Tana and I stood our ground for precious seconds before we realized we were no longer effective. The thing was on the move again, now slower than before as if mocking us and our pathetic attempts to thwart it.

I sensed that Tana was about to move bodily between the creature and I. Once again, she was going to intercede on my behalf. This time Sam beat her to it.

As we stood in that hallway, watching death bear down us, music filled the air. *Music* of all things. You might expect the music for a heroic last stand to be something like *Carmina Burana* or Holst's *Mars*. No, this was rock'n roll, an almost James Bond-like electric guitar grinding away with a sound that would have been at home in a movie car chase.

In fact, I recognized it immediately as *Rock Lobster* by the B-52's, right at the part before they started making animal noises. One of my favorites.

Tana and I turned to see Sam standing back by the cart holding a boombox in the air like he was in a John Hughes film. To our surprise, the Destroyer recoiled from the sound. Sam had cranked the volume up to maximum and flipped on the turbo bass booster.

Then I remembered the scraping table in the breakroom that had first made the thing emit that soul-piercing cry. *Loud noises*, I thought. *That must be it.*

Both of us rallied around Sam's sonic banner. The older man looked at me, and I knew what he was going to suggest.

"Go on, Johnny," he said as the music echoed through the hallway. "I'll hold it off. Take her and get out of here."

"No!" Tana said. "We stay together."

Sam shook his head.

"I don't know how long this is gonna last, sweetheart. Go," he said, then seemed to go grow angry. "Go! For the love of God, *go!*"

I took Tana's hand, and we left. The last time I saw Sam, he was advancing on the Destroyer and holding the boombox out in front of him like Perseus with the head of Medusa. We were soaked, but I could still feel my tears, warm and constant, as they mingled and disappeared into the artificial rain.

▲ ▲ ▲

We made it to the opposite stairwell. Yes, I understand that much of this story has taken place in or around a stairwell, but I guarantee you this is the last one. Tana and I hit the stairs at a run. By this time, my legs were burning. At first I could ignore it, but as we moved up, I began to lag behind her by half a flight. My heart was still heavy with the loss of Sam. The man who carried the sun with him, now gone, too. The futility of our actions started to weigh upon me, slowing me faster than my aching legs. I wanted to cling to Sam's 'do not go gentle into that good night' ideal. Most of me did, anyway. The part that was controlling my stair-climbing movement was not part of that *most*.

Tana realized that I was falling behind. She stopped and looked back at me.

"Come on!" She beckoned me to rejoin her.

My limbs felt leaden. They barely seemed to work of their own accord now. I was tired, so very tired. Tana was having none of that.

"Move your ass!" she barked like a Marine drill instructor.

The funny part of it was that I wanted to rejoin her; it was my body that needed convincing. Apparently her stern tone was enough to win the argument. Sluggishly, I ascended. She extended her hand. I reached for it...

That was when we both heard the sound. For the benefit of you, the reader, I will attempt to describe it. It had the *whooshing* sound of flooding water, but embedded within it was a strange hiss. It was almost as if a lion had tried to mimic a cobra sound, first low, and then at a full roar. The sound was echoing up from the stairwell.

We were less than two feet from each other when the stars below came spewing up like a Las Vegas fountain or Hawaiian volcano. They split the stairwell in half, separating us. Tana moved back from the abyss that had almost taken her. I did the same. Yet, fierce and bubbling as this star spray was, there was no solid base to it. These liquid spires were merely tendrils of what was below.

I saw one of the fronds reach out and touch the supports that held Tana's portion to the wall. The entire section shivered with her on it and lowered in space, putting the two of us on an even level. The violence of the shockwave propelled her toward and over the railing. Her reactions were superb, which is why she found herself hanging off the side rather than plummeting down into the starry depths.

I watched all of this in horror, which was only magnified when I saw two Disassemblers materialize on the landing next to her. They just seemed to step out of the wall. Tana saw them and screamed.

For the first time in all of this, I felt pure and unadulterated rage. That anger cast what was left of my world in red. My body was once again my own as I shrugged off the lethargy that had burdened me down. My rage was helpless rage, however, as I could not reach her.

Then I saw the cable that had dislodged from one of the flights above us, only slightly kissed by the stars' advance. It hung limply not five feet from where I stood and I knew what I had to do. I resolved to aid Tana or die in the attempt. At that moment, I was ready to lay down my life if it meant saving her.

I could almost hear the theme from *Indiana Jones* playing in my head as I ran, seized the cable, and swung around in a wide arc, the stars nipping at my feet. I planted on the landing, standing tall. It was a wonder I hadn't done myself in with that maneuver, but desperation had spurred me on, determination had been my fuel.

The Disassemblers both turned to look at me, their burning yellow eyes reflecting fear for the first time. I kicked one squarely in the chest and watched with a note of satisfaction as it tumbled down and was swallowed up.

I delivered a right-cross to the other one with a power I never would have thought I could muster, and it felt like hitting a strawberry crate with a baseball bat. The little creature literally came apart under the force of my blow until what was left was likewise consumed.

When I turned to Tana, she was in worse shape than before. I saw immediately that a tentacle had phased out most of the railing. Now she hung by a sliver of metal that was buckling. I slid across the landing on my belly and extended a hand out to her.

"Take my hand," I shouted over the roar-hiss around us.

She switched grips right as the piece she held gave way. Now I was holding her entire weight by one arm, while my free arm grasped the stubs of the railing. Now I should point out that trying to pull someone up with one arm is quite a bit harder than the movies suggest. Usually, all it takes it getting a hold of someone and they're saved instantly.

Right then, most of my body was just trying to keep me rooted in place, leaving only my right arm to pull her up. Her grip was like iron, though. I didn't have to worry about dropping her, but bringing her back up was proving difficult. She would have to climb my arm to reach the unstable ledge. I had no doubts that she could do so, I just had to hold on long enough, even if my shoulder joint was on fire at the strain.

There was another problem, however. From my vantage point, I could see the rising level of the stars. I couldn't gauge their distance exactly, but I was sure there was only a slight distance between its surface and Tana's kicking legs. She saw it in my face and looked down.

When our eyes locked again, she knew that it was too late. Despite my pulp-action heroics, I couldn't save her, not in time. Tears formed at the corners of her dark eyes. Right before she was taken from me, she said:

"Remember me!"

Then she was gone, and I screamed to the heavens. I had no idea that there was so much pain in the world, even in a world as small as mine. My emotions translated into sound as a I made soul-tearing wail. There wasn't much left in the way of sanity when I lost my sweet Tana. Only her final words kept me from surrendering. Now, I was the only one to bear witness that she had ever existed at all. For as long I remained, so would she, and Sam, and Gus, and all the others consumed by the stars.

I was on my feet and blindly climbing the stairs, only peripherally aware of what I was doing. I needed to make it to the roof. Enough people had fallen to bring me to this point, the least I could do was follow through.

Climbing, climbing, climbing was I.

And the stars followed, ever close behind.

⅄ ⅄ ⅄

The door to the roof slid into view. To my surprise, I ripped the door off of its hinges when I pulled on it. That same surety and strength I had felt when I fought the

Disassemblers burned within me, but it had also abandoned me when it came to saving her. At the time, I did not question my luck. I merely tossed the steel door aside as though it were made of styrofoam.

I stepped out onto the roof, my ultimate destination.

Things outside the L&H building were now worse than before. Orion's belt was even closer now, the three points of his belt were now the size of tractor tires in the sky. No landscape, no other buildings, just the roof on which I stood, strangled by the stars.

And no place left to go.

I centered myself on the roof to buy as much as time as I could. I imagined the flood from below as it boiled out of the roof entrance. I imagined the feel of cold fire as it touched me, as it finally erased me from existence. Would I feel pain at this passing? Would I join the others in some sort of great beyond, or would everything I was—my hopes, my dreams, my essence—know only the cold dark of oblivion?

I don't know how long I puzzled along these existential lines before I saw the yellow-orange of firelight spring up behind me. My stomach wrenched. I knew what I would find there even before I turned.

The Destroyer was there, walking through the empty space between the stars as though it were solid ground. Its slow, resonant steps towards me gave me the time to see the liquid black creep over the edge of the roof. Behind me, the roof entrance disappeared behind a starry veil. The black line continued outward over the air vents and air conditioner units. I was besieged in all directions, but again, there was no place left for me to run.

I watched as the stars took everything else until I stood on the remaining portion of the roof, which was no larger than a manhole cover. The Destroyer came to stand in front of me. It made no attempt to attack me. It merely stood there like a blazing statue.

"What do you *want* from me?" I yelled at it. "You've taken everything! Everything! There's nothing left for you to take from me! It's gone! Gone, because of *you!*"

The Destroyer was unmoved by my words, literally; it made no move or acknowledgment of me. Meanwhile, I saw the stars touch my shoes. I waited for the feeling of being disintegrated, but it didn't come. I wasn't sure, but maybe all that was left of the world was the space beneath the soles of my shoes. The stars were all around me now, in every direction, but I was still standing on *something*.

"It is done," said the Destroyer.

"Why did you do it?" I asked. "What was the purpose of destroying the world?"

Then I added in a small voice, "And why did you leave me to see it?"

The Destroyer looked down on me through its ghostly flames.

"Me?" it said, sounding confused. "I did not do this. *You* did."

"W-what?"

No sooner had I said that one word when the strange fires around its face parted briefly. The nearly human face that looked back from atop the mantis-like body was distorted, but somehow familiar. Then I was cold as space as realization dawned. *My* face lay behind the flames.

"It is time to come home," the Destroyer said. It reached down with one of its serrated claws and lightly touched my forehead.

"Remember," it said.

Memories filled my mind, and I realized they were not my own. They flashed by in a dizzying kaleidoscope, but I found that I fully understood each one in a kind of perfect fullness.

Tana's life played before me, the life that even she couldn't remember at the end. I found that she had been in training to be a gymnast before a sudden growth spurt made her too tall to be competitive. I saw how she had been assaulted at thirteen by her coach, and how that had tinted her view of men in general, seeing them as perennially slavering jackals, lusting after her because her outside shell happened to be attractive. I saw how she cut herself off from the world, insulating herself behind a fortress of her own making, and letting so very few ever in close. Then I saw me in her memories. At first, she dismissed me as just another would-be predator when she noticed the admiring looks I cast at her when I thought she wasn't looking. Of course she was aware; women have a sixth sense about that kind of thing. But in all of that, she thought my hands were beautiful, the hands of an artist in her opinion. She also felt that my eyes were exceptionally bright and joyous. When the world came crashing down, she was at first uncomfortable with me, but as events wore on, she came to hold me in a kind of reverence she could never show. Somehow she had known that the events around us centered around me, even before I did.

I stood there in front of the Destroyer, weeping.

Next, I found Sam. I saw the terrible things that had happened to his parents during the war, and how he had only barely escaped dying at a very young age. I saw him grow up, full of youth and vigor, marry, and the birth of a baby boy. I saw his hair start to turn gray, saw the wisdom, the joy of merely being alive well up inside him like a sun. I saw the death of his son, the victim of a senseless car wreck at the hands of a drunk driver. The light dimmed. There was so much doubt, doubt in everything he had been taught to believe about how the universe worked. Then I walked into his deli one day, and somehow I reignited his faith. There was something that he saw in me that was like his son, a tilt of my head, a turn of phrase, a hand gesture that so reminded him of the seventeen year-old he had buried. He had been overjoyed that I was among the survivors of the initial flood. In all of this, he had just wanted to see me get out, and noted the Adam and Eve-like quality that Tana and I seemed to represent.

Then there was Gus. I felt the empty part of him that yearned from an early age for some sort of purpose when the world told him he was worthless. I felt him put on the uniform for the first time and look in the mirror.

This was his chance to reforge himself in his own mold, to be something greater than the sum of his parts. I felt the General pin the Silver Star on his chest, and felt the pride of belonging. Then there was a dark well of pain. The roadside ditch in the desert, near a ruined and smoking Humvee. His blood was seeping out from a dozen wounds. The agony...the agony was overwhelming. I saw the chopper blades overhead, making a strobe light of the sun, felt the soothing medication take the pain away. The pain was a constant companion, and so were the drugs that kept it at bay. And pretty soon, the drugs dominated his world, taking everything else from him. Only when the world was ending was he able to finally feel that sense of purpose again.

Then there was Evelyn. Bookish and plain for most of her life, she sprang suddenly into the fullness of her beauty right as her twenties gave way to her thirties. Normally passed over for other, women, she once found herself on a cruise ship. There she found a tall, blonde man who had taken her in a way she had never felt before or since. He had made love to her with such ferocity that she thought she might burst from the sheer ecstasy he brought her. When the cruise ended, she never saw him again. She later married, had children, and settled down. She loved her husband, but her thoughts still strayed to the man who had made her feel like a goddess. When I smiled, it reminded her of him. That was why she had smiled at me back in the elevator.

Others followed, Brenda and Robert, even Steve, Monica, and Jerry. I lived their lives in instants, understanding them fully. The memories kept coming, spreading out all over the world. If that were not enough, my knowledge began to expand to various places and things. I was a blade of grass growing by a dirt road in Costa Rica. I was the pitted surface of a sun-baked concrete barrier near Long Beach, California. I was a tree on the savannah of Africa being nibbled at by giraffe. I was a sea anemone gently waving in the depths of the ocean.

All of this came to me, but my mind was not disturbed by this. If anything it was almost as though pieces from a puzzle, long absent, were now falling back into place. When I ran out of things on Earth, my mind spiraled upward into space. Planets, stars, and whole galaxies became known to me. Mysteries of existence I had grappled with my entire life became instantly clear. When it was all done, I realized the truth.

I knew *everything*.

Furthermore, I knew who I was.

I was God.

Yes, that's correct. I was God, as in the Creator of the Universe. Believe me, no one was more surprised than I. Now I won't go so far as to tell you which one I am, because it's really not that simple. You could say that I'm all of them and none of them at the same time. Let's not concern ourselves with that triviality, because, trust me, trying to pigeonhole me into one of your existing cosmologies is pretty trite and self-serving when you really think about it.

But, at that moment, as the mortal form I had inhabited gained awareness and power, there was still part of my old personality left, still stung by the part the Destroyer had played in the recent events. There was a somewhat surprised look on my servant's face when I reduced him to atoms, and then dismissed those atoms from the burden of existence. Yeah, it was a petty thing to do, of course; the Destroyer was merely playing his part, but I was angry. I've always had a bit of a temper, but that just comes from never being told 'no,' and being accountable to no one for my actions.

The truth is, the entire reason I chose to live as John was because there is a difference in knowing and *understanding*. I know everything, but my limitless nature had become a limiting factor. Sound contradictory? Well, it is to some point.

Let me see if I can clarify: I cannot die or be destroyed by any means I know of. You, on the other hand, can, and do, die quite easily. Yet, because you know of your own mortality, you possess a level of altruism that I could never hope to match. You can lay down your life for a cause, or sacrifice yourself for someone else with the full knowledge that there may be nothing else beyond the howling curtain of death.

I can't.

Because I can't truly die, I could never truly know the meaning of self-sacrifice. So I set about to live as one of you in order to understand these things on a level I could never have done just by watching from the outside. I wanted to *understand*. When I saw how unpleasant a place the world could be, even outside the arenas of war, famine, or pestilence, I realized it wasn't for me. John's unhappiness with the hollowness of his existence is what brought on the dissolution of the world with stars as my instrument.

So, lesson learned. I'll try to do better next time.

As I write these words, I sit in Fineman's Deli. I have restored the world, but not the people just yet. The streets and buildings are empty, but I have moved upon the stars and they have receded. I look like John did on his way to work that fateful morning. While John is a part of me, I may separate him out from myself so that he can live a normal life. Who knows, maybe he'll finally get to know Tana under normal circumstances. They won't have a memory of what has transpired here. Neither will you, for that matter. I have removed those moments of horror you felt when the stars came for you. Don't worry, you went out like a champ.

But before I repopulate the Earth, I have a few tweaks to make to how things work around here. I hope it will be for the better. Perhaps one of these days we'll bump into each other on the street or in line at the bank. Chances are you won't know it's me, but I'll know it's you, my reader. I can tell you one thing, though: If you're out there and wholly dissatisfied with the day-in-day-out, corporate cube farm office environment, well, I'm not a fan of it either.

It's a bummer, no doubt, but let's just say I'm working on it. The universe really is a giant work-in-progress, and you know what they say:

"If at first you don't succeed, try, try again!"

The last story in this book is also the oldest, and one inspired from a song. Years ago, I was part of the performing cast of Scarborough Renaissance Festival, also known as Scarborough Faire. Yeah, some of you just sang "parsley, sage, rosemary, and thyme" in your head, didn't you? You know who you are.

At the time I was on cast, there were two incredible a cappella singing groups out there: The Corsairs, an all-male, pirate-themed group, and Queen Anne's Lace, which was made up of wonderfully color-coordinated ladies. On rare occasions they would sing together, calling themselves, collectively, Queen Anne's Revenge.

Queen Anne's Revenge performed a version of the old song "The Minstrel Boy." (You might remember this song from the Star Trek: The Next Generation *episode "The Wounded," where Chief Miles O'Brien came into his own as he faces down his old captain, gone rogue). The difference here is that Queen Anne's Revenge sang "The Minstrel Boy" to the tune of "The Parting Glass."*

Magic.

"The Parting Glass" is already one of the most bittersweet and beautiful tunes I know. To then add the poignant, tragic lyrics of "The Minstrel Boy" is just a Hulk-punch right in the feels. There are other songs which made up a soundtrack to this story as well, largely from the group Gaelic Storm, and the violin stylings of The Last of the Mohicans score. Vivaldi put in an appearance as well. I had yet to discover Lindsey Stirling at this time, but I would retro-actively include her Assassin's Creed cover and "The Arena." Look them up, they're fantastic.

Astute readers may notice some historical simi-larities between William and George Rogers Clark. Placing the story within that structure helped give The Foeman's Chain some much-needed lift. At the time, this story was longest thing I had ever successfully completed, a few years before I finished my first novel, The Backwards Mask.

And it is within this story that Sector M first appears, though it is not called that by name. So, gentle reader, I leave you with the final installment of this anthology, which is more of a beginning than an end.

The Foeman's Chain

Cynics would have us believe that no one person can make a difference in the true scheme of things—that the individual is only given scope within the context of a greater whole. They are wrong. I've seen proof of otherwise firsthand, seen how the will of one man shaped not only the borders of our map, but of our lives. So long as I live, I will never forget it.

- BRIGADIER GENERAL NADIA CANTRELL,
MEMOIRS ON THE FRONTIER

The light cruiser, INV *Rampant Lion,* streaked through the dark enigma of space, a growing corona of gamma rays crowning her armored hull as she neared her destination. The next few hours and days would represent the culmination of years of events and mass concerted effort. The possibility of battle was less a likelihood and more a guarantee. It weighed on the faces of the crew as they went about their appointed duties.

Commander Vanya Thornton looked up as a soft chime sounded from the Captain's command chair. Captain Halycon peered down for a moment before shutting it off.

To Thornton, the ship's XO, this was nothing new. Each time they knew they were destined for battle the Captain would excuse himself for an hour at precisely four hours prior to their arrival. What he did or where he went no one, not even the XO, could say, but not once when he had kept this ritual up had they known defeat. An intensely reserved and private man, no one dared unravel the Captain's secret. And, spacers being a more superstitious lot than they would let on, took this is as a good omen.

The tension on the bridge lessened considerably at the sound of the chime. Thornton wondered if he actually did anything during this time, or whether it was a merely a response he had cultivated over time to raise pre-combat morale.

So it came as a surprise when Captain Halycon did not immediately exit the command deck, but rather came to stand by Thornton's workstation.

"Commander," he said, businesslike as usual.

"Captain?"

"Come with me." He turned on his heel to leave.

"Sir?"

He half-turned and spoke over his shoulder.

"There is something I think you should see." Something serious glittered in his grey-blue eyes that Thornton had never seen before. "Something that may never come again."

Thornton nodded.

"Lieutenant Clairemont," Thornton said aloud for all to hear, "the ship is yours."

Though it would have been protocol for the Captain to have relinquished mastery of the ship to him first, it was an unwritten law on *Rampant Lion* that when the chime sounded, Thornton was in command.

"I understand your concern, Commander," the Captain said as they exited the bridge, "but I believe a break from the norm, this time, is warranted."

Thornton knew better than to question where they were going. He'd seen the relatively diminutive man beside him work miracles, but as open as the Captain was about their work, he was just as closed off about his personal life. Now, before their most important mission to date, this was a rare glimpse into the Captain's mind.

They wound around through various supply stores and magazine compartments until they came to one of the three auxiliary sickbays. While it was kept in readiness, there were seldom any attendants here. Captain Halcyon walked purposefully across the room until he took a seat next to one of the medbeds.

"Take a seat, Commander," the Captain said. "It should be any moment now."

Thornton kept his features carefully neutral as he arranged himself in a chair beside the Captain. Silence reigned and only the quiet sighing of ventilating air and the thrumming white noise of the FTL engines reached his ears.

And then...

He heard a sound, soft at first, then growing louder, echoing from the vent just above where the Captain now sat. It took a moment for Thornton to fully realize what he was hearing, until the pieces of the puzzle clicked clearly into place.

The sound of a single violin, warmed by the gathering tones of a bow.

And then, it seemed like the sound filled the compartment as though the one playing it were in the same room. The music soared suddenly into the staccato rise and fall of Giancomo Reccini's immortal classic, *Salvatorio D'Aria*.

Not only was the piece itself evocative and soul-stirring, but the hand at the bow was unequivocally a maestro. The player made the music come alive in the way that only someone who understood music so completely, on such a fundamental level, could possibly accomplish.

The notes pierced Thornton and found their way to his heart. What he was hearing was no less than a flawless window into the musician's soul. There was a heavy Terran influence to the style, incorporating the haunting overtones of the Romani, and the bittersweet twang of the Irish. Imperial influence of the *chavari* school wound its way through it, and even a bit of the Fenri cyclical *G'vakon* note flourishes seamlessly melded in to a single transcendent voice.

When the song began its slow and sad climb towards the pinnacle, Thornton was sure this was the sound angels made when they cried. The emotion reached out and embraced him.

Thornton felt a lump spring up in his throat and his eyes began to mist over. As his control teetered on the brink, he looked to his Captain. Gone was the stern mask. In its place, a melancholy rapture. The man's eyes were closed as he too lost himself in the music.

Thornton mentally pulled up a deck plan of the ship. Whomever was baring their soul would be close by. He raised an eyebrow as he realized that the sickbay lay directly beneath Marine Country. Was it possible that the unknown virtuoso might be a ground-pounder, and one of the grim-faced Long Knives at that?

"Magnificent, isn't it?" The Captain spoke in hushed tones as though afraid to break the spell.

"I...I...don't have the words to describe it, except for perhaps—"

"Pure?" Halcyon finished for him.

"Yes, sir." That had been *precisely* the word he was going to say. "Who is playing?"

Halcyon closed his eyes again, soaking in the music as it came to a smoldering finale.

"The Prisoner of Zyi-Kang."

Everyone who was currently pitted against the Brotherhood of the Red Chain, civilian and military, was familiar with Hans Grünning's poem. It had practically become a rallying cry against the very tyranny that *Rampant Lion* was shortly to face, perhaps for the last time.

When Grünning's transport had been raided, the Brotherhood had no way of knowing that the man they had enslaved was one of the preeminent human poets living in Imperial space. Always a man accustomed to privilege and comfort, the artist had found the draconian conditions of the Zyi-Kang slave prison to be a gruesome essay in what a living hell was all about.

Thornton sometimes wondered what life had truly been like on that grim peak of Mount Ducane, or the horror that the Imperial Marines must have felt when they liberated the prison. The debasement and dehumanization—people treated as livestock in the hands of madmen.

Grünning, whose tenure at Zyi-Kang lasted six months, confessed upon his liberation that the daily regimen of torture, back-breaking labor, and ever-present degradation had eroded his will to live. But, just when things had seemed darkest, Grünning had heard a fellow prisoner playing a violin. The genius of the music, the emotion it conjured up, kept Grünning from giving up or trying to take his own life. Each night the music would float down from the upper level, and give him comfort. It served as an anchor for his sanity when all else around him was chaos.

When the Imperial Marines discovered the poet, the identity of his mysterious musician was still unknown. The Red Chain had decided that dead slaves were better than freed ones, even as Marines in powered armor stormed the ancient fortress turned prison. After that, Grünning had returned to a life of poetry and immediately set to work on what became his most well known opus, *The Prisoner of Zyi-Kang*.

And yet, the narrative didn't focus on the trials he himself had faced, but rather the music and sadness of the unseen player. The imagery of a single soul, locked in a horrendous stone tower, whose presence inspired others, found an emotional niche, made even more romantic as an unknown. Like the Unknown Soldier or the Man in the Iron Mask, the Prisoner had taken on a legendary persona, with books and historical forums rife with debate with theories on who he or she actually was.

The Captain nodded towards the airduct and Thornton's jaw dropped.

"Surely you can't mean...*that's* the Prisoner playing?" The Captain again nodded.

"You mean he's here, aboard the *Lion*?"

"Correct," Halcyon said, his hands idly straightening the tip of his handlebar mustache. "The song you're hearing is not only the same musician, but also the same tune that inspired Grünning."

The violin started up again, this time in a mournful lament that was overflowing with sorrow. But deep within the almost funereal sounds was a spark of hope. Both men stopped their conversations as the sound suffused them.

"I come here to remind myself of what *Rampant Lion* is really fighting for. At times when I feel that I can't move forward, I come here and listen. In that way, I know precisely what Master Grünning felt like in his cell, with that one voice to guide him."

This was a day for firsts, Thornton reflected. In the last half-hour he had learned more about the deep well of Halcyon's feelings than in four years of line service.

"Sir, I must know, who is the Prisoner?

The Captain told him.

▲ ▲ ▲

Lieutenant Colonel William Aidan Montgomery of the Imperial Marine Corps drew the bow across the strings in one final note of grieving melody. The sound faded from his ears and seemed to echo. For a moment he kept the violin to his chin before setting it down on the table.

He would never play it again.

For long years he had known this day would finally come, but now that it was here it seemed surreal and dream-like. His eyes traced the lines of the instrument, admiring now as always the glossy black lacquered wood with that distinctive golden laurel leaf pattern tracing down both sides like two halves of an hourglass.

He started to reach out to it, but instead stepped away. Deep down, he knew that as long as he lived he would want to play it once more, to lose himself in the divine bliss it gave him.

But no, this was how it had to be. He had loved that violin ever since the craftsman who made it had given it to him—the same luthier who had once been his wife. And now, it was all that he had left of her. He could still feel her love resonate with every note, no matter how sad those notes might become.

Forgive me, Valentina. You gave this to me in love—it does not deserve what I'm about to do.

From somewhere in the great beyond, her voice whispered to him.

Finish what you started.

Rampant Lion arrived precisely where she had intended, on the rim of the Maven system. Advanced stealth systems dispersed the gathering gamma radiation from announcing the *Lion's* presence like a royal trumpeter.

"Engage ECM and rig for silent running. All sensors to passive." Halcyon said as soon as the astrogator reported the good news.

"Aye, sir," came the reply.

"What was our read on the insertion point?"

Lieutenant Korahl looked at her sensor panel for long moments before looking up. "It's clean, sir. No contacts in our vicinity."

"Very well, continue monitoring."

There was no doubt about it—they were now in the heart of enemy territory. Their destination, the planet Vermillion, served as both the enemy's headquarters on the outskirts of the Imperial frontier and as the living space for the Overseer of the Red Chain Brotherhood himself.

Their task here was deceptively simple: *Remove the leadership of the Red Chain in detail.* Failing that, *Rampant Lion* was to inflict as much material loss on their infrastructure as possible. The latter was not a scenario any of them wanted to fathom, as detection by the enemy would almost certainly spell *Rampant Lion's* destruction. The slaver ring they faced had spent years building a fleet of ships. While the Red Chain's hulls were neither as advanced nor as numerous as the Imperial Navy, they were sufficiently concentrated so that a direct naval conflict would be costly.

In that sense, the *Rampant Lion* was poised to land the final blow. Since the conflict had begun, the *Liberator*-class light cruiser had been at the vanguard. Marines from this ship had liberated the Red Chain systems at Modi, Moran, and Mar-Kang. She had been the first to strike the foe at the Margolas Engagement, and had been the one to destroy the slaver flagship, *Inevitable*, amongst the silver rings of Murakhan. In short, the history of this conflict had been written with this ship.

The Brotherhood's fleet strength had been neutralized or drawn out of position in dozens of locations thanks to the stratagems of Naval Intelligence, which left only the head of the snake—which was where *Rampant Lion* came into play. Strike the source of the tyranny directly and the rest would wither on the vine.

But as much as Captain Halcyon would have loved to ram his ship down the slavers' collective throat in a flurry of missile fire and flashing lasers, that was not the mission profile. Much of *Rampant Lion's* laser batteries and magazine space had been refitted with improved ECM suites, sensor enhancements, and stealth, all of which made the light cruiser less like her namesake and more like a panther in the night.

Primary operations for this mission fell to the Marines. Too much depended on the leaders of the Red Chain, specifically the Overseer, being identified and dealt with up close. Considering the volume of slaves that tended to be in close proximity to high-ranking Brotherhood members, the collateral damage of innocent life was too high for a direct orbital strike. Certainly not when the man lead-ing the Marines was an ex-slave, fighting against the very establishment that had once shackled him in chains. For that matter, a large number of the Long Knives were freed slaves. For being a somber, efficient lot, Halcyon was sure they were the best damn Marines he'd seen in his sixty-plus years of wearing the uniform, and *that* was saying something.

Now the Long Knives would pay a visit to their former masters and thank them in kind. Halcyon knew it would be soon, and he could feel their anticipation in the air, even far removed on the command deck.

Stars know they deserve it.

⁂

Sergeant Major Nadia Cantrell of the Long Knives sur-veyed the organized chaos of the shuttle bay with a sense of pride. She had helped train most of these troops herself, many of whom had been newly liberated and knew little of the outside world.

She had reached down into their lives and hammered them into brilliant swords. Like a Spartan mother, she mar-veled at their mettle as they clustered around the *Nimbus*-class assault landers, knowing that she had only helped to sharpen and hone that which had already been beneath the surface.

As with *Rampant Lion*, the landing shuttles had been rigged for improved stealth, leaving only their dorsal batteries to cover a potentially hot landing zone. If they did their job right, however, the Marines would have no need for them.

She keyed up the operational parameters in her data display and let the glowing amber letters soak into her mind. She'd already looked them over more than a dozen times since the Captain posted them, but as the senior NCO, she had to have the details at her command in case the Colonel should need them. Not that he would; Montgomery would own the mission specs just like she would, but that didn't excuse her one iota in the performance of her duty.

Their mission here consisted of three goals:

1.) Avoid detection and open engagement with space-borne enemy forces.
2.) Capture the orbital defense platform intact without alerting any ground forces.
3.) Covertly strike the Overseer's Palace and eliminate all high-ranking Red Chain personnel.

As simple as that might sound in writing, each goal was totally dependent on the success or failure of the previous one. Luckily, the crew of the *Rampant Lion* was doing a bang-up job on the first goal. The plan was painstaking, and not without considerable risk, but now they coasted on a ballistic course without active drives. When they reached Vermillion's outermost moon, Cerulaan, they would take advantage of the moon's gravity well to finally bring themselves to a halt.

And that should be anytime now, Nadia thought.

That would put them in striking distance of their second objective, the orbital space platform, Helot Station. The real obstacle was not taking the station, for Nadia was sure that a battalion of Marines in powered armor could sweep aside whatever security forces they might encounter. No, they had to do all of it in such a way that the Overseer on the planet below would remain oblivious to the death about to descend upon his head. That meant they would have to jam the enemy's comm system, but for a short enough interval to avoid suspicion. Within that narrow window of time the Marines would have to completely secure Helot Station—a tall order even for them.

The door whirred open next to her, revealing the imposing presence of Lt. Colonel Montgomery, near resplendent even in his work fatigues. At over two meters tall, he was a giant among the normal rank and file of spacers. Immensely fit, Montgomery possessed the V-shaped torso right out of a recruitment poster, with the thick forearms of a construction worker. He did not, however, have the perfect jaw and teeth that might have gone along with the rest. Instead, his close-cropped red hair stood straight up on his head like flames frozen in place. He had a long nose that could only politely be called Roman, and looked as if it had been broken numerous times and never quite healed straight. His wide-set cheekbones and thick brow gave him an almost brutish aura, which was offset only by his delicately cleft chin and clear, ice-blue eyes.

All told, William Montgomery wasn't a pretty man, but what he lacked in looks, he made up for in sheer, unadulterated menace. Nadia had lost count of the friends and foes who had withered underneath that dread basilisk gaze. Once on Murzahn, a whole platoon of soldiers had spontaneously surrendered when that behemoth had burst upon them, face soot-streaked and hair smoking like an avatar of Hephaestus.

Perhaps many were keen to dismiss him at first glance as an ogre in uniform, but Nadia knew that the heart that beat in his barrel chest could have easily belonged to Lokain, Paganini, or Yeoh. Those hands that could crush an opponent effortlessly could also work sublime magic on a violin unlike any other. Often times, he had carried that musical instrument in the field, bolstering morale on the eve of combat with his own soaring battlehymns.

But not this time. The case was strangely absent from underneath his arm as he moved towards her. She came smartly to attention and saluted.

"At ease," he said in his usual laconic fashion. "Report."

"Sir, all twelve of the *Nimbus* landers are prepped and ready for immediate deployment. They have been customized for operations against Helot Station, per your orders, sir."

"And the troops?"

"Four hundred and sixty battle-hardened instruments of the Czar's wrath are hungry for action, sir!"

"The powered armor has been detailed out as I instructed

"Yes, sir. And the EW officer informed me that all the jammer drones are ready to deploy as soon as our shuttles are in position."

He held his hand out and Nadia presented the data display to him.

"Everything looks in order here, Sergeant Major," he said. "Carry on."

▲ ▲ ▲

Nadia departed from his presence, leaving him on an island amongst the sea of activity. He quietly took in the swirl of movement around him, noting the Long Knives going about their business with vigor and efficiency. His troops redoubled their efforts while he was in view of them, and this was not lost upon him.

The aft hatch opened and Commander Thornton strode in, the crisp lines of his naval uniform a stark contrast to the baggy Marine fatigues swirling around him. As though he knew precisely where William stood, his steps brought him unerringly into the Lt. Colonel's personal sphere.

"Ah, Colonel, there you are." If the XO had come in person to deliver news, then it must be important. By unwritten law, naval officers didn't venture into Marine Country all that often.

"Commander."

"We've evaded the outer picket screen. Our best ETA puts us at about eight hours from launch against Helot. I trust you will be ready for operations within that time frame?"

William glanced around the bay and his eyes flicked back to the XO.

"We'll be ready in five, sir," he said, adding the courtesy honorific.

"Splendid," Thornton replied. He did not immediately turn to leave.

"Was there something else, sir?"

"Yes, Colonel, there is," he said, taking a half step closer so that none could hear his words. "You and I have served on the ship for years, and managed to weather every storm we've encountered."

Thornton paused, before meeting's William's eyes in full.

"In all that time, I thought I knew you," The XO said, sounding almost ashamed. "I found out today how wrong I was in that assumption."

Thornton fished into the pocket of his tunic and removed a palm-sized velvet case. Snapping it open, he held it out for William to see. Inside was a gold and silver disk, polished to a mirror sheen. Embossed upon its surface was an enameled red lion in the upright rampant position surmounted upon a royal blue chevron. The motto upon the flowing scrollwork read: *Nobilis est Ira Leonis.*

"Your service placard, sir?"

Thornton nodded. "The Admiralty gave this to me on the day that I received the assignment to the *Lion.*" His eyes became distant, "One of the proudest moments of my life, both professionally *and* personally."

William nodded, admiring the clean, sculpted lines.

"I want you to have it."

"Sir?"

"It is my wish that when you leave this ship that a part of the *Lion* travel with you," he indicated the placard.

"I can't accept this, sir."

"You can, and what's more, you will," Thornton said in his officer's voice that left no room for a dissenting opinion.

"The Captain may be the ship's brain, the engineer her heart, but after today, I have found that you, sir, are her soul."

Reverently, William closed the cover and cupped it in both hands. "Thank you, sir."

Thornton extended his hand and William shook it firmly.

"And in this voice may we be found worthy of the courage to surmount any pinnacle…and aspire the stars," Thornton said, quoting *The Prisoner of Zyi-Kang* preamble.

William showed no surprise at the subtle revelation of his past. He merely tilted his head in acknowledgment.

"Godspeed, Colonel," Thornton said as he turned on his heel and walked away.

⏶ ⏶ ⏶

Twelve *Nimbus* shuttles hung in the velvety darkness of space, all but invisible. In their wake, *Rampant Lion* now concealed herself in the blue shadows of Cerulaan, waiting like a prowling predator.

Now it was up to them, and each man and woman in Imperial powered armor felt that crux of circumstance upon their shoulders. The fortunes of the whole endeavor hinged upon their actions. And yet, they bore the burden, each like an Atlas standing upright.

The shuttles arced out from Cerulaan in their parabolic course toward the floating fortress in orbit. Though the massive construct wasn't visible to the naked eye at this distance, readouts of the station flashed across every display and HUD.

Helot Station loomed above the planet like a dull silver barbell with a protruding central docking ring around its middle. Each end of the station was festooned with powerful weapon emplacements that rivaled those of a capital ship. The firing arc of each battery had been carefully set to overlap with its neighbor, allowing them to cover any point on its surface or surrounding space.

A direct confrontation would be impossible, but those cannon protected the communications array at either end. Any communications ability had to be silenced for the endeavor to be brought to a successful conclusion. The task of setting the jammers carried with it a high projected mortality rate, but there was no shortage of volunteers among the Long Knives.

"Coming up on Point Taurus, sir," Nadia said to William from her command station, her helmet racked on the back of her chair. "Shuttles 4, 5, 9 & 10 are ready for course correction."

"Confirmed. Signal departure," he synched up the onboard chronometer, "now."

In space, a single row of lights on either side of the Command Shuttle flicked from front to back one time. With that, four shuttles departed from the rest of the family to begin their dangerous errand.

"What's their ETA to Helot?" William said over his armored shoulder.

Nadia already had the information ready for him. "Looks like about seven hours, forty-seven minutes at present speed. Call it eight hours, sir."

"And ours?"

"About 30 minutes before that, sir."

"Very good," William replied and ran the numbers on his console. That would just give them enough time to cut their way into the main cargo bay. When the jammers cut in, that was their signal to start the attack.

The eight remaining shuttles sliced through the night, carefully avoiding the interwoven net of sensor drones laid out to prevent precisely what they were attempting. In that regard they were successful—an advantage gained by the simple fact that much of the slaver tech was either stolen or copied from Imperial originals.

Like ghosts in starlight, they continued inexorably on towards their objective. Hours passed as they crept slowly around the cobalt curvature of Vermillion, until finally the massive orbiting structure came into view of their sensor array. Powerful lenses that belonged more on a planet-born observatory reached out into the night and captured what they saw without an active sensor ever being fired.

"Sir, I think you should see these," Nadia said from her station.

"Patch them through."

As his repeater screen cleared and resolved into the first image, he knew immediately why Nadia had brought them to his attention. The gigantic oblong shape of Helot Station was there, outlined by the light of Vermillion's red moon, Rakaana, as though it were drenched in blood. Three vaguely cylindrical shapes occupied the space around the station. The resolution of the image tightened and refined itself until those indistinct shapes became the unmistakable forms of three *Inferno*-class destroyers. While the *Rampant Lion* was more than a match for the trio, each enemy ship carried enough firepower to destroy a *Nimbus* a hundred times over.

And they were directly in the way.

"Our flight path to the docking ring will take us right past them, sir," she said after William had a chance to digest what he'd seen. "Even with our stealth, their sensors are bound to spot us at that range."

William leaned back in his chair in consideration. The main strike force was dead in the water if they continued on its current path. And, there was no way to signal the four shuttles to let them know the plan had changed.

"Is there anything else on passive? Anything at all?"

If they had to abort this mission, *Rampant Lion* would be forced to show herself. There would be no way Helot Station would miss an Imperial light cruiser gunning for them, which would alert the planet below. In that eventuality, *Rampant Lion* would be forced to bombard the Overseer's Palace from orbit, killing all the slaves around them. William closed his eyes and took a deep breath. All that innocent blood would be spilled.

No, he could not let that happen. He would find a way.

"Looks like we have mainly unmanned sensor stations, two weather satellites, an independent missile launcher hovering over the northern pole," she paused for an interval, putting her hand to her earpiece. "And two transports on approach, sir."

The two converted troop transports openly burned their drives towards central processing at Helot Station, which gave a clear indication as to their cargo.

"They must've arrived in since we left the barn." Nadia said.

William stared down at the transports' positions relative to his command.

"All right, those transports are our ticket in. Put us on an intercept course. Try to hide our course correction in the gaps of their net if at all possible, and signal the other shuttles with us to follow the leader."

His face hardened at the thought of what they would find on those ships.

Twenty minutes later, the eight shuttles broke high and right from their original course and bore down on the oblivious slave transports.

▲ ▲ ▲

They never knew what hit them. Even when Nimbus shuttles began latching onto their hull like limpets, they still didn't react immediately. Apparently, the Red Chain hadn't thought much of these transports because they had stripped out all the military-grade sensors and replaced them with substandard civilian suites. These ships were as disposable to the slavers as the human cattle they carried. All of which made the Marines' job that much easier.

There had been token resistance from some of the crew, but the firepower at Montgomery's command was meant to assault the equivalent of a capital ship. They brushed aside the meager security forces like wayward insects. The scaled-down jammers the *Nimbus* carried were more than enough to keep them from calling for help, too. The two transports hadn't even changed course or altered their aspects in any way. The Marines continued on their course to Helot Station, and so far as they could tell, Helot Station was still completely unaware of their presence.

The crews of both ships had to be replaced, but luckily, there had been volunteers hand-over-fist when they had opened the slave pens. Qualified personnel were in abundance. But not all of them had been ripped freshly from their freedom. Quite a few had already been "seasoned," and the scars left on their minds and bodies were evident.

William had stood among them like a silver juggernaut in his powered armor. At first they shied away from his presence until one of the Long Knives made mention of his past. That had broken the ice. In their eyes, he had faced the same enemy and overcome. He was their savior.

Despite the horrendous conditions of the pens, smiles and laughter had resounded throughout the tight confines. The Long Knives took great pleasure in breaking the signature red chains with their servo-enhanced strength. Great piles of the crimson links littered the deck where they had been cast off.

Even though William had vowed to detach the transports at the first sign of hostilities, the overwhelming majority would have none of it. If anything, they shared the Long Knives' need to strike back at their captors. The Marines now had a support network, which freed them to the job at hand. At this point it made a difference since the action had put them six hours behind schedule.

That meant the sapper shuttles had already been at their objective for five and-a-half hours. What fate had befallen them was as yet unknown. The *Infernos* had not moved, nor even warmed their drives or primed their weapons.

The operation called for a specialist team to utilize the miniscule blind spots in the sensor cones at either end of the station, and go EVA to place the jammers and set governors on the weapon clusters. By now they would have either succeeded or failed. They wouldn't have waited on their tardy brothers to arrive.

Those destroyers could either be sitting there oblivious, or lying in wait to spring a trap. There was no way to know at this point. The shuttles were powered down, still attached to the transport hulls. It would depend on how closely the sensor tech on Helot Station had looked them over.

Tension on the bridge grew taut as the transport approached.

Finally, Helot Station challenged them, and one of their own crew, Lieutenant Brym Nagaavi, dutifully answered with all the correct passcodes and countersigns, while a Marine in powered armor stood just outside the comm pickup. The captured officer even added a humorous flourish to his words. William was well within his rights to cycle him out the airlock, and Nagaavi knew it. But before hard vacuum touched him, the slaves he abused were going to have their shot at him. Needless to say he was quick to turn coat on the Brotherhood and cooperate without hesitation.

"They bought it," Nagaavi said with no small amount of relief. "It did grab their suspicion that the Captain didn't answer, but I gave them the "all's free and clear" signal and they swallowed it whole."

"Congratulations," Nadia said, "You just saved yourself the death penalty. For now." Her hard eyes drilled into his soul. "Don't give me any reason—*any* reason—why letting you live is a bad idea."

Nagaavi shut his mouth with an audible *click*.

The two transports moved past the destroyer screen. The ships merely hung there in space like lethal decorations. As the transports fired their maneuvering thrusters to kill their forward momentum, the shuttles used that sensor flare to detach.

"Sir!" Nadia said sitting bolt upright, "I have confirmation that the jammers just went online!"

The sapper team had done it. Somehow they had waited it out in hostile territory and executed at precisely the right time. They were giving the infiltrators exactly the window they needed.

"The confusion should buy us a few minutes," William said, securing his helmet in place. "Make them count."

"Yes, sir!"

Magnetic grapnels shot out and reeled the command shuttle over to the access portal. Once contact was made, counter-electronic overrides cracked open the airlock. Silver-clad Marines poured through. The equipment was normally meant to move masses of slaves at one time, which gave the Marines a solid foothold in the station. Depositing all available troops on the station would still take time, but thirty-eight Marines in powered armor was quite a way to make an entrance.

"We're green to go, sir," Hoskins reported from the airlock controls.

"Open her up," Nadia replied.

The hatch opened to the compartment within.

What they didn't know, what they *could not* have known, was that a Red Chain troop had mustered their own troops there at that very moment. While the Long Knives had the element of surprise, they found themselves faced with almost ninety soldiers in crimson powered armor, plus a handful of regularly suited troops. Most didn't have their helmets on, or their guns loaded at the moment the Imperial Marines stormed the bay, but however clunky and third generation they might have been, they still outnumbered the Imperials almost three to one.

What had been the opening gambit of a lightning strike turned into a fight for their lives before the first shot was fired.

The Long Knives drew first blood as the front ranks opened fire and advanced into the bay. Firing teams fanned out and took cover, allowing the back ranks to move up behind them. Flechette rifles growled and found their mark, but the fusillade of soft plastic anti-personnel rounds were not meant to pierce that kind of armor. Since the Red Chain soldiers were gearing up for boarding actions of their own, they boasted similar weaponry.

But the Red Chains had the home field advantage, and were not limited to just the weapons they brought with them. In mere moments the room was a warzone. Shining silver and red figures lunged at each other, sometimes in hand-to-hand combat, a battlefield shared between demons and angels.

Nadia crouched down behind a pallet of machine parts and replaced her magazine with more potent armor piercing rounds. It wasn't your normal kit for taking a station by force, but nothing about this operation could be called *normal*. She came up firing and two hostiles withered under her barrage.

That was when she heard the high-pitched whine of heavy weapons being primed. Glancing to her right, she saw an APC's pulse laser battery swivel towards their lines. Barely-seen lines of magenta energy sliced into them with deadly effect.

Their forward momentum stalled. A few more seconds and the situation would go from dire to untenable. Months of planning, and they wouldn't have made it past the front door.

William's comm buzzed in her helmet.

"Nadia, give me some covering fire." His voice was the calm in the storm.

"Yes, sir!"

William broke from their lines flanked by two Long Knives. His goal was obvious, even from where Nadia stood. He was after that APC, which was *behind* the majority of the enemy.

Unstrapping her bandoleer of shock grenades, she armed them and let fly in the path that he would follow, adding her own weapon in tight bursts.

"Marines, clear him a path!" she yelled over the combat channel. Her HUD prioritized objectives. Their combined firepower focused down on one area, but cost them precious seconds of their own.

Nadia had always wondered how such a big man could move that fast, particularly one in powered armor, but there he was, always surrounded, fighting with the fury of an archangel. Both the Marines with him died, protecting their commander, but their effort gave him the edge he needed to make it to the APC. Even then, anyone else wouldn't have made it.

At full stride he lifted his rifle and put a steel-jacketed osmium round right through the gunner's armored visor. Cutting in his repulsors, he bounded up the side of the black vehicle and shoved the dead gunner out. In one easy motion, he settled into the gunner's couch and traced the lasers across the *enemy* ranks.

Critical moments passed as the enemy reeled from the blow. Nadia had brought up heavy weapons, some of which had been in crates and used for cover moments before, and tightened the noose. Right then the second wave of Long Knives arrived on the scene, two shuttles' worth who had entered the next airlock down and forced their way into the compartment.

Now the enemy was sandwiched between two waves of Marines, one in greater numbers attacking from behind, and the other a bunch of resolute survivors. Together they formed a pincer that through grit, determination, and sheer gall finally met in the middle, closing like the jaws of a vise.

By the time the third, fourth, and fifth squads arrived on the scene, the Lt. Colonel was tearing up the deckplates getting to the command center as Nadia and her team headed to the "lower" half of the station to secure the reactor. The narrow corridors negated much of their numerical advantage, but William pressed on like a man possessed.

Deck by deck, the Long Knives overwhelmed the enemy with the force of a tidal wave.

Outwardly, William was cold as liquid nitrogen, but inwardly the fire that burned in his veins was the heart of a star. And yet, it did not paralyze his mind, it liberated him. The fire showed him just how to move, just how to fight, like the call of a Spartan *aulos* over the battle. He stepped in time with the notes, becoming an elemental part of them, the violin he loved soaring in his head as the fight raged around him.

Only the armored doors sealing off the command deck gave him the slightest pause, but one shaped charge later he burst through the still smoking hole the thermite had burned. The white hot splinters of the door framed him like some kind of jagged alien mouth.

Small arms fire ricocheted off his armor as he entered the smoke-filled command deck, but his flechette rifle snapped up and began to sing its destructive song. To his right a steel toed boot lashed out and caught the end of his rifle barrel, propelling it upward. A giant of a man, fully as big as William himself out of his armor, charged the Marine in an attempt to wrest the dreaded rifle away. It was a desperate maneuver to pit flesh and bone against alloy and servomotor.

For a moment the huge man would not be dislodged, as he stood near nose-to-visor with an Achilles in armor. Then William's silver gauntlet closed around the man's thick neck and, with a shove, tossed him into the air as though the man's 160 kilos were nothing.

Those frightened few who raised a weapon died where they stood. As the other Long Knives fanned out on the command deck, William pressed forward. He had learned long ago that the only way to truly lead Imperial Marines was from the front as Alexander, not cracking the whip behind them as a taskmaster.

All around the two-tiered command deck, weapons clattered to the floor and hands flew up. The Long Knives honored this, but the liquid crystal blue of their visors conveyed a universe of pain should intentions prove less than sincere.

William panned his gun barrel around the room, his HUD filtering out the smoke. The situation was nearing a resolution…except…

"Behind you!" a Marine yelled.

Bloodied and battered, the man William had tossed reached towards a fire control panel for the laser emplacements. The blinking yellow indicator lights told William it was still operational. If the battery fired, the destroyers would notice, jammers or no jammers.

In one smooth, practiced motion, William wheeled around and fired, surgically removing the offending hand with his rifle. At first the man's face registered only confusion at the sudden disappearance of his arm below the elbow. Mercifully, shock engulfed his senses just as the realization began to dawn in his eyes.

If the captured crew had been docile before, after that they tried their best, their *very best*, to be microscopic under the dread scrutiny of the Long Knives.

An unnatural hush fell over the command deck, with only the crackling of burning computer panels and the liquid hiss of fire suppression systems going off.

William moved towards where the large man lay, only now seeing him clearly. The torn, burnt, and bloody uniform was now clearly visible as that of an officer. The gold pin made of tiny interwoven chain links marked him as the commander of Helot Station.

"Jeffries!" William shouted.

"He's dead, sir," Private Khardon said.

William's azure visor turned to face Khardon. "See that this man is stabilized and secure the rest of the command deck, ASAP."

"Yes, sir!"

"Colonel Montgomery," Nadia's voice came over the comm, "we've secured the reactor room and crew quarters. What's the status on your end, sir?"

"Status secure." William looked around the shattered room and the terrified captives, his gaze settling on the inert form of the station commander.

"Helot Station is ours."

⋀ ⋀ ⋀

William cracked his helmet seals, the contained atmosphere escaping with a sharp hiss. He removed the helmet from its connections and placed it on the desk in front of him. Sitting behind the station commander's black glass and steel station seemed wrong. How many lives had been decided, how many fates sealed from this very chair?

His eyes hardened at that thought. Helot Station had served as a processing station for newly arriving slaves before being either taken to the planet below or to the auctions. So many lives stolen...

He shook it off. The fatigue was getting to him, compounded by the news Nadia had brought him a few moments before. The operation had been a success, so far as they could tell. The Overseer had no idea of the events that had transpired in the heavens above him. But the cost had been high.

Aboard the station their casualties had tapered off dramatically after their deadly encounter in the docking bay. Their losses outside the station, however, were considerable. The four shuttles had done their duty, even in the face of the other eight shuttles arriving hours late. The sapper teams had gone EVA while the shuttles hid in the sensory blind spots, narrow cones extending out from each antenna. Others had planted the jammers while their brethren had quietly bypassed many of the laser batteries, right under the noses of the three *Infernos*. There they had waited patiently for some sign of the other shuttles. By the time the transports had arrived, those Marines were out of air, and it had been an educated guess on their part that the incoming ships were not as they seemed. If they hadn't thrown the switch when they did, no one would have been left conscious to do it.

So William's entrance had been paid with the hard currency of his people's lives. Nineteen had been too far gone when they were finally recovered, another eight had somehow survived, but were either comatose or out of action.

But that had not been the worst of it. Once the jammers had been activated, a last act by their operators, the three destroyers became suspicious as to why their communications were likewise jammed. Unable to raise either the station or planet, the three ships opted to move in to get a better idea of what was going on. Each destroyer had carried a sizeable compliment of armed troops. Without hesitation, the four shuttles had gone out to meet the destroyers and prosecute a boarding action against them. Shuttle 9 had been blasted out of existence, along with thirty-eight Marines plus a pilot, destroyed by the only shot fired in space during the whole engagement. What followed had been bloody mayhem as the three remaining shuttles took an understrength squad against each a ship.

True to their unyielding nature, the Long Knives had done it, even though it had been gauss rifles at twenty paces, a gauntlet of shocking brutality and violence. But where might would have despaired at their losses and faltered, the Long Knives had pressed forward, always forward, into fray.

In the final tally, the Helot Station operation claimed the lives of 141 Long Knives, leaving 319 left to carry on in their stead. While those numbers were paltry in the grand scheme of things, the Long Knives were a small, close-knit strike team. To them, the losses were staggering, shocking.

There were 141 faces that William would never see again, nearly a third of his command, already gone.

In light of those circumstances, they had won a victory against the Red Chain Brotherhood, a *real* victory. Whether their upcoming strike against the planet was successful or not, they now possessed two of the enemy's transports, three of their destroyers, and Helot Station itself—a sizeable portion of the Overseer's capital—none of which would ever be used in the tyranny of slavery again. William would see them destroyed first, and appropriate scuttling charges were already in place.

In the meantime, those hard won assets could work for them. The required personnel were once again drawn from the ranks of freed slaves from the station and ships. Even with the haunting numbers of the absent, William still had to prepare for his ultimate objective—an assault on the Overseer's palace.

And it wasn't going to be easy.

Helot Station's memory bank had been captured completely intact. It had confirmed that the Overseer was indeed on the planet, along with his six most senior lieutenants. And yet, the same memory bank had told them that the defenses of the Overseer's palace were far more advanced than they had believed. The madman's paranoia showed in the layers upon layers of protection he had constructed around his personal domicile.

While the palace itself was overly fortified—just the way William had envisioned—the real problem was the densely packed sensor net that extended out more than a

200 kilometers from the palace in every direction. While a *Nimbus* might have enough stealth ability to fool the net, the use of any of their other heavy equipment, including powered armor, would warn them of an approach in a heartbeat. A direct orbital drop was likewise out of the question—the palace could withstand a direct nuclear blast or stand up to the machinations of even a modern siege.

No. Their numbers were far too few to risk a direct assault. Everything up until now had depended on misdirection and stealth. The final leg of the mission would, it seemed, have to follow suit, now with the clock ticking.

The majority of Red Chain ships had been drawn out of the system by Naval Intelligence's skillful manipulations. Likewise, the units they had in orbit around the planet had been either captured or bypassed. The real problem was the patrol units further out in the system, many of whom *Rampant Lion* had avoided on her way in. According to their captured schedules, the next rotation would bring a *Myrmidon*-class heavy cruiser into Helot Station for re-supply within the next two to three weeks. The Long Knives had access to Red Chain code protocols, but the illusion that they were now enacting for the Overseer's benefit could not be maintained indefinitely.

They would have to bring actions to a close within that window. All it would take was one false transmission from that cruiser or the planet to bring every ship in the system down on their heads. While *Rampant Lion* was a deadly combatant in space, even she could not stand against *everything* the Red Chains had left, however thin their forces might have become.

William grappled with this knowledge, but was resolute. He would never turn back. This was their best chance to break the chain once and for all. The practice of so base an institution as slavery was a cancer on the soul of humanity and here it would be ended, that much William vowed the heavens. The very act of taking a sophont and subjecting them to forced servitude was such an anathema to William's nature that he himself would not, *could not*, ever think of slavery as anything but a manifestation of evil. The same spirit given flight upon the wings of music could never understand why anyone would wish to so belittle another as to chain them.

William blinked away the memories. Though he might not know the hearts of those who would perpetrate slavery, he *did* know how to stop them. His will was set, now more than ever.

He reached over and thumbed the comm panel. "Sergeant Major?"

"Yes, sir?" Nadia responded at once.

"I want a full assembly of available Marines in the docking bay in four hours. Additionally, I want each *Nimbus* fueled and ready to fly, loaded with the equipment manifest I'm about to post."

"Yes, sir. I'll see to it."

"That is all."

▲ ▲ ▲

Some ten hours after Helot Station's fall, its liberators departed again, leaving behind only a handful of their own to make sure the hundreds of freed slaves kept their sanity. The last thing the Long Knives needed was to have their *de facto* support team exacting revenge on those station personnel the Marines needed in place.

After piggybacking a signal to *Rampant Lion* through Helot's sensor net, thee hundred Imperial Marines disembarked for the blue planet below. Those shuttles which were now empty were loaded to capacity with weapons, provisions, and heavy equipment. The majority of their cargo was going to be next to useless where they were going, but William Montgomery was one who planned ahead.

The nine *Nimbus* shuttles made planetfall on the far side of Vermillion from the Palace and carefully crept around the curvature of the planet towards the spiked dome nestled among an endless sea of forest.

After the ablative shielding retracted from the viewport on Shuttle 1, Nadia couldn't help but be moved by the scenery. Aside from the blight that the Overseer represented, the planet was not industrialized at all. A vast, unspoiled garden sprawled out before her in every direction. In the northern hemisphere, it was early spring and the budding fronds of trees uncounted shook off the cruel chains of winter, assaulting the senses with a beauteous array of color and life. There was something primeval and innocent about this place that she read in each branch and bloom that blurred beneath their passage.

Hours passed as they crossed the placid surface of the Middle Sea towards the wide expanse of the Mohin continent and the dark mind that dwelled there. The sun began to slip below the horizon, its golden light fading to crimson, then to brilliant marigold orange, marbled through with indigo. When the sun had passed the rule of sky to the three moons, the shuttles arrived at their destination some 320 kilometers from the Overseer's palace.

The sounds of chirping insects greeted them as they made camp and sorted out their individual kits. Unlike most of their operations, the Long Knives would be operating without the benefit of powered armor or powered vehicles. Though they would carry modern weaponry, it was not to be switched on lest the Red Chain detection net herald their presence. No, the Marines were going to traverse the entire distance on foot. Some of the shuttles would stay behind at base camp, while others were being fitted with less conventional means of movement.

Aside from being outside the net, William had chosen this place for another reason. The LZ was adjacent to a mighty winding river that flowed clear and cold down from the mountains. In order to transport the shuttles and equipment as close as possible to the palace without detection, they were being fitted with IR shrouds and pontoons to use the river's strong current to bring them within striking distance of the enemy.

For the sake of speed, however, the Long Knives would cut across country and rendezvous with the skiffs in the woods just outside the palace grounds. The plan was worthy of any pre-space commander, using what was at hand to press forward when all indicators said to turn back.

There would be no turning back. Not now.

The Long Knives busied themselves in sorting out their kits. They wore the black, tactical body armor over camouflage fatigues. Green, brown, and black face paint covered their stern faces and they wore their unpowered helmets like crowns. Finally, each draped an IR shroud made from chameleon fabric over their battle-hardened forms.

Once assembled, they were still an impressive sight to behold. The armsmaster distributed as many powder burning firearms as they had, which wasn't nearly enough, all told. Sidearms which used no electronics at all were antique and rare, but in the strange situation where they found themselves, each was worth its weight in platinum. However, each Marine also carried the signature double-edged long blade responsible for giving the unit its name.

William's eyes swept across them, seeing every gap in the ranks that now existed, but also seeing the burning determination in each Marine who remained.

He motioned them forward as he took to a small hill at the edge of the glade.

"Long Knives, we have arrived at last," he said, a weight to his words. "Though it was not without its price, our ultimate foe lies there." He motioned in the direction of the palace.

"Let's not keep him waiting."

A rumble of laughter rippled through the crowd.

"All of you know what's at stake here, for many of you carry one of these," he reached into a pouch and produced a length of slaver's chain that was blood red. He held it out for all to see. "The time has come to give these back. But to do so, our road will be hard. Just remember who lies at the end of our journey. I will demand nothing less than the best from each of you."

He wrapped the chain around his massive hand and then it disappeared into a pouch.

"I know you will not disappoint."

He turned towards Nadia who stood at the base of the hill.

"Sergeant Major," he said, still projecting his voice.

"Yes, sir!"

"Are we ready to move out?"

In answer, a sea of silver blades flashed from their sheaths into sharp salutes.

Nadia looked out across the flashing steel with pride before she turned looked at William with fire in her eyes.

"We are ready, sir!"

"Very well then. Long Knives…move out!"

⅄ ⅄ ⅄

By noon the next day, Nadia had a new appreciation for armies in the pre-radio era. Even with a group of disciplined soldiers, getting everyone moving in the same direction was an enormous challenge. There was no way that they could march in formation given the thick forest they had to move through, but each squad had been given a map and an old-fashioned compass should they find themselves separated from the main body.

Progress was physically demanding, but the chilly breeze of early spring cooled them down from their exertions. Each Marine's breath sprang from their nostrils like smoke as they pressed forward on foot.

William himself was the calm at the middle of storm. Even when the Long Knives were tempted to vent the myriad of frustrations of being on the move, they had only to look at the aura of rock solid stability William and Nadia radiated. Eternally alert to their surroundings, neither seemed concerned with the rigors their journey placed on them. For leaders in adverse conditions there was no greater gift they could give to those under their charge than to project strength.

At 1800 hours that day they reached an expanse of craggy blue cliffs, which sat at the foot of imposing, cloud-capped mountains. Since their departure from the LZ they had followed the river, but here was where they must diverge from it. The Marines took one more drink from its cool depths before contemplating the climb ahead. One look told them that a good set of repulsors would have cleared those rocky heights in moments. The climb with old-fashioned hammer-in pitons and crampons would surely take hours of backbreaking exertion.

The sun was already starting its slow descent to dusk. They would need to be up there by nightfall.

"Be just like basic, sir," Nadia said to William as she checked her gear, just loudly enough where others could hear. "Then again, I think I was the only one that thought boot camp was *too* easy."

For any officer, having an NCO like Nadia was a rare gem. She could play the disciplinarian, or the comrade, each with equal acumen. She kept the Long Knives sharp and ready for him to wield at will.

Their most able climbers, including Nadia herself, led the way up the stone face, guiding the others up. Chill wind washed over them as they ascended, numbing hands and feet. Ropey tendons stood out in William's arms as he went hand-over-hand. Sweat beaded on his forehead. Even though his neck felt like it was on fire, the wind grew worse.

Like a parade of spiders, the Marines moved with remarkable speed. Mid-way up, William felt a tremor go through the line at the same time a rain of small rock and debris floated down, stinging his eyes. Shaking it off, he looked up to see one of his Marines dangling upside down as one of the pitons near the cliff edge gave way. To his credit, the Marine did not cry out as he flailed to regain control.

"Grab him!" William bellowed. The Marine's unsupported weight was threatening to dislodge other pitons, which could add to the number in jeopardy, if gravity didn't slay them all.

The guide rope slipped from the Marine's harness. For a moment he was in freefall, but another Marine snatched him out of the air with hands moving like a striking snake.

Another vibration in the line told William that the sudden shock had sent the pitons into a chain reaction.

Then, from the top of the cliff, Nadia appeared without her jacket or backpack. She leapt from the top, going straight for the problem's heart like a diver. William's heart jumped at first before he saw the rope tied to the back of her harness. She jerked to stop, but merely grunted at the shock of stopping. Bending in the air, she scissored her legs to hold herself upside down, freeing up her hands.

"The rope!"

The next Marine in line reached out from his perch, his fingers grasping at the wind-tossed life line. Tense seconds passed until at last his hand closed around it. With one deft toss the black thread sailed upwards and into her hands. She twisted herself around and reset the piton.

"Everyone hug the rock as much as possible," she yelled out. She looked back at the top. "Give me some slack."

Like a spider at the end of her web, she descended, securing the faltering guide line. Finally, satisfied with her handiwork, she hooked her arms under the fallen Marine's armpits and hauled him to the top herself.

William took in a long breath of mountain air. Stars, that had been close!

The day wore on, and by nightfall the last of the Long Knives had made it to the top without further incident. Private Khardon was a little shaken by his near-disastrous climb, but was quick to cover any sign of fright from his peers. Even here, the Long Knives had a reputation to uphold.

The three moons rose larger than life in the night sky as they made a cold camp. Nadia herself had to marvel at the striking starscape that came into view as the sunlight faded away. She was no stranger to sight of the sparkling motes, having worked in space for years, but seeing them atop this precipice made the night sky seem crystal clear in its immensity. Of all the hot zones and operations she'd been dropped into, none had ever held the magic of this scenery. She drank it in.

William stood at the edge of the cliff, silhouetted against the moon, staring off into the distance. Cerulaan was clearly visible tonight in the sway of her elder sisters. Somewhere in the cool shadows of that blue moon, *Rampant Lion* was on the prowl. Seeing it planetside was different, like a cosmic light show put on for their benefit. Nadia departed from those around her and came to stand by him.

"What do you see?" she said at his shoulder.

"The end of the road," he replied. "You were exceptional today," he added after a moment. He did not often compliment someone directly.

"Just doing my job," she said. "The Knives wonder why you don't play for them. They see it as a bad omen. Tell me, did you bring it this time?"

"No."

"May I ask why?"

"It's complicated," William said, still staring at the horizon. "Suffice to say, I couldn't run the risk of it falling into *their* hands. Not again."

Nadia was one of the few among their ranks who had never known slavery firsthand, though she had liberated enough camps to know the wretched hell of those souls who had been subjected to it.

"I think I understand. Still, it is a pity. Your song is… irrefutable to those who hear it."

He made no response, but somehow she knew he had accepted her words. She left him just the way she had found him, and snuggled into her thermal bedroll, while gazing up at the stars once more. Whatever was to come, whatever this planet had in store for them, she felt fortunate to fight side-by-side with the likes of William Aidan Montgomery.

▲ ▲ ▲

They moved out shortly before dawn, just as the eastern sky began to trade black for baby blue. When they left, no vestige remained that a camp had ever existed there. The ropes had either been retracted or dissolved.

By the time the sun crested the mountains, the Long Knives were working their way through the foothills, clinging to the sparse tree cover. Meals were taken quickly and on the march. Luckily, advanced combat rations had made a science out of getting the most nutrients for the least amount of effort.

At 1100 hours they reached the final ridge before the sloping rocks gave way to forest again. The view this spot commanded over the valley was breathtaking. A vast knotted green carpet of treetops greeted them, shot through with threads of gold and crimson more finely woven than the richest tapestry.

The river they had quit before their climb snaked sinuously down into the valley. The snowmelt of spring ran down the mountains, feeding into the larger river in a thousand clear streams.

They stopped to rest at one such stream. The water cascaded over the rocks, forming a small, perfect waterfall. Its constant low whisper was enough to sooth the knowledge of the six or seven day trek to come. They would have to push hard and move fast. Bone-deep fatigue had yet to seize them, but after they reached the far end of the valley, it might. Each of them knew the confrontation that lay at the end of their travels. They had to be in fighting shape when they arrived.

Several days passed, with each successive one becoming harder and harder to maintain. Nadia felt it, but tried her best not to show it. William seemed immune to the elements, and as always, he pressed on like a hunter closing in on his prey.

At the rising of the moons, they would collapse and draw as many hours of rest as they could until they were once again moving before the sun had its dominion of the morning sky. The thick landscape was a constant impediment. Some squads became separated from the main group and had to be retrieved at the day's end.

But if their muscles were sore, the spirit of the Long Knives burned brighter than ever. Nothing brought out the fiercest of camaraderie like shared hardship. It became a living aura that enveloped each of them. Being counted among their number, just like being a member of *Rampant Lion's* crew, meant something sacred to them.

They kept the pace William set for them, even at times when the elements, terrain, and fatigue all worked against them. Will alone sustained them.

At the close of the ninth day, they reached the rendez-vous point on the far side of the valley. When the advance scouts reported in, they brought two pieces of unfortunate news. First, the place where they planned to cross the river into Red Chain territory had burst its banks. Fueled from an unseasonable amount of rain and fed by the streamers of melting ice from the mountains, the shallows of the river had become a lake. Where they had originally expected a crossing of 120 meters of ankle-deep water, now it was more than 300 meters, and up to their chests.

The second, and perhaps worse, part was that the shut-tles hadn't made it on time. In fact, once the scouts had taken a vantage point atop a mountain, the *Nimbus* convoy wasn't anywhere within a day's journey. William had left instructions for the shuttle group to send a messenger to meet them if things went awry.

No such messenger had arrived.

That meant that unless they arrived soon, they would have to cross the near-freezing lake and proceed just as they were without any kind of modern support. William toyed with the idea of sending a burst message to the con-voy, but quickly discarded it. After all this way, he couldn't risk showing their hand. That was, assuming they had a hand left to show. If the convoy had been captured or compromised, they could be walking squarely into a trap. And without the modern backup their chances of storming the palace shrank into near nothingness.

But, he had to admit, that *storming* the palace had never really been an option for them with the resources available. What they were looking for was really a surgical strike right at the heart. If they could find a way to pick their battle, to find that balance point of crisis and exploit it to the fullest, then William had faith that his Marines could turn the tide even if they had only their long knives.

He ordered the Marines to retreat back from the lake a few kilometers and make camp early. They would take a few hours rest until 01:30 when they would cross the river into occupied territory with or without the supply train.

Nadia never hesitated as she facilitated his orders, but even he could tell that there was some apprehension buried deep inside her. William couldn't blame her, for this would tax their reserves to the limit before ever confronting the enemy.

Hours crept by and the Long Knives sat in silence. The moons rose to dominate the sky once more. More than one set of eyes looked to Cerulaan as if trying to draw strength from the friends around that moon. Nadia surely did, and so did William. *Rampant Lion* had been their home and the knowledge that she was still out there blunted the bitter edge of their circumstances.

Then the moment arrived and they were away. They slowly waded out into the ice-cold water. They couldn't just plunge in, they had to walk in increments, holding their rifles and other sensitive equipment over their heads. The sensation of shock began just as soon as the water filled in their boots. The water was so cold it almost burned. Then, as the water level rose to the knee, it became many times worse. For both men and women, the water around their waists was torturous. Waves of shivering engulfed the company, involuntarily trembling like leaves. And then when the water reached chest, or even neck deep in some cases, the real pain began as the freezing cold water was like a thousand tiny daggers eternally stabbing into their flesh. And when the numbness started to take hold, their limbs grew leaden and lethargic. The existing current in the water course was a constant barrier.

To their credit, not one faltered or cried out. They were troopers of the highest order and it showed. Since their inception, the Long Knives had always been a strictly volunteer unit. Task Force-1171 had brigades of Marines, but these were individuals with a personal stake in events. At that point, when even breathing felt impossible, they pressed forward when all instincts said they should bolt.

Voices floated across the water from the far side of the lake. The Marines stopped in the water without command or signal. On the far bank six men materialized from the edge of the forest. The moonlight glinted off their weapons and red body armor.

"This graveyard shift business is killing me, Paulo," one voice said.

"You should talk to the boss," another said as he lit up a cigarette, "maybe he can get you transferred back to Processing when they've just come off the boat."

"I hope so," the first one said. "There's not nearly as much fresh meat on this beat."

The others laughed harshly.

As cold as the water was, William was surprised the lake wasn't boiling over with the combined rage of his troops. Here they were caught out in the open. If those guards looked too closely at the surface of the water, they could be found out.

"I guess you'll just have to amuse yourself with the natives," the one called Paulo said, flicking an ash to the wind. "It'll get you by for now, at least."

A splashing sound echoed down river from the Marines.

"What the hell was that?" Paulo said.

Beams of light lanced out towards the surface of the water as electronic torches lit up. William glanced over to see a long, sinewy shape cutting through the water towards their position.

"Night Python," the other man said. "Big one, too. Don't worry, they hate bright light," he said to the rest of the men who had taken an involuntary step back. Their beams tracked the mammoth ophidian for a few seconds, clicking off only scant yards from the first Marine in the water.

"Let's get back to base, guys," One of the others offered. "There might be more of 'em."

"Yeah, not a bad idea," Paulo said, flicking his cigarette butt into the river and exhaling the last of the smoke through his nostrils.

The patrol turned and disappeared back into the woods. Nadia held her breath as a cold, scaly shape brushed over her shoulder. She didn't move a muscle. Neither did William as the twisting form passed within arm's reach of him, its yellow eyes glowing in the night.

For long moments they held still in that frozen hell of a lake. Then moved again, holding steady, until at last the first ranks reached the shore and drew themselves out of the glacial depths. As the Long Knives made their exit, discipline broke down temporarily as they collapsed, clawing at the soft ground.

Some of the Marines in the back ranks were immobile as the delay had sapped their reserves with a nearly insurmountable distance now between them and safety. William gritted his teeth and blackened his face with dirt before plunging into the icy depths to retrieve them. Nadia followed suit and so too did many others.

Going back in was worse, like escaping hell only to go back of your own volition. Timing was critical before hypothermia set in. The next while became a swirl of activity to Nadia's mind. Then, she was back on the shore with her boots off and swaddled in thermal blankets. Her short black hair was slicked back on her head.

Men and women came up to where she sat, thanking her for pulling them out. Numbly she accepted it, not even remembering the very act for which they praised her. She had been on autopilot until her mind had thawed enough to switch back on.

Across from her, William sat like a troubled king. He might have been chiseled from stone, for he sat unmoving, eyes dark, lost in thought. Crossing could have irreparably damaged their ability to prosecute this attack, but what other choice did he have? He had to press ever forward. No one had died from the cold, and miraculously they were across the river, but what could they do now?

An idea occurred to Nadia as her faculties returned in full. She hated to break his chain of thought, like the regret that comes from throwing a stone in a placid pool. Still, it had to be done.

"Sir, I have an idea."

His eyes flicked towards her and instantly she held his attention.

"Those men are more than likely stationed at an outpost around here. If they run patrols in this area, then we're probably going to run across them at some point." She swallowed, marshaling her thoughts. "We could take a small team and track them back to that base to clear it preemptively. That would allow us forward passage as well as access to some of their equipment that apparently doesn't disturb the sensor net."

William immediately saw the utility of her suggestion. Her plan of action would do everything she stated, but also allowed the Long Knives more time to recover their strength. More than that, it would be a chance to strike at the enemy and possibly win a victory face-to-face against the foe. Nothing could drive a unit to excellence faster than a taste of victory after hardship and ordeal.

"Excellent thinking," he said after a moment. "Find six candidates that are in fighting shape and equip them with our best weapons. We move out at first light."

"*We*, sir?"

"Yes, I'm going with you."

"Very good, sir. I'll take care of it."

William nodded towards her.

"I know."

▲ ▲ ▲

As soon as it was light enough to see, William, Nadia and six others set off into the forest. The patrol, as it turned out, wasn't hard to track since they made no real effort to disguise their passage.

They didn't have far to go either. The outpost was only about four kilometers from where the Long Knives were camped at that moment. The squat grey building surrounded by a razor wire fence came into a view a short time later. Men in red armor stood about lazily with very little to do except torment the aboriginal slaves around them.

Each member of the strike force looked daggers at the dark debauchery unfolding before their eyes, but held true. Not one of them would fly off the handle in a fit of rage. No, they would save it and focus on the enemy when the time came.

"I can get us in there, sir." Nadia said.

"How is that?" Khardon said next to her.

"I'll be extra charming."

"Do it," William said, his eyes never leaving the camp. "We'll be ready."

Nadia stood up, adjusting her IR poncho over her body armor, dusted herself off slightly and strode down the hill towards the front door as if she belonged there.

"Olivar, Sharo, you take out that antenna when the time comes," William said indicating the comm dish on top of the structure. "The rest of you are with me."

Below them, Nadia walked right up to the front gate in full view of everyone.

"Open up," she said imperiously.

One of the men on the other side turned around, surprised. He took in the hard curves of her body and the luxuriant black hair, falling from a central part. A lascivious smile began to form on his face until her hard brown-green eyes bored into him.

"I haven't got all day, open this fucking gate *now!*" She was using her drill sergeant voice that gave the hint of all kinds of pain and suffering if her demands weren't carried out. The man was easily cowed by it. He did as she said.

"Who are you anyway?" he said as she passed.

"You better pray you never find out," she hissed at him. "Now tell Paulo to get his ass out here, and I mean yesterday." The polar ice-cap quality to her voice had turned the bones of even Imperial Marines to jelly in the past.

These men were just two-bit thugs with guns. They had no defense against her unassailable aura of authority.

A crowd began to gather around her. One man could not resist eyeing her muscular form from top to bottom, albeit hidden in her cloak. He thought he was out of her peripheral vision. He was wrong.

Her long blade materialized at his throat before he could blink. They all took a step back. "I'm not one of your meat whores, so you better just keep those eyes in your head or I'll carve them out. You get me?" He nodded hastily. With her free hand, she cracked him hard in the face, sending him sprawling to the ground.

"Now, does anyone else want a closer look?" She glanced around. They were terrified, just where she wanted them. "The next one of you who so much as glances at me like I'm one of our *products*, so help me, I will field castrate you right here."

She gestured with her knife and they jumped. "Now where the hell is Paulo?"

"Right here," a voice said from the door of the building. Paulo was half-dressed and struggling to put on his armor. His eyes went from the man with the broken nose to her unfamiliar face.

"Who is this?" he asked of his men.

"I'm your one-way ticket out of this life if you don't listen up," she growled. "The boss wants to see you and your team, stat." she eyed him not hiding her disgust. "So put your pants back on, grab your team and let's go."

"What's this all about, anyway?" Paulo said while sealing his tunic.

"Can't say, but I doubt it's about a comfy position over at Processing. The boss sounded *really* pissed off when he sent me, so let's hope you've been behaving yourselves out here." There were guilty looks all around.

Nadia snorted. "But from the looks of this outfit, you'll be lucky if there isn't a red chain with your name on it." She let that soak in for a moment. "Now, do I need to tell you again? Get moving!"

In just a few minutes the bulk of the Reds were moving out the door with Paulo and Nadia in the lead. All told, there were only ten of them around, with another three remaining behind to man the monitoring stations.

As they exited the gate, Nadia walked a few steps ahead. Before they had a chance to react, she drew her antique sidearm and jabbed it underneath Paulo's chin. As she did, seven other figures materialized from the undergrowth like specters, surrounding the Red Chain men.

"Drop your weapons," William rumbled, pointing his submachine gun at them. They were dumbfounded and hesitated. They didn't draw their guns, but neither did they put them down.

"Tell them," Nadia said almost face-to-face with Paulo, "or I will splatter you all over them right here and now."

"St...stand down, everyone," Paulo stammered out. A tense moment passed as Nadia's finger curled around the trigger until modern rifles and equipment thudded to the ground all around them.

"Congratulations," the Sergeant Major said as she backed away, keeping the pistol level. "You just saved yourself the death penalty...from us at least." She motioned back towards the gate. Paulo turned slowly along with his men to see a phalanx of seven natives, five of them women, who all had blood in their eyes.

"Sorry to break it to you, Paulo, but it doesn't look like you made many friends here." she tossed a few plastic restraint bands in their direction. "You know the drill. Step away from your weapons and bind yourself." She'd heard that the Red Chains often made their soon-to-be slaves bind themselves when they were first captured.

"Olivar, Sharo, get inside and secure the comm system along with the operator. We need him alive." As the Reds made the transformation into prisoners, William turned towards the assembled natives and raised one hand towards them.

"I am a friend, do you understand my words?"

One impressively built specimen stepped forward with a pick-axe in hand.

"I know your words."

"I am William of the Empire, what is your name?"

"Mon-Dra-Kai," the man said flatly. He looked William over with his aquamarine eyes before waving his other tribesmen down. "Our meeting is good, Wil-Li-Am. You are a friend, this I know."

William shouldered his rifle and came forward. "We're here to free your people from their chains and stop the man who did this to you."

Mon-Dra-Kai made a sweep of his hand to encompass his people.

"This is good." The man's weathered face looked perpetually calm, even serene. His tan skin was leathery, but it lent his face a remarkably wise character. Though older than those of his compatriots, Mon-Dra-Kai was fit even by Marine standards.

Olivar ducked his head out from the structure. "All secure, sir."

William acknowledged this and turned back to his new ally.

"You and your people are safe for now. I must ask for your help to keep it that way. Will you join us?"

Mon-Dra-Kai turned and exchanged words in the musical language of his native tongue. Each responded in kind to him.

"We will help," he said. "But, we wish the blood of these men." He pointed at the newly minted prisoners.

"I give you all but their speakers in there. Those we need," William said, pointing to the building. "These men here have wronged you. It is only right that you seek their blood. If it is your wish, they are yours."

"This is good."

Across the way, the captives were mad with terror, and from the near demonic look that had settled upon Mon-Dra-Kai's calm features, they had every reason to be.

"Sorry guys," Nadia said. "Looks like this isn't your day after all."

The enraged native went to the pile of captured weapons, and produced a modern hatchet that had been carved and decorated with tribal markings. He went first to Paulo, roughly grabbing him by the hair so that he could look him in the eyes.

"This one lashed me until the ground ran red," he spit in the man's face. "He took my daughter so that now she may not bear children!" He was yelling to the air and the other natives stalked forward like cats. "He burned my son so that he would scream. He did not. He killed him for keeping his pride!"

One clean swipe with the hatchet and Paulo was no longer among the living. With that the others joined in, screaming a catalogue of wrongs done to them in the air and exacting tribute in life's blood.

Almost any other officer in William's place would have tried to halt the savage reprisal being enacted before his eyes.

But William was hardly *any* officer.

⏶ ⏶ ⏶

When they returned, the mood became almost festive. The recovering Long Knives and the freed natives, some thirty-eight in all, became fast friends, each having suffered under the yoke of the Red Chain. Once the chains in question were removed, the natives began wearing them as jewelry in bracelets, anklets and hair locks, but never around their necks. The Long Knives showed them their crimson links with a certain pride of escaping their servitude.

The natives even built a great bonfire, which Mon-Dra-Kai assured them was perfectly normal in this area. The Red Chain would think nothing of it. The warm orange glow bathed the camp as night fell, and its warmth was heavenly to the half-frozen Marines. Their combat rations mixed with the wild herbs and berries of the natives. From this an impromptu feast was created between the two peoples.

Nadia marveled at it. Seeing an Imperial Marine dressed in battle armor laughing with a native wearing little to no clothing seemed perfectly natural, and the company was exactly what the Long Knives needed to bring back their crippled vitality.

Overlooking it all were William and Mon-Dra-Kai who sat next to the fire speaking of many things. Once again the native was placid, as though the bloody revenge he'd wrought that very day had never happened.

Several of the natives made garlands and floral offerings to Nadia for the part she had played in their ultimate emancipation. She accepted each with the earnestness in which it was given. One of the women had even worked flowers into her short hair, but she did not refuse. These people had been made to endure something she never had and to deny them something as simple as giving thanks was abhorrent.

William waved her over to where he sat. As she approached, Mon-Dra-Kai stood and bowed to her.

"My thanks, Na-Di-Ah," he said, touching his hatchet in salute as he sat back down.

"I believe Mon-Dra-Kai has given us the critical piece we need," William said, motioning to the other man to speak.

"Many of the Yakonoi Tribe are held in the Overseer's home. Many are made to serve him," he spat on the ground. "Several seasons ago, I was one of them." Both of Nadia's eyebrows shot up.

"There's more." William said.

"There is a door into his home that only slaves use. I can show you the way."

"Best of all, the door is largely unguarded," William said, his voice rumbling. "It seems the Brotherhood doesn't see the Yakonoi as a threat."

"Well after what I saw today, that's a costly way of thinking."

"They wish to believe my people have no spirit left in them. They think they have destroyed it in us. We make them think this, though it is not true." Mon-Dra-Kai said.

"Perhaps it is the folly of all slavers to believe their captives are truly broken," the firelight reflected in William's eyes like dark mirrors. "At times all we can do is show them they are wrong."

"This is good, Wil-Li-Am. You understand my mind."

Olivar walked up just then with his hands behind his back. "Uh, sir?"

"Yes, what it is?"

"Um…we found something today at the base. We didn't believe it at first, but there it was just sitting there."

Clearly, Olivar thought he was presuming upon his CO to approach him like this. "Well, sir, I was wondering if you would play it for us."

The Marine presented the item in question that he'd been holding behind his back.

A violin.

"We heard you didn't bring your normal one for this drop, and it's something of a good luck charm for us...so we...uh...were hoping we could get you to play this one."

"I know of this," Mon-Dra-Kai said. "It sounded like a dying sand cat when the man in red played it."

William took the violin in his huge hands, reluctantly. The piece was actually of good quality, probably stolen during one of their raids. The lacquered golden brown wood caught the light as he turned it over in his hands.

"This will do." William said, placing it under his chin and set about tuning the instrument. He drew the bow across the strings. The bow still bore its rosin. The tone he brought forth was rich and melodious. Immediately he was on his feet with the violin singing its beautiful, bittersweet tune.

All activity in the camp immediately stopped as the Long Knives heard the welcome song that had for so long been sought but never found. The notes found and caressed them one by one.

The song that flooded from his hands was not one that would have sounded in opulent concert halls, nor in the marbled porticos of the privileged few. No, this song was as rustic as the setting, one that was meant to be heard in the presence of nature. The song, played for centuries on the wharves and docks of ancient, salt-sprayed ports, found new meaning by echoing through the unspoiled glade by firelight. The notes became an urgent staccato that William kept impeccably, closing his eyes and tapping his foot, giving himself fully over to the music.

Nadia stood by his side, and as the music soared in introduction, she let her own sweet soprano join it in song. This old traditional song was one of her favorites, only slightly changed to suit their circumstance. She sang:

> *The Lion is a ship me lads,*
> *For the Davis Straits she's bound*
> *And the Quay it is all garnished*
> *With bonnie lasses round*
> *Captain Halcyon gives the orders*
> *To sail the ocean wide*
> *Where the sun never sets me lads*
> *Nor darkness dims the sky.*

> *And it's cheer up, me lads*
> *Let your hearts never fail*
> *For the bonnie ship the Lion*
> *Goes a-fishing for the whale!*

> *Along the quay at Peterhead*
> *The lassies stand around*
> *With their shawls all pulled about them*
> *And the salt tears runnin' down*

Oh don't you weep, my bonnie lass,
Though you be left behind
For the rose will grow on Greenland's ice
Before we change our mind.

And it's cheer up, me lads
Let your hearts never fail
For the bonnie ship the Lion
Goes a-fishing for the whale!

As the reawakening strength of the Long Knives felt this song work into their sinews, their collective hearts were kindled into a great roaring flame, as if the exertion and hardship had been suddenly erased. The bonds of camaraderie were forged anew by the one true voice of that violin. Even the natives were taken aback by the song speaking to them so. When Nadia's song was concluded, William still played on, reaching those upper heights of one born with such propensity of song as to unite generations and worlds.

Then at length the tune was played out, exiting at last with one final transcendent note that seemed to touch the stars before descending back to the earth. When it was gone, it seemed the entirety of breath among the camp went with it. Moments passed before a cheer echoed in every throat before him.

As his eyes scanned the assembled ranks, one indelible truth became apparent to William.

They are ready.

He stood among them for several minutes, letting their attention turn towards each other in their revelry before setting the still-warm violin upon the stone. As the attention waned upon him, so did he seek comfort in the dark outskirts of the camp.

Nadia and Mon-Dra-Kai watched him go, giving him a polite space before following. As they approached they saw that he stood staring up at the moons with something gold and round faintly glimmering in his hand.

"That was…amazing," she said as she came up behind him. "How many times have we sung that song? A dozen, perhaps more? I felt the difference, and I guarantee you *they* did as well."

William turned towards them with a face much changed from normal with a wetness in his eyes. She saw that he held the placard of the *Rampant Lion* in his hand.

"I wonder about that song, Nadia," he said with a catch. "I wonder if the whale it speaks about is the Overseer. Now that I can see its end, I look back upon my road and wonder if it was traveled at too high a price." His gaze drifted over her shoulder towards the Long Knives, as if seeing every gap and absence in their ranks.

"You are wondering if you are Ahab, sacrificing everything in an all-consuming quest for revenge, is that it?" She didn't even need his confirmation to know she was right.

"That's not true, William," she said, taking his hand. "You give hope to so many that I wonder if you hold any in reserve for yourself. You have pursued the Overseer, yes, but you've done so with honor and integrity." She looked him squarely in the eyes.

"You've kept yourself."

Mon-Dra-Kai raised his hand in a sweeping gesture.

"When I first saw you, I knew that you were a friend not only to me but my people," he said in his sagelike manner. "Do you know how?"

William shook his head that he didn't.

"There is a spirit you carry with you. From her you draw strength to meet the foe, and to stand where others might fall. I saw this as clear as in a mountain stream."

William covered his nose and mouth with his hands, as the native pierced deeply into his heart of hearts.

"My friend, she is your song. Your love for her makes you strong, just as your love for them," he gestured towards the Long Knives, "is the same. They follow you into fire because you fight the way you play, with this." He laid a hand across his heart.

At his words, William was undone. There, on the eve of facing their ultimate enemy, beneath the light of three moons was the first and only time Nadia ever saw his tears fall like spring rain. The bottled-up torment of years of pain welled to the surface from places deep in his soul. In a flagrant disregard of protocol, Nadia held him close until they abated as Mon-Dra-Kai spoke words of blessing over him in his seemingly magical native tongue.

It came, the final catharsis, the final realization of truth that had been so long in coming. Any weight or baggage that might have lingered on was finally released in that outpouring, freeing him from the shackles of his own self-doubt and recrimination, and none too soon in coming.

The next day, they would come upon the foe at last.

▲ ▲ ▲

As the horizon slowly lightened, outlining the tall trees against the distant mountains, William woke as a new man. He purified himself in the same waters that only hours before had tormented him. They did not hinder him now. He breathed in great breaths of the fragrant forest, borne to him on the gentle hands of the wind.

Ceremoniously he donned his armor, taking utmost care and attention to every detail of his kit. Those who saw this couldn't help but think the qualities of the man seemed somehow magnified in the early blue-grey light. Nadia took note of this transformation with approval. Whereas in the past he seemed to wear a near-scowl, his features were at peace, in many ways like Mon-Dra-Kai standing at his side.

They were underway within a half-hour, with each member of the procession alert and acute. They passed by the captured outpost and made for the broken trail that led them another seventeen kilometers to the edge of the forest and within sight of the mammoth dome, adorned with soaring spikes radiating outward as though an infant sun had turned to stone.

The plan had been laid out for them. A small team would seek to enter the slave entrance and gain access to the lower halls while the greater part of the Long Knives would begin their assault on the outer defenses, seeking to divert attention away from the strike team.

Not one among them balked at having traveled this far only to serve a role of misdirection. Many were more than willing to keep their order of battle for the chance of giving the Red Chain Brotherhood their just due. It would be a bloody affair for the Marines, however, as they knew they would trade their lives for mere minutes of diversion against the advanced defenses of the foe.

Khardon was left in charge of the greater bulk of the forces, while the five of them set out towards the slave entrance with Mon-Dra-Kai as their guide. He had even gone so far as to replace the red chain around his neck to preserve the illusion.

As the sun climbed ever higher in the sky, the group circled the outer palace grounds until at last they arrived at a humble entrance bored into a slab of red granite. No guards stood in vigilance or challenge.

They entered into the dark corridors, and the smells of slavery assaulted their nostrils - filth, sweat, and the rusty smell of too much spilled blood. But aside from the members of the team, the halls were completely empty. Their guide led them to a long spiral staircase hewn from the stone. Down they went, descending the stairs, and down further still until they came upon a metal corridor.

A rumble went through the ground, followed by another, and another, each at too regular an interval to be natural.

"That's their weapons firing," William said, feeling another ripple through the ground. "The fighting has started."

Nadia turned to Mon-Dra-Kai. "Is it far from here?"

"No, we are close. We must pass by a room of windows and then on to his chambers."

They followed the labyrinthine tunnels around through several intersections and turns, their guide never faltering in his forward progress. Down the way, the corridor terminated into a large control room with a multitude of monitoring stations. Inside there seemed to be a flurry of activity, just barely seen.

"On my mark," William said to the team. "*Go!*"

They charged the room and found it in utter disarray. A voice was near frantic as it yelled into the comm system.

"Helot Station, Helot Station, commence firing on these coordinates at once! Do you hear me? Why aren't you responding?"

The Marines exploded into the room. Many of their foes were merely technicians, but several thugs in body armor realized what was happening and drew down on them.

Before their weapons cleared holsters or came to bear, they were put down. The technicians, already half-mad with fear, were now almost catatonic at the formidable company they faced. Those who were not overcome put their hands up pleadingly.

"Sir, look at this!" Olivar said, as he studied one of the panels. William's tall bulk maneuvered close to the screen to see what had raised his trooper's interest. What he saw was enough to lift his heart into the clouds.

On the monitor, reproduced in startling fidelity, were the forms of the Long Knives attacking the base with unparalleled courage and audacity. Weapons discharged in a deadly fusillade with fury akin to a river bursting its banks. And each one of his troops was shining silver in their pristine powered armor. Nimbus shuttles filled the sky with missile clusters firing off and lasers flashing like lethal fireworks.

Somehow the overdue party had arrived in time to equip their brothers for the battle. Even though the fortifications of the Palace were still superior, the Long Knives fought on with fierce determination. The comm chatter sounded in the control room, bearing witness to just how much of a surprise the band of armor-clad Imperials suddenly appearing in their midst had been. Members of the Red Chain began appearing in powered armor of their own, but were scattered in their direction and unity—easy prey for the Marines who fought as never before.

"You see that, sir?" Nadia said. hefting her rifle in one hand. "That is what your song can inspire. They are fighting for you out there."

And, at least for the moment, they were winning. The secondary defenses had yet to go online, thanks in part to their timely capture of the nerve center, where those orders would have been issued.

"We can't let them regroup," William said with resolute calm, "not now when the advantage is ours." His eyes glanced over the controls for a moment and lit like flame. With a motion, he had Olivar quit his seat so that he could squeeze in. Those deft hands, able to draw out the highs and lows of emotion upon the violin, began to unerringly play across the controls, weaving a song of cunning.

As Nadia watched, William created false sensor images directly into their system. Those monitoring elsewhere in the palace would have looked at their display with pale faces as the number of armored Marines grew from below 300 to well over two-thousand with an additional 50 assault shuttles bringing up the rear. Her smile was wolfish as the maestro put the master stroke on his symphony.

"All units! All units!" he said putting just the right amount of fear in his voice. "Helot station is overrun! We are under attack by superior Imperial forces converging on our position! Recommend immediate withdrawal or surrender, or be destroyed in detail! Good luck!"

He turned back to the glad faces of his troops. "Now, piggyback a coded signal to Khardon and detail what I just did. Have him form up accordingly and run the troops back and forth in full view of the enemy so that they believe our numbers are as great as their sensors tell them. Tell him to accept surrender if any is offered."

Olivar got on it quickly, and in a few seconds gave the all-clear signal.

"Done, sir."

"Let us go then," William said, turning towards the door.

Mon-Dra-Kai, who had watched this with his usual implacable tranquility, once more led them forward, this time to a reinforced door. To their surprise, he punched in the code on the keypad. The door bleeped faintly before allowing them access.

"Great is the Overseer's folly for making a chief of the Yakonoi his slave!" Mon-Dra-Kai said with steel.

The door opened into a long corridor that could have been transplanted from some Archduke's manor or other immensely opulent dwelling. Rich tapestries lined the hall, along with polished mirrors reflecting the graceful vases that were set among them.

The vaulted hallway stretched out before them, terminating in a set of overlarge double doors fashioned from red metal, surmounted by the device of the Brotherhood—a circle of unbroken chain. Mon-Dra-Kai darted towards them as swiftly and surely as an arrow in flight.

And yet, some preternatural awareness or sense turned him at the final moment as a lone figure stepped from around the corner, bearing death. The tell-tale whine of a heavy gauss rifle roared down the corridor. William witnessed Olivar fall as he stepped quickly into an alcove, pressing his back up against the wall. His shots answered the opening gambit, but did not deter their attacker.

From a canted mirror, William saw the reflection of the hideous spectre that had come upon them. The figure was encased from head-to-toe in a crimson suit of powered armor, whose lines had been made to resemble the terrifying form of a demon. Even the helmet had been altered to resemble the fearsome visage of a fire Oni.

There was no mistaking the warrior's identity, burned as it was into William's mind. The man they faced now was the Overseer's champion to the cause, the man whose nature more closely resembled a demon than even the armor he wore.

The Taskmaster.

In short order this infernal image was completed as a gout of fire reached out from his top-mounted flamethrower and caught another of the Long Knives in its fiery grasp. Using the reflection as a gauge, William wheeled around low and took aim. Burst after burst was turned aside by the seemingly invincible armor. The hellfire seemed to spread until the delicate adornments of the hall became twisted and black.

Across from where he crouched, Nadia and Olivar stood reloading their weapons. They were pinned down— by a by hardened, implacable foe.

At once a blood-curdling warcry resounded in the hall. Mon-Dra-Kai sprang from his place of concealment, facing the armored malevolence with a hatchet and force of will. Brave as he was, the native was no fool. His first swipe severed the hoses to the flamethrower, fouling it. The second chop descended towards the power cell housing contained within the backpack. But the armor that could turn hypervelocity bullets proved effective against the hatchet, despite the determination of the hand that drove it.

As the native brought his hatchet around towards the neck joint, the Taskmaster shoved him hard with the butt of his rifle. Mon-Dra-Kai sprawled back, but landed lightly as a whisper. The muzzle of the rifle turned towards the native with deadly intent.

Fast as thought, William was there, his steel-toed boot catching the end of the barrel, snapping it up as it discharged the shot over Mon-Dra-Kai's head. William stepped closer to the face whose mouth was frozen in a hideous snarl, fully remembering the fate of the last one who sought the steely embrace of powered armor in such a fashion.

Nadia materialized at his side and her hands joined in to wrest the massive weapon from their opponent's grasp. To the Taskmaster's surprise, they held him at bay for the barest of seconds, the servomotors whining against the strain. But the metal sinews won out quickly. With a toss of his shoulder he flung Nadia off of him, though William's heavier bulk remained firmly grappled on.

Another burst of ululation split the air and Mon-Dra-Kai drove his hatchet into The Taskmaster's gauntlet with surgical precision. The shock of the blow made the blood-red hand palsy, relaxing its grip ever so slightly.

William seized upon it, driving his knee up and caught the weapon in the middle, knocking it clear. Nadia snatched the end of the rifle and twisted her body to wrench it from his grasp. Then William did a strange thing. His hands flashed up to the demon's neck as though he sought to strangle the man through his armor. But once again, there was a method to his madness.

The Taskmaster's armor had been modified extensively to grant him extra protection in battle, and yet the basic framework was built upon Imperial designs, with which the William was chiefly familiar.

With the same swiftness that made the bow dance upon the violin strings, William broke the seals on either side of the helmet. Before the tyrant could divine his intent or react, William deftly twisted and the demonic mask came away with a hiss of escaping air. The fiery eyes of a zealot found beneath the red mantle did not stare long at William as he flipped the armored helmet up, caught it surely under the lip, and smashed it into The Taskmaster's exposed face.

The slaver champion stumbled back, his grizzled visage now as red as his armor. With nerveless hands, he sought the whip at his side that was wrought from the all-too-familiar red chain. Nadia lunged forward and drove her long blade through his neck with such unrestrained force that the blade snapped. When she pulled back her hand, she held only the jagged hilt and guard.

The Taskmaster clawed frantically at the wound, then collapsed to the ground in a pool of his own red blood, never to rise again.

William threw down the helmet with disgust, sparing only the briefest look at the contorted face of a man who had claimed at least two of the Long Knives, and countless others during his brutal career.

Olivar came limping up finally with a layer of combat bandages over the area where shrapnel had viciously torn up his calf.

"I wouldn't have believed it possible," the wounded Marine said as Mon-Dra-Kai moved to support him. "When I saw powered armor, I thought we were all dead, sir."

"We're not out of this yet, Marine." Nadia said with iron.

"Indeed," William seconded. "There is one tyrant who still remains."

The leader of the Marines retrieved his weapon, primed it in one motion and strode purposefully towards the double doors. He pushed them open forcefully like the harbinger of ill tidings and they parted before him like the Red Sea.

In contrast to the demolished hallway, the interior of the Overseer's private sanctum was undisturbed and tranquil. The Overseer's den was lined with leather bound books. A fireplace burned to one side of the room, guarded by two suits of armor. Only the faint, haunting tune flowing from an antique phonograph broke the silence.

"So, my prodigal son has finally returned home," a dead-calm voice said from behind the enormous desk. The light fell upon the albino features that seemed at once human and inhuman in their luminance. The nearly translucent skin was a stark contrast to the black business suit he wore, its only conceit being a small lapel pin in the form of the circle chain emblazoned on his door.

At first Nadia believed the Overseer intended that comment for Mon-Dra-Kai, until she saw the set of William's jaw. "Oh, yes, I remember my guest of honor. Has my chain been so long absent from your neck that you yearn to feel its kiss again?"

A tremor of pain rippled across William's face, but disappeared as quickly as a wave on the water.

"I am a prisoner no longer," William said. "I have come to end you."

The Overseer stood and his pallid features looked almost ghostlike in the orange light about him. "Then by all means, take my life, but realize the price your vengeance will require."

Something cylindrical in his hand glowed faintly red at the top. William's finger hovered over the trigger, ready to strike his foe down.

The Overseer's lips curled into a horrific smile that seemed almost feverish. The pale blue irises burned red in their center like furnace doors thrown wide. They gleamed with madness as he languidly strode over and took the needle from the record with a dull scratch.

"I have equipped myself with what you colloquially call a 'dead man's switch,'" he said with a casual mien. "Should you kill me, you will set off a thermonuclear device of many hundred megatons. You will be instantly consumed in the fiery torrent of my funeral pyre, along with your soldiers who even now attack my home. Perhaps it is a small matter to me that my attendants and living property would also perish, but I'd wager the stars that it is of great import to *you*," he said as he poured a drink from a crystal decanter.

"If you take me from this room, the result will be much the same. I have ensured that I cannot be kidnapped from my own home." He downed the black liquid with one drought and let forth a crazed burst of laughter. "And, should I tire of this conversation, I can always activate it myself at will."

"Slayer of children!" cried Mon-Dra-Kai brandishing his hatchet dangerously. "A river of blood must flow from you that the Yakonoi can sleep once more in peace!" His normally serene voice was now terrible in anger.

He advanced two steps and Nadia laid a restraining hand on his shoulder. One look from her eyes told the native the volumes of understanding as to their peril. Mon-Dra-Kai bit back upon his rage, his hand repeatedly flexing on the hatchet's haft with all the coiled anticipation of a cobra about to strike.

"Control your dog," the Overseer said with nonchalant disgust, "now that he is yours and no longer mine." For a moment he seemed regretful of that fact, but it passed. "A river of blood you say? I have started this for you, my old friend, even before you arrived." He motioned a pale hand towards a curtain at the back of his office. As if on cue, the long black cloth retracted back to reveal the still forms of four men and two women, each in black suits similar in cut to his own.

"My lieutenants," he presented them proudly. "I took the liberty of culling them myself. I would rather that I be the one to take them from this world, having loved them as a father, than have them lost by the rude hands of a native or soldier." His proud expression faded to almost pathetic sadness. "They were also planning to betray me," he noted with a shake of his head. "They always do. Something about our noble enterprise breeds that among them."

As slowly as she dared, Nadia began moving to her right so that she would ultimately face their foe at a perpendicular angle from William. Olivar used his wound to limp ever closer and close the noose from the other angle. Mon-Dra-Kai nearly quivered with anticipation next to William.

To all this, the Overseer seemed indifferent. The madness in eyes seemed directed inward as if the outside world no longer concerned him. His thumb still hovered menacingly over the kill switch, however.

"It is fitting that so many have returned home at this hour," the Overseer said. "There is one truth that binds us together. It doesn't matter whether you are slave or slaver, servant or master, the chain I've wrought upon the world is unbroken."

"That is not the way of it," William said coldly. "Many have escaped your tyranny and been the better for it."

"Is it truly tyranny," the Overseer said with a sneer, "for the strong to subvert the weak? Have those in my red embrace found it so easy to return to their banality once I have shown them their destiny? Can you, William, say with all certainty that you are not still in that cell upon Mount Ducane, eternally playing a lament for the wife I gleefully took from you?"

At this William grimaced, and through his haze of insanity the Overseer knew his blow had struck home. "Don't you see, it is as I said," the tyrant said with fevered certainty. "The chain is unbroken."

At these words the Overseer stumbled slightly, grasping at the bookcase for support.

"To this truth you will bear witness," he said with a cough, "now that I have taken the same medicine I administered to my lieutenants." He pointed towards the dark liquid of the decanter. "I have perhaps one hour left upon this world, even if I didn't wish to shorten it further."

The Overseer took in their widening eyes and shocked expressions, returning a sickening smile.

"Why did I do it, you ask?" the lord of slaves said as though the answer should be apparent. "Weakness...or vanity...perhaps both. It should be by my hand that my house is consumed, not yours. The medicine was only to ensure I would not turn back."

He let out a gout of soul-chilling laughter.

"But I suppose that since we are all assembled, there is scant reason why I should delay us further from our fate."

Before the word *our* had passed the Overseer's lips, Mon-Dra-Kai divined his intentions. With the sureness of a lion, the native struck. His hatchet flew from his hand, whistling end over end through the air until it hewed the hand which held the deadly device.

Nadia rushed forward and made a crisp snap kick to the mangled hand, whereby the detonator sailed into the air as if in slow motion. Nadia stretched forth her hand into the air to catch it. It descended down, down, down... her hand opened to receive it when another hand closed over it in her stead.

The Overseer stared down at his broken hand with several emotions playing out across his face, until they settled on something close to curiosity. His eyes lifted from his hand to the one who now held his prize.

"The burden is now yours," he said to William. "And a heavy burden will it prove to be." An ominous humming sound began to fill the air, emanating from the detonator in the Marine's right hand.

"The device you now hold is keyed to my DNA alone. In your grasp it will begin to gradually heat up by increments. Should you at anytime release it, or try to take it from this room, it will activate." The Overseer's tone grew grim. "Your fate, along with mine, is sealed."

The hum grew louder as the cold metal began to grow warmer against William's skin. Already it was uncomfortable.

Nadia's gaze met William's, and she knew that the foe they'd come to kill spoke the truth. Anger surged in her veins and before she realized what she was doing, she had elbowed the albino hard in the stomach and sent him falling into his large armchair. She lashed out with her fist to shatter his face when it was blocked now by the strong arms of Mon-Dra-Kai.

"Our time grows short, Na-Di-Ah," he said mournfully. "Come, we must warn the others."

"Not yet," she said, tearing away from him. She ran to the door where she produced the Taskmaster's chain whip. In seconds she had bound the curiously blank Overseer to his chair while Olivar poured skin sealant over the slaver lord's bleeding wound.

"Never thought I'd be trying to prolong this bastard's life."

"That's life in the service, Marine," Nadia barked. Her bravado was only there to prolong the inevitable look at William, who now literally held all their lives in his hand.

When she finally looked to him, she saw that he stood straight and tall in the middle of the room like a titan. The muscles in his jaw seemed tense, but his eyes showed no pain. She opened her mouth to speak, but he spoke first.

"It's up to you now, Nadia," he said in a calm voice as though he were marshaling all his monumental self-control into it. "Get them out of here. I will make sure you have the entire hour."

With his free hand, he removed his own long blade from his belt and gave it to her. "This is yours. Show it to Captain Halcyon. He will honor my wishes." He also withdrew the placard marked with the seal of the *Rampant Lion*. "Give this to Commander Thornton. It is his by rights."

Tears scalded her cheeks as she threw her arms around him in an embrace. Fate had dealt this brilliant man its final card, and the reality that she would never lay eyes on him again began to dawn.

"Go now," he said as she pulled back. "Farewell now, my friends, may the stars shine for you alone."

With that, Olivar, Mon-Dra-Kai, and Nadia dashed from the room to see to their charges. Her last sight of him was as he removed a small length of red chain from his belt and bound it to his burning hand, as he sought to trade his life for their freedom.

▲ ▲ ▲

When they were gone, William turned to face his foe, who now sat looking at him without emotion. The detonator in his hand sang its harsh song, as it grew ever warmer in his hand.

"They are lost, as we are," the Overseer said at last.

"No, Nadia will see them clear," William said defiantly. "Of that I have no doubt."

Of all the times in his life, now was when he required the pinnacle of his will. Everything he had endured, every lesson he'd learned, and even the final catharsis of the previous night was all in preparation for the ordeal he must now suffer. Every ounce he could muster was directed towards keeping his hand closed.

Would even that be enough? It had been in his hands no more than five minutes and already it was all he could do to keep a hold of it. The pain was increasing, and would only continue to grow until either the Overseer expired from the poison, or he could no longer hold it.

He had to hold out.

He began pacing to distract himself from the screaming nerves of his hand that blazed with pain. The Overseer watched this with a certain cold amusement as William took his stolen comm unit out and set it down on the desk. Nadia's hard voice gave orders to all stations, sounding the evacuation. The pain grew in intensity and a spasm ran through William's body.

"It grows heavy, does it not?"

William ignored him and kept pacing…until his eyes fell upon a familiar shape, sitting on the table behind the row of decanters. One look told him not only its purpose, but also its creator.

With his free hand, he picked it up by the slender neck. The bow sat next to it, forged from red metal. The adornments upon the hourglass shape were similarly made from red links that jutted sideways from the reddened wood. Fitting it under his chin, he carefully wedged the bow into his captured hand.

"Now is the time of my final performance. Strange that you of all people should be my audience."

It came to life with sound as he drew the bow across the strings, and there could be no doubt that this violin had also been made by the hand of his wife. He whispered her name reverently as the first few notes of *Salvatorio D'Aria* drowned out the dread humming, and began their climb towards apotheosis.

Higher and higher the music took him, until he was ascendant. The music bolstered him, dulling away the pain and giving him the center point on which he must revolve in these final minutes of his life. Even when the metal of the bow began to fuse together with the chain that encircled his hand, he never missed a note. Even when he was sure he could see the glow through the back of his hand, he played on.

Lost as he was in the music, he didn't realize that the Overseer was not the only one to listen in on his final concert. The comm channel beamed the song out for all to hear. Aboard the *Rampant Lion*, now around Helot Station, Captain Halcyon recognized it and switched it on for all the crew to hear.

The Long Knives too could hear their leader's hand speak in song with that one true voice and it fueled their efforts. Not one among them, after hearing that heavenly resonance had any doubt that William Aidan Montgomery had, in fact, been the Prisoner of Zyi-Kang.

Far from distracting them, that muse's voice fired their efforts and drove them to heights of excellence that even they had never expected. Lives were saved that might have been otherwise lost. By the end there had been more acts of personal courage and heroism than could be ever be recounted.

William let the song take him over fully. Even when the Overseer began to fade, expressions of beauty continued to pour forth like a waterfall. In his mind, he saw the angelic shape of Valentina, radiating with love, beckoning him towards her. A smile, the first real one he'd had in a long time, beamed from him. She returned it and revealed to him visions of wonder. As the white light took him, a single sight filled him with immeasurable happiness and peace.

A broken chain.

▲ ▲ ▲

They had done it. In such a small space they had worked miracles. All remaining members of the Long Knives, along with all the captured slaves and natives had been whisked away before the palace went up. Fortunately, the immense fortifications had contained the blast somewhat. They had sailed by on a razor's margin, but they had done it.

The impact of their victory at Vermillion was already being felt. Many of the Red Chain ships in the system had bugged out when they heard of the Overseer's spectacular end. Even more ships had surrendered. Not long after a scout ship, the *Hawkeye*, transited out of superluminal speeds announcing that the other elements of the Imperial fleet had been successful. At every engagement, the Imperial cannonade had proven victorious. The back of the slaver fleet had been broken.

Because the Red Chain Brotherhood threat was gone, it was possible that some of the clusters of separated Imperial worlds in the region might now be brought into the whole of the Empire proper. The mission at Vermillion would one day move the borders of the map.

Nadia and her company were once again home aboard the *Rampant Lion*. There was celebration at every station. She didn't feel as ecstatic as the others. The world seemed emptier somehow, immeasurably diminished now that he was gone. She found herself wandering the corridors, as if trying to hold on to that shard of William which had become part of the ship. So many times, she turned around expecting to see his face or hear his voice, only to find echoes and air instead.

Captain Halcyon, upon seeing William's long blade in her hands, gave her a field promotion to lead the Long Knives. Pending finalizing of OCS, she would make the seven-league stride forward to become an officer, with Olivar as her new senior NCO. Brevet promotions like this hardly ever stuck, but Halcyon was convinced that having the position willed to her by the last act of the Prisoner of Zyi-Kang would carry the necessary gravity to make it permanent.

Commander Thornton had reluctantly taken the placard back, now knowing that it had traveled with the man all the way to the end of his journey. If the crest had been sentimental to him before, it was now holy.

At last, she found herself putting on her dress uniform, complete with her new rank, and joining the solemn group that stood parade still in the hangar bay. Many of the other Long Knives who had fallen had already had their hour of remembrance, but now they came together to bid farewell to the man who had been the truest part of *Rampant Lion*'s spirit.

His coffin was laid in a place of honor, covered with a richly embroidered Imperial flag, a five-pointed star crowned by laurel leaves upon a field of space black. There had been no body to commit to the depths, but the coffin was not empty. It held three items that had been found in his austere quarters. One was a selection of his service medals, each telling the tale of his virtue and courage. The second was a length of red chain that had been inscribed with a single letter "V." The last was the black violin whose beautiful song would never be heard again.

They had found it in his quarters just as he had left it, with its strings cut and its body smashed. While it had been a shame to destroy an instrument of such excellence, Nadia found it didn't matter. No one could have ever made it sing the way he did.

Nadia and five other Long Knives served as pall bearers as they lifted the coffin and moved it towards the airlock. When it was arranged within, the flag was folded and presented to the Captain, who would act as its custodian.

It came time for her to honor him her own way. She strode forward to the spot where his coffin rested. In perfect *a cappella*, her voice rose in the chamber to give her last goodbye in song. The melancholy tune, ancient as it was, was filled with an enduring hope for the future. As she sang *The Minstrel Boy*, the iron demeanor of her companions began to falter. Her words were made all the more poignant as she changed the melody to that haunting song of goodbye, *the Parting Glass*. When she reached the second verse, not an eye in the room was dry, including the Captain's. She sang:

The Minstrel fell, but the foeman's chain,
Could not bring that proud soul under.
The harp he loved never spoke again,
For he tore its chords asunder.
And said: No chain shall sully thee,
Oh soul of love and bravery.
Thy songs were made for the pure and free
They shall never sound in slavery.

Acknowledgements

Oh—you're still here! Good! I was afraid you were going to duck out before the credits roll. Since you're still reading, let me talk about some folks who helped make this book a reality. Depending on how much you liked these stories, you may commence with either singing their praises or cursing their names.

<u>My Parents</u> — They both loved (and continue to love) science fiction, and passed on their mutual love *Star Trek* at an early age. My Mom read to me constantly and my Dad played word games to build up my synonym game. Both of them have been there to encourage me, and prompt to me to keep feeding them reading material.

<u>My Uncle</u> — All those conversations led to so many books I might never have found otherwise. He gave me some of the best birthday and Christmas presents in the form of a sprees at the local bookstore. Many of those titles collectively formed the catalyst to tell stories of my own.

<u>Steve Ross</u> — One of the most creative guys I've ever met. Whether it's humor, impressions, digital and free-hand illustrations, or social satire, it's the true professional who can make it all seem so effortless. He designed the sweet cover art for this book, as well as the Sector M logo.

<u>Beth Mashburn</u> — My nerves-of-steel editor, she's been with me since my first manuscript. She is critical in taking a bunch of words on a page and ensuring that that they transform into something readable. Patient and eagled-eyed, I appreciate how she uses a blue or pink editing pen rather than red.

<u>The Good Folks at CreateSpace</u> — And speaking of patience, a shout-out to the folks at CreateSpace who helped me on the technical side of this project. A dream of mine has been to hold a physical copy of my book in my hands. Achievement unlocked!

<u>Rusty Bentley</u> — A calm at the center of the storm, Rusty is a canny and smart beta-reader, always quick to point out when I'm not making sense, or when I'm out of bounds. His support in every literary project I've undertaken has been critical to making it a reality.

<u>Miranda Vahle</u> — My First Reader and the voice of reason when yours truly bites off more than he can chew. As a veteran of the United States Navy, she doesn't even bat an eyelash when I ask random questions like "What's the unrep (underway replenishment) time for a supercarrier?" or "What's the name of the channel the Captain uses to address the crew?" It's the 1MC, by the way. Thanks for that, and for everything you do. Every. Day.

<u>You</u> — Maybe it's cliché to thank the reader on a project like this, but I'm all in for it. Writing is just half of the equation. Without a reader to give it a go, my work is just smeared ink on a page or patterned electrons. By reading this book, you are supporting my work. And that, gentle reader, is the greatest gift you could give me. So, from the bottom of my heart, thank you! Onwards!

Oh, And One Last Thing...

Before you put the book down, consider connecting with me online, won't you? Here's where you can find me:

Official Website: Go to **TheSectorM.com.** This is the hub to all my other platforms, and your place to see what I'm doing, find links to my other works, as well my blog and all my social media.

Cool Stuff: Want to get your hands on a sweet Sector M T-shirt, a mug, or smartphone case? Check out **TheSectorM** on Redbubble.com!

Patreon: Consider supporting me on Patreon, for cool fan rewards and benefits! **patreon.com/ TheSectorm**

See You Around The Sector!

After graduating from the University of North Texas, Matt Carson worked as a writer in journalism, advertising, and other assorted fields. His first love, however, has always been fiction.

Carson describes himself as an unrepentant fanboy and gamer with a deep interest in etymology, acting, and naval history. A geek and nerd from back when neither was considered cool, Carson has been fully enjoying the current "geek awakening" and contributing to it with his own stories, including his military science-fiction novel *The Backwards Mask*.

Made in the USA
Monee, IL
30 March 2022

93828313R00198